A WOMAN'S WORLD

BOOK 1

THE WOMAN'S WORLD SERIES

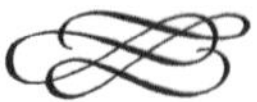

LYNNE HILL

Future Classics Publishing

1st Edition

OTHER BOOKS BY LYNNE

The Lords and Commoners Series

Of Lords and Commoners Book 1

Of Princes and Dragons Book 2

Of Gods and Goddesses Book 3

A Gods and Goddesses Novelette

A Woman's World Series

A Woman's World Book 1

Lost Powers Book 2

A Collision of Worlds Book 3

This book was written for Fatima, Khadijah and Ayat.
I hope you found love and happiness.

PROLOGUE

Childhood Memory

No moons shone in the night's sky. Such a night only occurred once a year in Pathins.

Something gently shook Baya from her sleep.

"Wake up, little one," Rus whispered. "Your mother is about to give birth."

The little girl threw back the covers, leapt to her feet and ran out of the room.

A pain-filled scream came from her mother's chambers, causing Baya to stop short in the hallway. "What's wrong?"

"Don't worry. Your mother is strong and the midwife says that everything is fine. Her baby is due any minute. Come see what your mother is capable of creating. She can bring the miracle of life into this world — a gift from the Great Goddess Herself."

"Wow," Baya said. Since Rus appeared to be calm, she decided that everything must be fine. Slowly, she ventured to peek around the door to her mother's chambers. The blood drained from Baya's face.

Her mother, Aga, was pale and covered in sweat. Another scream rang out. The midwife placed a damp rag on Aga's forehead.

"That's it, Aga … just a couple more pushes and this will all be over." The midwife spoke in a low soothing voice.

Baya's head felt light as she held her breath in anticipation.

The midwife guided the baby into the world and wrapped it in a white blanket that was soon smeared with dark blue blood. Baya was wide-eyed and too scared to move. She had never seen so much blood.

Rus carefully took the baby from the midwife. "Why hello there," he cooed at the tiny bundle in his arms.

"Is the baby okay?" Baya's tiny voice shook as she spoke.

No one answered.

Rus studied the baby who had begun to fuss.

"I'm sorry," the midwife said. She moved around Rus and headed for the door.

Rus was left alone to tell Aga the bad news.

"Sorry … why? Don't tell me …" Aga's weak voice trailed off.

"Yes. It's a boy," Rus whispered.

"No," Aga gasped. She glared at Baya, as if this were somehow her fault. Then she rolled over, turning her back on Rus, Baya and the baby.

Rus moved to the washbasin to clean the newborn.

Baya's frustration came out in an angry outburst. "What's wrong? Is the baby okay?"

"He's healthy," Rus said.

Even after being cleaned and wrapped in fresh blankets Aga refused to hold or even look at the baby. She kept her back to her family.

Rus walked over and sat in a chair in the far corner of the large room and held the baby close.

"May I see him?" Baya asked.

Rus shifted the baby so that Baya could crawl up on his lap. He placed the newborn across her legs and they held the baby together.

"He's beautiful." As Baya spoke, the newborn opened his large eyes and stared up at her. "Rus! He has your eyes, too." She tilted her head to the side as she admired the baby's light brown eyes with the sunburst of green running through them. The baby's eye color turned to bright gold in a narrow band that surrounded the black pupil. To top it off, his eyes were surrounded by generous dark lashes. His head was covered in soft dark hair and his skin was a lovely golden-brown.

Baya furrowed her brow in concentration. "How come we have eyes like yours?" Baya asked. The dark hair and skin were common but the tri-colored eyes were not.

Rus shrugged. "The Great Goddess works in mysterious ways. I wish I was smarter so I could better answer your questions."

"But … it's like we are your children … somehow. I mean Aga is our mother … and maybe you are our …" there were no words in her language for what she was trying to say.

"There are only mothers. Men have nothing to do with the creation of new life."

Baya frowned. "Then how come we look like you? I mean, Mother's eyes are a common brown."

Rus smiled. "Always with the questions." He gently poked her tiny nose. "I honestly don't know, Little One."

Baya sighed in resignation as she turned her gaze back to the baby. A smile crossed her lips and the faint lines that creased her forehead disappeared.

"What will you name him?" Rus spoke to Aga's back.

"I don't care what he's called. It doesn't matter."

Even young Baya recognized the sorrow in her mother's voice, yet she didn't understand why. Her mother should have been happy that he was healthy. At least Rus didn't seem to mind that he was a boy.

"Well, Baya, you will have to be the one to name him," Rus said.

Baya's eyes widened. "Me! Really?"

Rus nodded. "It's always the woman who names the baby." He frowned briefly at Aga's back. "I suppose the job falls to you, as the next oldest female in the house. You said you wanted a baby brother, remember?"

Aga let out an irritated snort.

Baya studied the baby's perfect round head, as he slept peacefully in her arms. "Bek. It starts with a B, like mine."

"That's a good name. Bek it is. Bek will make a good theo someday."

"That is all he will ever be — a manservant." Aga's voice was bitter and full of sleep.

Baya frowned. She waited until Aga's breathing grew heavy, indicating that she was fast asleep before whispering, "It doesn't matter that you're a boy. Rus and I will always love you."

CHAPTER 1

Baya's entire body jerked as she woke from an all too common nightmare. She had been alone and lost in a vast unfamiliar land in which every shadow seemed to have eyes — stalking her. She had caught a flash of something at her side, as a wild beast lunged for her.

Sometimes Baya dreamt about giant beasts with three elongated noses that hung to the ground, beasts so huge one of them could stomp her into dust with a careless step. At other times her night terrors consisted of large mouths filled with countless sharp teeth that could swallow her in one bite. In the world beyond the island of Pathins, humans were nothing more than tender morsels — at the bottom of the food chain.

"Maybe the stories of Ameris are not the best bedtime stories," Baya mumbled to herself. Ameris was the Great Goddess and her adventures in the wild were legendary.

Baya shook her head to help brush way the dream.

Yellow sunlight poured in her window and the familiar sight of her room set her at ease but then Baya remembered what day it was. "Oh no!" She bolted upright.

It was a day she had been dreading for years. Her hands trembled as she pulled the covers off and crawled out of bed. Today was her eleventh birthday.

Baya watched Rus from her window. Rus was her mother's theo, the man who raised her children and tended to the household. Birds flocked around his feet, pecking away in a frenzy, as he spread feed from a bucket tucked under his arm.

A soft knock came at the door. Bek popped his head into her room. "Good morning, big sister!" Bek looked a lot like Baya. He had thick dark hair and light brown skin. Their most unusual feature was their tri-colored eyes. They were light brown mixed with green, and gold surrounded their pupils.

Baya quickly wiped a tear from her eye. "Hey, baby brother."

Bek moved to stand beside Baya and he also peered out the window. He kept his arms tucked behind his back. "I always thought birds were ugly."

She chuckled. "That's because they are."

"But Rus sure knows how to cook them up good," Bek said.

"Thankfully they don't taste like they look. Birds must have been Ameris's most hideous creation. She must not have liked them, for some reason, if she made them so ugly and yet so delicious to eat."

Even the wild ones were fleshy, as if they had been shaved. Their wings consisted of a veiny almost transparent membrane that carried them through the air. They came in the dullest of colors — various shades of gray or black. On land they were particularly awkward, as they had to hop around on one spindly leg.

Baya eyed Bek. "Why are you standing like that — with your hands behind your back?"

Bek revealed a bouquet of orange and red flowers. In his excitement to give them to his sister, he almost smacked her in the face with them.

The sweet scent of the flowers accosted Baya. She took a step back to place them at a safer distance. The flowers had broad soft petals and long yellow stems.

Baya frowned. "Did mother make you get these for me?"

"No. It was Rus's idea. He thought they could be braided in your hair, or something — you know, for your big day."

An eleventh birthday was indeed an important day — for a girl. "Thank you. They're lovely." Baya's eyes swelled with tears. Today she would be moving into the Palace of the Unawi to continue her education. Una' meaning one and, 'wi' refers to a female, so the Unawi was the ruler of Pathins — which included all of womankind.

The only time Baya would be allowed to see Bek and Rus was for the most important holidays — the time of No Moons and the time of Four Moons. Otherwise, she would not be allowed to come home.

Her stomach turned at the thought of Bek and Rus being left alone with Aga and Tash. Their mother, Aga, served as a high priestess on the council of the Unawi. Tash was the youngest of Aga's children. Tash looked nothing like the rest of the family. She had long flaxen hair and bright blue eyes the color of the sea.

Baya's hand shook as she took the flowers from Bek. "I don't want to live with the other daughters of the priestesses."

Bek lowered his head and ran his big toe in an arc across the stone floor. "I don't want you to go."

Baya wrapped her arms around his tiny shoulders. A sharp intake of breath accompanied the terrible thought that popped into Baya's head. "Bek, I won't be able to give you secret lessons anymore." A sob stuck in her throat and almost stopped her from being able to continue. "Your education ... We didn't even get to solving equations or —"

"It's okay." He still gazed at the floor. "I don't know why I would need to know all that stuff anyway."

A sad smile crossed her lips. "Remember when Mother caught me teaching you to read?"

Bek laughed. "She was so mad. She grounded me for a week and sent me to bed without dinner."

"I thought her head was going to explode." Baya chuckled. "I kept arguing with her, telling her that you were learning everything I taught you but she said, *'Bek can't light a candle with a wave of his hand, now can he?'* As if that proves anything. So what if boys don't have powers. You're still very smart."

Bek frowned. "And Tash was going on and on about how I'm nothing but a stupid boy."

Baya growled. "I wanted to pull every piece of golden hair out of her head."

"You've always been a good sister. You snuck bread to my room that night."

Baya sighed. Who was going to look after Bek while she was gone?

Bek forced a smile. "We got smarter after that and never let Mom catch us again."

"It was like a fun game, just between us."

"Our little secret." Bek chimed.

Baya shook her head in dismay. Aga had even blamed her that day for Bek being born. Aga had said, "You wanted a brother more than anything. You are the reason my household is burdened with a *boy*."

"When I come back for the holiday," Baya said. "I will teach you all the new stuff I've learned, I promise."

Bek nodded. "It'll be just like old times."

Tears were about to spill out of her eyes when Aga entered the room. Baya had to quickly pull herself together. Her mother despised crying. It was a sign of weakness that she wouldn't tolerate from her oldest daughter, especially now that she was eleven.

"The flowers will be a nice touch," Aga said. "You can go, Bek. I must see to it that Baya is ready to meet the Unawi."

Bek left the room quickly with his eyes on the floor.

Aga braided the stems of the flowers into Baya's thick brown hair. The braid hung down the length of her back. Aga had bought her daughter a special gown for the occasion. She helped Baya into the full-length tunic. It was white with gold trim. The finishing touch was a gold belt that hung loosely around Baya's waist. Once it was fastened Baya spun on tiptoes to test the light fabric. The gown flowed elegantly around her legs. It made her feel older and prettier — important even — like when she used to play dress-up with her mother's clothes.

Aga studied her daughter.

Baya shifted uncomfortably under her intense stare.

"Today you are no longer a girl, you are a mistress. This is the stage between childhood and womanhood." Aga's face softened. "You are positively lovely. You'll grow to be more beautiful than I ever was. You simply must become the next Unawi."

Baya could not help the smile that crept across her face. She hated that her mother's praise meant so much — but it did.

"Are you ready?"

Baya's stomach did another summersault. She wanted to say no. But instead she found the strength to give a slight nod.

CHAPTER 2

Baya's family lived in Una Sitka — the First City, also called the Ruler's City. Shema was their current ruler and Una Sitka was located in the far South of Pathins. The large island was the only land inhabited by humans. Even the Northern part of the island was difficult to reach as it was separated from the South by a high mountain range that could only be crossed on foot and in the Time of Daylight.

The weather barely fluctuated from warm to steaming hot in Una Sitka. Although, Baya had been told, the mountains in the North could become miserably cold.

Pathins had roughly four seasons. The longest was the Time of Daylight. This was when at least one of the planet's suns shone in the sky at all times. The Time of Daylight would give way to a brief season when there would be a couple hours of darkness each night. Next came the Time of Darkness. This was when both suns would set, casting the planet into a darkness that lasted as long as the day. The nights would quickly grow shorter as they headed back into the Time of Daylight, when they would not see darkness again for many months.

Both suns were high in the sky by the time Aga and Baya made their way to Unawi Shema's palace, which could be seen from Aga's home, but being up close was an entirely different experience. The black stone structure had a wide base that held the diamond-shaped palace high into the sky. The palace looked as if two massive pyramids had been placed together at their bases, balanced on the point of the bottom one.

Baya examined the walls angling upward above her. She fought the urge to run out of the shadows of the building before the stones overhead came crashing down. "How come the walls don't fall?"

"There is no need to worry, my dear," Aga said. "This is the best-built structure in all the land. It has stood for many centuries."

The fact that it was really old didn't help to put Baya at ease. Now she was certain the structure would collapse at any moment. "It's just that the base doesn't look like it could support such large stones. It's like a tiny neck trying to hold up an oversized head."

Aga chuckled. "Take a look at the Unawi's grounds." Aga opened a large wooden gate in the tall stone wall that surrounded the palace grounds, thus revealing an oasis of colors and life.

Flowers and plants burst into a sea of every imaginable shade. Baya's lips parted as she took in the scene laid out before her. "This puts Rus's garden to shame."

Water flowed from many small streams around the base of the palace. It cascaded down steps and sprayed out of stone fountains creating soothing sounds.

Baya exhaled and her shoulders relaxed.

Flowers of every color grew from the earth and hung off bushes. Numerous ponds held yellow leafy plants. Above all else, blue and purple flowers with petals that spiked outward in every direction caught Baya's eye. They were the most unusual flowers she had ever seen, she had no idea what they were called. She wanted to pick one but refrained. Surely it was a punishable offense to pluck one of Unawi Shema's flowers.

They passed two gardeners who were bent over, hard at work. Aga kept her head held high, ignoring them entirely. But Baya's attention was drawn to the younger one, a boy, whose black skin glistened where the hot sunlight touched it. His golden-brown eyes briefly met hers.

Baya smiled.

He quickly put his head down and expertly plucked a weed — roots and all.

She continued to watch him. He was about her age, or maybe a bit older. High cheekbones and a strong jaw made him rather nice to look at. His eyes weren't round like hers, they were dramatically almond-shaped. She hadn't seen anyone who looked like him before. The feeling that came over her was something she didn't recognize. All she understood was that she wanted to talk to him.

Baya had stopped walking altogether.

"Keep up, Baya," Aga snapped. "We can't be late."

Baya reluctantly pulled her eyes away from the boy and ran toward the palace entrance. Her gown caught around her foot causing her to stumble forward. She wasn't used to such a long dress. She managed to right herself before hitting the ground.

The boy had jumped to his feet as if to help her.

Baya turned away from him to hide her embarrassment. What a stupid, clumsy mess, she thought.

Aga waited at the entrance. The tall wooden doors were covered with carved pictures from Ameris's time on this planet. They depicted her casting away wild beasts as she sat high upon her throne.

Baya couldn't resist the urge to look back one last time at the strange and handsome boy. To her surprise, their eyes met briefly before he turned away again.

"Don't waste a second of your time on a garden boy." Aga frowned down at her daughter.

"Wh … what do you mean?" Baya's cheeks turned a shade of purple as the blue blood rushed to her face.

"You will choose your theo from one of the sons of the priestesses, as I did." Aga gave a crooked smile. "Unless you become Unawi. Then you could have the garden boy as one of the many theos who would serve you."

Baya shuddered. "You mean the untheos?"

Aga nodded. She made this sound like a good thing. As if having many men was the prize you won for becoming the ruler. Something about that was … not right … disgusting even.

"I just …" Baya's nervousness made it difficult to speak — after all she was about to meet the ruler of the entire world. "I mean … he looks nice. … Like we could be friends."

"Friends." Aga chuckled but there was no humor in it. "You still have much to learn in these upcoming years — that is why we're here. Come."

A man pushed the heavy doors open for them and Baya followed her mother into the building. "Besides, you will have plenty of girls to befriend. The daughters of the high priestesses will make worthy companions."

Baya frowned. She doubted this. There would be entirely too much competition between her and her new peers.

The first thing Baya saw was a wide set of black stone stairs leading out of the neck and up into the large head of the palace above. The stairs were dimly illuminated by torchlight.

"Now remember, no matter who or when the next Unawi is chosen, these girls will be your companions for life. One will become ruler someday and many others will become priestesses who will offer counsel to the Unawi. So …"

"Make a good first impression," Baya recited. Even though she had no idea how to accomplish this. It felt as if she were the tiny base that was holding up the palace they now walked through. The pressure was unbearable.

CHAPTER 3

The black stone walls made for a dreary atmosphere, as Aga and Baya passed through the dark hallways of the palace. Aga came to a stop before two tall wooden doors — also carved with exquisite detail depicting the Goddess's ancient adventures.

This had to be it, Baya thought. The ruler was on the other side of this entryway.

"Okay. Chin up." Aga pushed Baya's chin higher. "Shoulders back." She pressed on Baya's shoulders until she was standing exactly the way Aga wanted. "Deep breath." Aga inhaled sharply and Baya did the same.

Baya's stomach fluttered and she hoped her breakfast would stay down.

A theo swung the doors open. Aga marched confidently into the Great Hall. Baya tried to emulate her but wasn't sure if she was successful. She largely felt ridiculous taking long strides with her nose in the air.

A vaulted ceiling rose high above them. Baya blinked as her eyes adjusted to the sunlight that flowed in through the high windows. Her lips parted in awe, as she realized that they were actually skylights. They had to be in the uppermost part of the palace.

Many thick pillars lined either side of a wide walkway. The columns consisted of a smooth white stone. Baya thought her mother's home was large but most of it could fit inside this one room.

In the center stood a large fountain. Four stone women, over twice the size of real women, stood in a circle in the middle of the structure. They held their arms permanently outstretched to the sky, in prayer to the Goddess. A thick spray of water shot up between the stone women, rising high above their hands. Eventually the water cascaded down, soaking the statues.

At the far end of the Great Hall, Shema lounged on an overstuffed divan, which sat atop a handful of stairs. The bright white fabric of the divan seemed to glow in the sunlight.

Shema watched with mild interest as her guests approached. At least fifteen untheos surrounded her. They seemed half-dressed to Baya. Only their midsection was covered in a white cloth wrap. Baya thought that there was entirely too much brown skin showing. The sight of all the lean male chests made her blush.

The men appeared to be taking turns fanning Shema. They stood or lay around on the stairs. No doubt they were waiting to fulfill any order the Unawi might have. Shema slowly stood. The men fidgeted and moved with her, trying to anticipate what she might want.

Shema, too, was barely clothed. Her tiny top left her large breasts half exposed. Her skirt showed off her long tan legs. Thin golden strands of light see-through fabric flowed behind her as she moved forward. Some of her theos openly gawked at her large hips as they swayed more than necessary when she walked.

Baya looked down at her own body. She was a skeleton — all skin and bones — in comparison to Shema. Baya bit her lip. Even her mother's beauty faded when compared to the Unawi.

A large beady-eyed creature crawled up Shema's leg. It disappeared as it crossed Shema's back securing itself around one side of her waist while it rested its upper body on her opposite shoulder.

Baya had been so enthralled with the ruler that she hadn't noticed the creature at first. The thing could have passed for a third arm. Its long body was brown and segmented, with numerous thin legs that moved like a wave as it positioned itself to get a better look at the newcomer. It appeared to gaze intently at Baya with four solid black eyes.

Shema gave Aga a genuine smile and Aga returned the gesture. A spine tingling sensation passed through Baya when Aga embraced Shema. The creepy creature didn't appear to bother Aga in the least. The hug ended with Aga kissing Shema's cheek.

"It is wonderful to see you, as always, Madam Unawi," Aga said.

But like the large insect, Shema's eyes scarcely left Baya. "It's about time you brought your eldest daughter to meet me."

Baya was not sure which one was more intimidating, the giant insect or the ruler of the world. It took everything Baya had to keep her head held high under the inquisitive stares. Yet Baya somehow managed to stop herself from lowering her chin to her chest.

Shema moved in close, presenting her cheek to Baya.

Oh no, Baya thought.

Everyone was expected to kiss Shema's cheek. This was how people showed the ruler her due respect.

Baya hesitated. In order to kiss Shema, she would have to get incredibly close to that thing on her shoulder — almost kissing it as well.

She hoped it didn't bite. Why hadn't her mother warned her about Shema's … pet … or whatever it was?

Do it quick. Don't be a sissy, Baya scolded herself.

Closing her eyes tight, she gave Shema an awkward peck on the cheek. She thought she heard the creature make some sort of noise, as if it were trying to tell her something. Baya studied the four beady eyes, then shook her head. She must've imagined hearing the sound.

"Baya turns eleven today," Aga was saying. "She is to start her official training for the priesthood."

"Excellent," Shema said. "She is quite tall for her age. I'm sure she will become a lovely woman." She gave Baya a tight-lipped smile. "Welcome to your new home, Mistress. Your mother is the most skilled and powerful of my priestesses so I'm sure you will do well with your training."

Baya swallowed hard. She was certain that her stone base was cracking under the immense pressure. "I will do my very best, Madam Unawi," she managed to squeak.

"Of course you will." With the slight wave of Shema's hand one of her theos stepped forward. "Show the young mistress to her new living quarters."

Baya looked at her mother with wide eyes. Was that it?

She didn't want to leave her mother — the only familiar thing in this odd place.

"Don't worry." Aga seemed to read Baya's mind. "I will be around. After all, I work here, remember? We have to join the priestesses for our morning rituals but I'll be instructing some of your sessions with the other girls."

"When?" Baya tried to keep the panic out of her voice but the last thing she wanted was to be alone in this strange place.

"Soon."

"Soon, as in an hour, or tomorrow or one week?"

"Go along, now." Shema gestured for Baya to follow the man.

Aga gave her a reassuring smile. "Go with the theo. I will not be far."

Baya choked back the knot in her throat. She couldn't be so weak as to cry in front of the Unawi. Slowly, she turned to the large doors. The servant held them open, as he patiently waited for her to follow. She ventured one last glance at her mother before she disappeared around the corner.

The theo led Baya through many dark halls, barely lit with torches, and down several sets of stairways. She was completely disoriented when they finally came to a stop. He opened yet another door for her. Baya entered only to find a room full of girls. The room was modest compared to the Great Hall — low ceilings, no windows, obsidian stone walls. Every girl stopped what she had been doing to stare at Baya.

She issued a nervous smile.

No one smiled back.

The clang of the door slamming shut behind Baya, echoed in her ears. The theo had made his quick retreat.

Baya felt a bead of sweat form on her brow as she scanned the faces of the twelve or so girls in the room. It appeared to be a common room, as the center was arranged with many divans. Girls sat about casually. They had most likely been talking freely amongst themselves before Baya entered.

They all had various tones of brown skin and long brown hair. Most of them wore frowns, while some even glared at Baya. What Baya thought was pity could be seen on some of their faces.

This was going to be even worse than she'd imagined.

CHAPTER 4

Baya stood frozen in the entryway to the girls' chambers. If she were to move, she was sure her feet would carry her swiftly out of the room. An intense longing for home hit her in the gut.

Rus ... she thought. All she wanted was for Rus to comfort her, the way only he could. If only she were still small enough to curl up on his lap. He used to wrap his strong arms around her and whisper, "Everything's going to be fine, Little One."

"So, you must be the daughter of the great *Aga*?" One of the older girls stepped forward to stand directly in front of Baya. She made the word Aga sound like an insult. The girl was only slightly taller than Baya but much more shapely. Her black hair hung loosely around her shoulders.

Baya thought about answering with a *no,* in the hopes of being accepted by these girls. Yet, the truth would come out eventually. Instead, she nodded and offered her hand in greeting. "I'm Baya."

Her hand was left untouched.

The black-haired girl crossed her arms in front of her chest. "And you think you can come in here and show everyone up, don't you?"

"No." Yet Baya knew that was what she was expected to do — to be the best, most powerful girl here, as her mother had been. "I'm just a regular girl — nothing special."

"That's right. You're nothing special while you're in these living quarters. You see, this is *our* world."

Baya was sure the girl meant *her* world.

"Understand?" the black-haired girl said.

"It's perfectly clear," Baya whispered. She wanted to explain that she didn't want to be here, that she didn't want to become Unawi. Someone else could have the job as far as she was concerned. Yet, there was a part of her that didn't want to disappoint her mother and she couldn't let Tash become more powerful than her.

Baya's eyes widened as it occurred to her: What if she wasn't the best and Tash was? Her sister would become the next Unawi. Then Baya would become one of her advisors, only a priestess on her council — beneath her. She couldn't let that happen!

But Baya had a bigger problem at the moment.

The girl moved closer. She towered over Baya. "I can't hear you."

"Yes. I understand."

"Understand what?"

"That you're in charge."

Baya could feel the tense silence in the room around her, as if every girl held her breath, not daring to move until the confrontation was over — until dominance was established.

The black-haired girl reached for Baya.

Baya flinched even though she had never been hit before. In fact, she had never heard of someone actually hitting another. It must have been a natural reaction to jump at an approaching hand.

The girl's hand didn't hit Baya, instead it plucked one of the red flowers from Baya's hair.

"What's this? Some foolish attempt to impress Shema — this common old flower. I'm sure you saw, Shema has much prettier ones in her garden." She held the flower in the palm of her hand and stared at it. The flower lifted into the air. A ball of fire grew from her other hand. The fire shot toward the flower, sending it up in a burst of flames and a puff of smoke.

Murmurs of awe came from the girls in the room.

Baya refused to respond, she didn't even blink. She kept her head held high and her shoulders back.

"She's got it, Lua," a smaller girl spoke up. "She knows what's up around here, so if you're done with the new girl, I'll show her to her room."

Lua glared at the younger girl, who pushed Baya through the common room and toward a long hallway on the far side.

"Thank you," Baya said, as they walked down a long narrow hall with average-sized doors lining either side.

The girl said nothing.

"Well, Lua is really something, isn't she?" Baya hoped to recruit an ally.

The girl stopped walking and looked at Baya. She appeared to be about Baya's age yet shorter. She had large brown eyes and long brown hair. "Lua won't let anyone be your friend. So, you might as well give up. No one here will cross her."

"Why? What's so great about Lua?"

"She's the oldest mistress here and obviously powerful."

"So someday we'll be the oldest and —"

"Then we'll be in control." The girl started walking again.

"You mean then we'll be the bullies." Baya saw the cycle clearly.

"Oh yeah. Payback time. I hope to become Unawi just so I can make mean girls like Lua pay."

This didn't sound right. "But…" Baya couldn't find the right words. "Then you'll be just like Lua."

"Yeah, that's the point."

"But Lua is … mean."

"So?"

Baya shook her head in disbelief as she followed after the girl. All she understood was that she did *not* want to be like Lua.

The girl stopped at the very last door at the end of the long hall. "You're the newest, so you get this room. When we come back from the Holidays, they assign us new rooms. The longer you're here, your room will move farther down the hall. Lua's room is the one closest to the common room."

That made sense, Baya thought. She opened the door and the girl turned to leave. "Can I at least get your name?"

"Fay."

The next thing Baya knew, she was alone in a tiny room. A single bed and a simple wooden desk lined one wall and … not much else. The walls were black stone, like everywhere else in the palace. A slender rectangular window on the far wall let in some light. In only a couple of paces Baya was peering out of it, or rather, *up* through it.

The girls' quarters were in the top part of the diamond-shaped palace. Not as high up as the Great Hall, which was in the very top but still in the upper half. So, the wall was slanted at the far end of her room and when she peered out the opening all she could see was the purple sky above.

Baya sat down hard on the bed and gripped the mattress until her knuckles turned white. She was trapped in this small dark space, unable to see out. Her mother's home was spacious and open, a place where she could always see her surroundings through numerous large windows.

Rus and Bek had always been there to reassure her, to care for her, to make her feel loved. Even her mother, in her own way, cared deeply for her. But now she was on her own.

Hate seemed to pulse through this place, from Lua all the way down to Fay. Baya's legs were telling her to run — run home. It was only just over… Baya frantically looked around.

With all the twists and turns she had taken in the palace she had no idea where home was. "What if I can't find my way out of here?" she whispered.

Pulling her knees to her chest, she sat on the bed in a tight ball. She had managed to keep her head held high during all she had been through that morning but now she dropped her forehead to her knees and rocked.

Back and Forth.

Baya didn't know how much time had passed when she finally

looked up. To her surprise there were two doors. The one she had come in and one right next to it. A closet.

She ran to it, stumbling over her gown, and threw the door open. Her trunk! Of course Rus would have packed it for her and it would have already been delivered to her room by one of Shema's theos.

There was barely enough room in the tiny closet for her wooden trunk. She opened it straight away. Her best gowns lay folded neatly inside. She hung them on hooks. As she pulled the last gown out, she noticed that the bottom of the trunk contained many objects.

One item was her favorite orange blanket that she used to always sleep with. In fact, there was a time when she couldn't sleep at all unless she had it. The trunk also contained a pillow that Bek had made. It had been his first sewing lesson. It was crude and now well-worn but it was the best pillow in the world — to Baya.

Wooden figurines, roughly resembling animals, were also included in the contents of the trunk. Rus had carved them many years ago. The paint was chipped in places as she and Bek used to play with them a lot.

Numerous scrolls were in the bottom of the trunk — many of them were the drawings she had hung on her walls back home. Plus, she found some new ones — drawings and scripts from Bek. One of the new ones contained the symbol for longing. He was telling her that he already missed her.

Baya's eyes burned with tears, as she traced the lines of the simple, yet elegant symbol. The last item was a small jar filled with a golden amber substance. It was a sticky tree-sap mixture used to fasten parchments to walls.

Perfect!

In no time, the black walls were covered with colorful scrolls. She lined the figurines on top of the desk and spread the colorful orange blanket across her bed. She took out what remained of the flowers in her hair and hung them upside down on the wall, like she'd seen Rus do with plants in his kitchen. They would dry nicely and add even more color to the bleak room.

The last touch was her pillow. It had once been a bright blue but had since faded to a greyish color. She held it to her face and inhaled deeply. It smelled of home, which was a stark contrast to this stale place.

Baya smiled with great satisfaction, as she placed the pillow on her bed and looked around her new room. Much better — livable anyway. It was not as nice as, or even close to the size of, her old room but she could feel Rus and Bek with her. Her mother and even the Unawi had once occupied this room. This offered some comfort.

This time when she looked up to the skylight, she was grateful for the light it let in.

Baya imagined that Rus was looking up at the same clear sky. She could almost hear his voice, "You can do this."

"Can I?" she asked the sky.

CHAPTER 5

The next morning Baya followed her fellow mistresses to a spacious room with long wooden tables and benches, where they were served breakfast. Dim torchlight glistened off the drab obsidian walls.

Would she ever get used to this gloomy place?

Baya sat alone and poked at her porridge with her spoon. She had no idea where to go for her lessons so she waited for what seemed like an eternity for someone to head to class.

In silence, she followed the first girls to leave the refectory.

They led her to another large room that was arranged with rows of numerous wooden benches — no tables. The ceilings were low and one wall was lined with many windows. Real windows, not skylights.

This must mean that she was in the middle of the building. The bases of the two pyramids joined to form a thick belt in the middle of the diamond-shaped palace. This allowed for normal windows that looked out over Una Sitka.

Baya immediately took a seat in the very back. As more girls trickled in, no one sat next to her. The other girls talked loudly and freely with one another and every one of them acted as if Baya was not there — which Baya was surprisingly fine with. At least they weren't being outright mean to her.

A handful of them threw balls of crumpled parchment at one another as they giggled and laughed.

When Unawi Shema entered the room the mistresses transformed into silent statues. They sat with straight backs and their hands folded in their laps, chins up. Baya glanced around and quickly emulated them.

"Praise to the Almighty Ameris," Shema greeted them.

Every girl got to her knees and raised her arms to the sky. "May She always protect us from harm and provide us with another blessed day," the mistresses chanted in unison.

Baya had barely gotten to her knees when the girls returned to their benches. She had all but missed the brief morning prayer ritual.

How embarrassing. She would have to get the hang of that.

"Older girls, go with Priestess Aga for your inflection practice. The younger girls will stay with me, for a history lesson."

One of the girls seated in front of Baya moaned. "Not another boring history class. I can't wait to learn inflection," she whispered to her friend.

Baya looked around for her mother and found her standing in the doorway. She wanted to run to her and throw her arms around her, which was something Baya had never done before.

Aga greeted Baya with a slight nod before leading the older girls out of the room.

Not even a hello, Baya thought. An icy loneliness moved through her. She supposed that it was best if Aga didn't draw attention to her. Baya tried to brush away her disappointment by turning her attention to Shema. The lonely feeling was replaced by envy, as she listened to the lovely woman. She wondered why the Unawi didn't have her pet wrapped around her today.

"The first Unawi to rule Pathins was indeed the Great Goddess Ameris herself," Shema began her lecture. "She purged this island of all predatory beasts by filling the air with smoke from her hands —

driving them into the sea. She then placed a protective shield around our land." Shema paced in front of the class.

"My priestesses and I continue this tradition by maintaining the protective shield. That is what keeps us safe from the wild and dangerous world that lies beyond Pathins." Shema eyed the class critically. "Can anyone tell me how we create the shield?"

Baya knew the answer. This was the most important part of Aga's job. But Baya was not about to open her mouth. The last thing that would help her would be to come across as a know-it-all.

"It takes a morning and an afternoon ritual. This must be performed every day." Fay's smug expression made it clear that she was proud of herself.

"That is correct. And how many does it take to accomplish this?"

"Nine," another girl blurted.

Fay glared at the girl, as her mouth had been open — no doubt Fay was about to give the answer.

"Very good. It takes eight priestesses as well as myself to accomplish this task. The safety of the entire island depends on it. That is why I keep twelve priestesses on hand at all times, in case one is absent." Shema let out a heavy sigh. "That is a luxury that I do not have. The Unawi must be present at every ritual — two times a day. And that is every day out of every year ..."

Shema shook her head. "But that is a small price to pay in the service of the Great Goddess ..."

Baya felt a twinge of pity for Shema. Being the Unawi must be difficult.

Her mind drifted as Shema preceded to cover the origin of life. She couldn't believe that this needed to be taught. Everyone knew how Ameris created life, didn't they? Aga had first taught Baya this when she was five years old. The memory flowed back ...

* * *

"WHY CAN'T I be outside with Bek?" This was how most of Baya's lessons would start.

"Your education is vastly important," Aga would say. "Now tell me what this symbol means." She pointed to a rough-drawn figure of a shapely woman on the unrolled scroll.

But Baya gazed out the window. Bek was making mud pies, while Rus tended to the garden. She longed to have her hands in the gooey mud.

"Baya! Focus."

Baya sighed and turned her attention to the scroll laid out before her. "That's Ameris's symbol."

"Very good. And who is Ameris?"

Baya moaned before answering. "The Creator of all womankind."

"Correct again. What does it say here?"

Baya struggled to make out the ancient text. "Something about women coming from … dirt."

Aga chuckled. "Yes, Ameris shaped the first women from the earth and gave them life. She created us in her own image. But the merciful Goddess didn't want her beloved daughters to be alone so she created men from the sea. You see, it says that right here." Aga pointed to the text. "From the day men were created they were meant to serve women," she read out loud.

* * *

BAYA SHOOK her head to bring herself back to the present. The backless wooden bench was uncomfortable. She forced herself to listen to the Unawi but Shema was still covering old material. At least none of it was new to Baya. A yawn threatened to give her boredom away.

It was all she could do not to move to the window. She desperately wanted to get her bearings. This place was suffocating. Baya was lost — imprisoned — in this palace and she still had no idea where her home was or how to get out of here.

Yet, she didn't dare get out of her seat for fear of drawing unwanted attention. Her mind wandered again, as she pondered inflection and what that would entail. She still had much to learn and sitting in this lecture was a waste of time.

CHAPTER 6

When Shema finally finished speaking, Baya's lower back ached from sitting on the wooden bench. She all but jumped to her feet when Shema dismissed them. The other mistresses steered clear of Baya as they left the room. She didn't know where to go or what to do next, so she followed the others, keeping her distance.

They headed back to the large eating room. As soon as the girls sat down, theos brought in large platters of food. Silverware and a plate were placed in front of Baya. The nearest girl sat at least three feet away.

Baya picked at her food. It wasn't anywhere near as good as Rus's cooking.

As soon as a couple of girls finished eating and headed out of the refectory, Baya followed after them. She remained several paces behind. Never before had she felt like she didn't belong but the feeling of being an outcast couldn't be ignored.

They led her down many different stairs and hallways. Baya tried to memorize the path. When they came to the palace entryway, Baya's heart leapt.

The gardens!

Relief flooded through her as sunshine hit her face. The clear purple sky and fresh air consumed her — instantly melting away the feeling of being confined and lost.

She wandered the gardens alone for a time. In the distance she watched a group of girls chatting away. Their merriment caused Baya's jaw to tighten, so she headed for the other side of the vast grounds.

At least she could get away from everyone — even if only for a little while.

Baya stopped to admire the blue and purple flowers with their spiky petals that jutted outward in every direction. They were by far the most beautiful thing in the garden, which was really saying something, as every plant was glorious.

Baya felt someone watching her. She turned to find the handsome garden boy staring at her. He stood twenty paces away. His head instantly lowered and he spun on his heel.

"Wait!" Baya's heart jolted as excitement consumed her. Perhaps she could find someone to talk to in this place after all.

The boy stopped immediately. He would have to do as she asked. Yet he kept his back to her.

Baya ran to him. "I'm Baya." She moved to stand in front of him.

"I … know."

Baya waited for him to offer his name but instead received awkward silence.

"What can I get for you?" he finally asked.

"Get? … I don't need anything."

He gave a stiff nod. "Then I'll be going." He sidestepped her.

"Okay, there is something …" Baya spoke quickly, anything to get him to stay.

The boy stopped again.

"Well … as you can see, I don't have any friends in this place and well … you look like you're alone."

He raised his eyebrows, waiting for her to get to the point.

"Umm …" Baya didn't know what else to say. She didn't have much experience talking to strangers.

"I'm not alone. I have Azod."

"Who's Azod?"

The boy shifted uncomfortably. "He's the head gardener … and my caregiver."

Baya exhaled, relieved that he was talking. "And he does an amazing job."

"The best in all the land," the boy's almond-shaped eyes sparkled with pride.

"Obviously." Baya looked around at their immaculate surroundings. Spotting the lovely spiky flower she pointed to it. "What's that called?"

The boy stood frozen where she had last stopped him as if he were not allowed to move unless she said so. "It's a waset."

"Thank you. See? Talking to me isn't so hard, is it?"

"Do you like flowers?" His shoulders seemed to relax a bit.

"Of course, who doesn't?"

"But you seem really interested in plants. I mean, more so than most girls."

"I would love to know more about plants. I used to spend lots of time with my mother's theo in his garden … when I was younger. That was before my schooling, back when I had more time. Anyway, I enjoyed it."

"But women don't garden."

"Well. Maybe I'll become a gardener someday." She gave a playful wave of her hand. "The first woman gardener!" Baya laughed.

For the first time, the slightest smile crossed his full lips. "That would really be something, the daughter of a priestess gardening." He pointed to a flower. "That one over there, that's a saper. And over there … those are called hanu." He appeared to like it that he knew more about something than she did.

Baya smiled at the light that shone in his honey-colored eyes. "What's that one?" She wanted to keep him talking and keep that light in his eyes.

He gave her a tour of the grounds, telling her all about the different plants. "There are two major types of plants, those valued for their beauty and those that hold purpose."

"Purpose?" Baya asked.

"You know, we make teas, medicines and spices out of them."

"Oh, right." Rus always had plants drying in the kitchen that he used to make their morning teas and as seasonings for their food. It truly was a man's work. Baya knew very little about the herbs and plants that Rus grew.

"Yet some plants are very special."

Baya looked at him with wide, interested eyes. She noticed that his breath hitched as he studied her.

"What is it?" she asked.

"It's … your eyes. They're brown … no, they're green … or gold?"

Baya chuckled. "They're actually all three colors." She cleared her throat, even though she didn't need to. "You were saying some plants are special."

He shook his head. "Oh right, because they are lovely *and* they serve a purpose or even several purposes. Like Lav." He pointed to a patch of thin stemmed plants with an elongated tuft of purple flowers on top. "Lav is ornamental and has several uses. It's most often used for its potent smell in soaps, or in fragrance bowls for the home. And it can also be used to flavor teas."

The boy continued on about the different plants for some time. Baya's head spun with all the new information. She knew she would not be able to remember all he had told her, yet she tried to take it all in.

A loud gong sounded. Baya's heart dropped into her stomach. "That must mean it's time for me to head back inside for my afternoon studies. I wish I could spend my days outside like you." She looked into his eyes. "So are you going to tell me your name?"

He appeared reluctant to pull his eyes away from hers but a boy shouldn't be so bold as to stare at a girl he'd just met.

"Vic … Vicaroy."

"Vicaroy. How unusual." She rolled the name over in her mind. It was quite a mouthful for a name. "I like it." She gave him a smile and a quick wave as she ran off. When she rounded the corner where the other girls would be, she looked back. He had not moved an inch. "Will I see you tomorrow?" she called back to him.

Vicaroy nodded and continued to stare in her direction long after she was gone.

CHAPTER 7

After meeting Vicaroy, Baya felt like she was floating high in the purple sky. She'd succeeded in making a friend, despite Lua's efforts to make sure no one talked to her. Baya's loneliness eased, or at least it seemed manageable.

The next day Baya made sure that she sat as close to the windows as possible. She studied the view until she spotted her home in the distance.

She wondered what Rus and Bek were doing.

Aga entered the room, bringing everyone to attention. Just like the previous day, Aga barely acknowledged her. Baya was not surprised this time, yet it still made her feel cold enough to shiver even though it was always warm in Una Sitka.

Baya managed to get through the morning prayer better than she had the first day.

"Today's lesson will be a review for some of you," Aga began. "But we have to make sure you all have the fundamental essentials before we can move on."

Baya stifled a moan. She knew it would be material she already knew and she would be bored to the point of going crazy — until the mid-day break where she could finally go outside. She prayed that she would get to see Vicaroy.

Aga gracefully hung two long scrolls on the wall. Sure enough, they were ones Baya had read years ago. Baya's gaze shifted to the window and she was soon lost in her own thoughts. At first, they were about Vicaroy and all the amazing plants in the garden.

Soon, her thoughts drifted home. She hoped that Bek and Rus were doing okay without her. Hopefully Tash wasn't bossing them around too much.

Baya could almost hear Tash's squeaky childish voice. "Bek, fetch me my favorite blanket," or, "Bek, I need more coloring paints," or "Bek, get me ..." Tash's needs were endless.

"Get it yourself, you lazy brat," Baya would yell. This would result in a wrestling match between the two girls. Being older, Baya could easily pin Tash to the ground.

"Mom!"

Aga would come running. "Baya! Stop that this instant and Bek, do as your sister says."

To make matters worse, Aga was always carrying on about Tash's golden hair and her beautiful blue eyes — so rare. She was simply perfect ... as far as Aga was concerned.

However, Tash's unique appearance only reminded Baya of the odd-looking man from the North who had visited them briefly a long time ago. In fact, the only other person Baya had ever seen with blues eyes and blond hair had been this stranger.

These thoughts took Baya back to the time before her sister had been born. It was one of her most significant childhood memories — when *he* came to town. She didn't remember his name, only how different he looked from the people in her household. He was tall, with pale hair that hung down past his shoulders. In fact, everything about him was pale. His skin looked sickly to young Baya. Even his eyes were pale, a watered-down shade of blue.

What surprised Baya most was her mother's reaction to the stranger. Aga's high-browed serious demeanor changed whenever he was around. Her smile turned radiant and she laughed with ease.

Before Baya knew it, the man was staying in their home.

One night she curled up on Rus's lap as she always did before bed. She sensed that something was wrong — terribly wrong. "What's the matter? You don't like that man either?"

"Women will do as they please." Rus's eyes were open, yet he saw nothing.

"Does this mean you will find a new wi, too?"

Rus snorted. "Your mother would have me castrated or at least imprisoned for life if I did any such thing."

Baya didn't know what castrated meant but she did understand what imprisoned meant. "That's not fair."

"Life's not fair ... for men." Rus tried unsuccessfully to smile down at her. "Besides I could never leave you and Bek." Rus wrapped his arms around Baya and she snuggled into his chest.

Rus was never quite the same after that and Baya had vowed that if she were ever to have a theo she would never do that to him.

The pale stranger from the North left town as swiftly and mysteriously as he had arrived. Aga appeared not to be upset about his sudden departure. She also seemed oblivious to Rus's diminished mood. He continued to meet her every need but without any of the kisses on the forehead or previous affections he had once shown her.

Not long after the stranger left, Aga's belly grew large and round once again. This time the midwife merrily announced, "Praise Ameris! It's a girl."

"Thank the Mighty Goddess," Aga breathed.

After washing the baby and wrapping her in fresh blankets, Rus handed the crying infant to Baya and quickly exited the room.

The baby was pale. Baya's first thought was that she was sick. The newborn was completely bald and she stared up at Baya with blue eyes. It might as well have been an alien. "She can't be one of us. She doesn't look anything like us," Baya said.

"Let me see her." Aga held out her arms for the baby.

Baya gently handed the newborn to her mother. She watched Aga coo over the little bundle for a time. Baya's heart was heavy and she didn't understand why.

Baya headed for the door as Aga said, "I will call her Tash."

Baya nodded solemnly and left her mother and sister alone.

* * *

BAYA VAGUELY HEARD HER NAME, jolting her back into the present. Her head snapped to the front of the classroom. "I'm sorry. What?"

Aga glared down at her. "I said, 'Are you too good for my lesson, Baya?'"

Giggles came from her classmates.

CHAPTER 8

All of Baya's classmates stared at her, their eyes full of expectation.

"No. It's not that I'm too good for your class." Baya's heartbeat drummed in her ears. "It's just ..." She looked at her mother with pleading eyes. "I need to be challenged," she implored her to understand.

Aga crossed her arms and continued to glower. "I do not allow daydreaming in my class, Baya."

Baya's body sagged like a water bladder that had just been punctured.

A tight-lipped smile crossed Aga's lips. She turned to the other girls. "Well I'm sure everyone is familiar enough with these scrolls. If, for some reason, you are not then you can study them on your own time. Now we will move on to writing. Everyone stand."

The girls instantly obeyed.

Aga raised her arms — palms facing upward. With a deep breath, she closed her eyes. Faint yellow wisps floated from her hands, like smoke but more colorful. The substance spread out around the classroom.

The sound of wood creaking filled the air. The bench in front of

Baya began to rise. Looking around she saw that half the benches in the classroom were … growing!

Aga lowered her arms and opened her eyes when the benches reached the desired height. Now there were perfect writing desks in front of the students.

Baya bent down to examine what was now a desk in front of her. Each of the legs had been extended with an amber substance. It glistened like it had shiny metal flakes inside. "It's lovely," she whispered.

She tapped on the new part of the leg with her fingernail. It was hard but it wasn't stone or wood. It was something else entirely, a foreign substance. "Where does the new part of the leg come from?"

Aga sat down as if she needed to rest. "It comes from inside us. We make it, perhaps it is like how we form a baby or how a spider produces endless webbing."

"I can't wait until I can do that," one of the girls whispered.

Wow, Baya thought.

"It's called the Creation of Matter," Aga said. "It's one of the most advanced skills that you will master in the years to come. Well, most of you anyway. Now, take a blank scroll from the pile."

A number of girls moved toward the stack of parchment at the front of the room.

"Not with your body. Using your feet is the easy way. Use your minds instead. Levitating objects with your thoughts is much more difficult. Baya, you first."

Baya's stomach churned, even though she had done this before with other light objects. A scroll should be easy enough to summon. She took a deep breath.

What if I can't do it? Baya thought. People will say, "The daughter of Aga can't even lift a parchment with her powers."

"Clear your mind," Aga instructed.

Baya's gaze narrowed as she focused on the stack of paper. The room disappeared around her until only the parchment remained. The top piece shot toward Baya. She had to duck so that it wouldn't hit her in the face.

Chuckles rippled through the class.

"Nice concentration. Lots of power. You'll need to work on your control," Aga lectured.

Baya bent down to pick up her parchment by hand.

"Who's next?" Aga asked.

"Me. Me." Fay said. She gave a mocking glance to Baya before she turned to the stack. The paper gently floated into the air, crossed the room and landed squarely in front of Fay.

"Very impressive, Fay. That is how it is done." Aga said. "Next."

Some of the older girls lifted the scrolls to their new desks with apparent ease. Most of the students could lift the paper with their minds but Aga had to help a couple of them steer it toward their desks. Another girl sent pages flying all over the room. This brought about much laughter, while Aga re-stacked them into a neat pile by using her thoughts. One girl struggled to lift the paper at all. Baya had the feeling that Aga finally did it for her.

"Which of the ancient texts should we copy?" Fay asked, once everyone had paper in front of them.

"You can copy any text you choose or if you'd rather, you may write whatever you wish," Aga said.

Fay's mouth fell open. "Pardon me, High Priestess, but are you saying that we can ... write freely?"

"Yes. I am."

"We can write home or even a letter to friends?" another girl asked.

Aga briefly glanced at Baya. "That's what I'm saying but don't grow accustomed to it."

Baya smiled. She was sure her mother was doing this for her. Aga was intentionally giving her a chance to write to Rus and Bek — completely changing the curriculum for Baya. Writing home should be done in one's free time and studying the religious texts should be done in class. Yet here Aga was letting them write about whatever they desired.

Fay giggled with the girl sitting next to her. They were most likely glad for the break from another boring lecture.

In no time, Baya had the parchment covered. She thanked Rus and Bek for packing her stuff in her trunk. She described her new room and talked about how none of the girls liked her. She almost mentioned Vicaroy but stopped herself. The time flew by and she gave her parchment to her mother when they were dismissed for the midday meal. Not only would Aga have to deliver it to Rus and Bek but she would also have to read it to them.

Well, Bek could read most of it but Aga didn't know that. In the margins Baya had drawn a couple secret symbols that only Bek would understand. Their own "language." Aga would think they were meaningless doodles but Bek would know better. Baya chuckled to herself, as she headed for the door.

"Wait a minute, Baya," Aga said.

Baya reluctantly turned around. She was overly anxious to get outside — to see the garden boy. She sighed.

"In your room tonight work on controlling your powers. You can do better."

"Okay. Yeah, sure." Baya looked at the door. Most all the others had already left.

"Baya, this is serious. You saw the girl today who could barely lift the paper?"

Baya narrowed her eyes. "What about her?"

"This is her second year and she will not make it."

"What do you mean, she won't make it?"

"In your seventh year, each of you will go through a series of trials."

Now she had Baya's full attention. "What trials?"

"They will test your abilities to the fullest and if you don't pass you're ... out."

"Out?"

"Yes and that girl will not even be allowed to go through the trials. She will never be a part of the priesthood, let alone become Unawi. I have known of girls whose skills seemed up to standard, yet they did not pass the tests. You can't afford to be mediocre and survive."

"Survive?" Baya whispered.

"I mean, graduate to a powerful position in society." Aga searched Baya's eyes for confirmation that she fully understood.

That familiar pressure was back, threatening to crack Baya's tiny base, like the one the palace sat atop. Baya swallowed hard and nodded.

"Good. You must practice every spare second."

"Yes, Mother."

"You are to call me High Priestess."

Baya's shoulders slumped. "Yes, High Priestess."

"Hang in there, Baya. Some lessons will be boring for you but you'll learn many great things in the years to come."

Baya nodded. Her mother was always serious but this was a whole new level of intensity. Her knees felt week as she pondered what these trials might entail. Surely they were not life-threatening … were they?

CHAPTER 9

Baya stopped in the refectory to grab a quick snack before she headed to the garden. As she reached for a bag of nuts she overheard one of the girls saying, "Did you see Aga get mad at her own daughter — 'Are you too good for my lesson, Baya?'"

This was followed by a course of girlish laughter.

"Yeah and Aga was *so* disappointed when Baya's paper went flying across the room completely out of control."

More laughter.

Baya knew that they were talking loudly on purpose, so that she was sure to hear them. She snatched the bag of nuts off the table and left. Her head swam with thoughts of failing tests and ... what had really happened in class that morning? Baya didn't think she had disappointed her mother. In fact, her mother may have changed the entire class for her.

Baya's brow was furrowed with worry as she stepped into the garden. She stopped in her tracks when an overwhelming feeling hit her. She could all but hear a voice, a woman's voice. It whispered, *None of that matters.*

She glanced back at the high palace doors and over her head to the monstrous building above. It didn't matter what other people thought. And those petty girls certainly didn't matter.

Not even what your mother thinks matters. The thought popped into Baya's head as if it, too, came from someone else. She was not completely convinced that this last part was true. Nevertheless, she felt free and the lovely garden helped her to forget her troubles. She could think more clearly out here.

The wrinkle in her brow disappeared as she took in the fresh air. She set out at once for the other side of the garden, away from where the other students gathered.

Vicaroy waited for her on a stone bench. Baya's face brightened when she saw him. She ran to close the distance and plopped herself down beside him.

He sat with one arm across the back of the bench and rested a foot on his knee. Baya was glad to see that he seemed relaxed. He was not as guarded as he had been when she first tried to talk to him.

"What's your favorite flower?" Vicaroy said by way of greeting.

"The … what's it called. The wa …"

"The waset. I knew it."

"How did you know that?"

"It's the flower you're most interested in. You pause at the waset bush the longest and it's the first flower you asked me about yesterday."

Had he been watching her — studying her every move? The thought made her cheeks hot. She was sure they turned a shade of purple.

Vicaroy swiftly moved to the nearest waset bush. He reached for the large purple and blue flower.

"No!" Baya almost shouted when she realized what he was doing.

"What's the matter?" he said.

"You can't pick one of Shema's flowers."

Vicaroy chuckled. The sound of his happiness made Baya tingle inside.

"That's odd because I do it all the time," he said.

"You do?"

"Sure. Azod and I harvest the purposeful plants and we make bouquets for Shema almost daily. Of course, she would be upset if someone picked all the waset flowers or dug up the entire bush. Heck, that would make me mad. But one flower doesn't hurt anything." He plucked the flower and handed it Baya. "You can use it to decorate your drab black walls."

That was exactly what Baya would do with every colorful flower he would give her.

* * *

MONTHS PASSED and Baya tolerated her studies. The only bright point in her life was her limited free time, which was spent outdoors with Vicaroy, not practicing, as her mother urged. He was the only thing that added any joy to her life, well that and the thought of the upcoming holiday.

The time of No Moons was quickly approaching. This was also Bek's birthday. She couldn't wait! She'd already drawn him some pictures for his room. It would also be a relief to get out of the drab palace and be in her normal room with real windows.

The three days before the night of No Moons and the three days afterward were a time for family and prayer. This meant that Baya had seven full days at home. There would be a large feast held at Aga's home on the night of No Moons. Neighbors, friends and family would join in the celebration. This was Baya's favorite time of year.

At the start of the sacred holiday, Aga walked Baya home after the day's lessons. Baya ran circles around her mother, whose slow pace seemed designed to annoy her daughter.

"Come on. I can't wait to get home." Baya laughed as she ran ahead.

"Slow down," Aga hollered after her.

Baya's first sight when she ran into her home was Tash and Bek hovered over a scroll together. Baya's mouth fell open with a sharp inhale — her excitement instantly vanished.

"Baya!" Tash stood and ran to embrace her.

Baya's body went rigid when her sister wrapped her arms around her. She had never hugged Tash before and she wasn't about to start now.

Why was she happy to see Baya? What was her game? She must want something. "What were you two doing?"

Bek was next to hug Baya. This time Baya returned the gesture even though she was no longer in the mood for affection. She felt betrayed, replaced, irrelevant.

"What were you two doing?" Baya repeated with more emphasis.

"Well, after you left, it was just me and Bek. Rus is always so busy, you know. So we often study together. You were right, Bek *is* really smart. You taught him well. Sometimes he even teaches me a thing or two."

Baya's two younger siblings giggled when they looked at each other. This made Baya want to scream. It was supposed to be Baya's secret with Bek. It was her job to teach him, not Tash's.

Tash appeared to be oblivious to Baya's disapproving scowl. "Bek even taught me about your made-up symbols — very clever," Tash beamed.

Baya's hand flew up to cover her stomach, as if Tash had just punched her in the gut. "Bek, those were supposed to be our secret, just between us. Why would you tell her?" Baya felt tears well in her eyes.

Aga entered the room with Rus in tow.

Tash quickly rolled up the scroll on the table. "Fetch me some water, Bek." She gave Bek a quick wink as he hurried off.

Baya wanted to yell at Tash, *You can't steal him from me. He's my brother not yours*. Baya scarcely recognized the error in her logic. They were all Aga's children, after all. But this didn't matter. It had always been Baya and Bek against Tash. Tash was an outsider. She didn't belong here; well, in Baya's mind anyway.

Now she was the outsider. This thought came with a sharp pain in the stomach. Baya choked the tears back. All because she had to be away at that stupid school, sitting through endless lessons that she already knew. Now she was being forgotten about at home — replaced.

Baya considered telling Aga what Tash and Bek were doing but that would only get Bek in trouble — big trouble, as in grounded to his room for life.

"Baya! You look like you've grown a foot since I saw you last." Rus moved to give her a welcome home embrace.

But Baya moved around him and stormed out of the room, she could no longer keep the tears from falling. She couldn't let her mother see her cry — the ultimate sign of weakness and vulnerability — not acceptable for a woman or even a mistress.

"Baya. What's wrong?" Rus called after her. He looked to Tash for clarification but she shrugged, not knowing the answer.

Baya shut herself in her room. It was cleaner than she had left it — Rus always kept the house tidy — but otherwise it was just the same as always. The first thing she did was gaze out her window at the black-diamond palace in the distance. She wondered what Vicaroy was doing. A weak smile crossed her lips. Walking in the garden with him was always so pleasant.

She shook her head at the irony. It was strange how everything had changed in a hand-full of months. Baya had thought she wanted to be home more than anything but now that she was here, she wanted to be at school. Well not in class, but in the lovely royal gardens.

More tears fell as she thought of her time spent playing and laughing with Vicaroy. Then it turned to sobbing as she thought of her brother. She pictured him spiraling further and further away. Every time she would return home he would be more distant until he no longer needed her or missed her.

Baya was utterly stuck between two worlds and she belonged in neither of them.

A soft knock came at the door. "Baya, can we talk?"

She thought about telling Rus to go away. Which he would do if she ordered it. Then the worst thought of all came to her, What if Rus loved Tash more than her? She swung the door open and threw her arms around Rus. He was the only person she could cry in front of. And that's what she did.

When the tears stopped they were sitting on the edge of her bed. Rus had an arm around her shoulders and she lay her head on his tear-stained shirt.

"Now. What's going on? Are the girls at school mean to you?"

"They don't even talk to me but that's not the problem."

Rus waited patiently for her to continue when she was good and ready.

"It's just that … Bek and Tash have grown close and I have to be away and …"

"Ah. I see. You feel like you are no longer wanted."

"You and Bek are fine without me."

"We missed you so much, more than you know. Change can be hard but no matter how much time we are apart our love for you will never fade."

"What if I were gone for an entire year?"

"We'd still love you just the same."

"What about twenty years?" This seemed like an eternity to Baya.

"Even then. No matter how much time passes or how far you go, and you will go far, our love will never waver, not even a smidge."

Bek slowly stuck his head around the corner, peering into Baya's room from the doorway. "Baya, are you okay?"

His genuine concern caused Baya to smile through the tears. She held out her arms and he ran to give her a hug.

Rus wrapped his arms around them both. "It's wonderful to have you home, Baya."

* * *

DOWN IN THE STUDY, Tash frowned at the scrolls spread out before her. "Mama, why does Baya hate me?"

Aga looked at Tash with raised eyebrows. "Don't be silly. Baya doesn't hate you." As usual, Aga "fixed" everything with a simple dismissal.

CHAPTER 10

During Baya's second year, Lua passed her trials and received her call to the Priesthood. To Baya's relief she was stationed in a neighboring region. She was to join the leaders there. Some of the girls tried to befriend Baya, since Lua was no longer there to stop them.

However, Baya's trust had been permanently destroyed. They had already proven themselves to be terrible friends. Many of them were petty and mean to one another in deceptive ways. Baya had seen enough her first year to know that she wanted nothing to do with them. The only peer she trusted in this place was Vicaroy.

As usual, Baya grabbed her mid-day meal to go.

"Oh, come on Baya," Fay said. "Why won't you sit with us instead of running off to the garden?"

"Thanks but I'll pass."

"We won't bite. Remember I was nice to you on your first day."

"Yeah, thanks for showing me to my room." That was all Fay had done. She hadn't stood up to Lua like a true friend should. Baya had seen enough of Fay the past year to know that she did "bite." She loved to play games, only being nice when it suited her and turning on her "friends" at a moment's notice. Not to their face, of course. Baya knew better than to fall for Fay's nice act.

Baya bounded out the door with her lunch in her hands but not before she overheard Fay …

"She's so weird."

The girls around Fay laughed.

Baya rolled her eyes. The only reason Fay was "nice" to anyone was if she thought they might be of use to her. As the daughter of Aga and showing promise with her powers, Baya might be a good ally to have. She imagined herself becoming Unawi and Fay telling her, "Remember all those times I was kind to you. I tried to be your friend."

"Yeah, only to stab me in the back the second I turn around," Baya said under her breath.

* * *

BAYA SEARCHED for Vicaroy in their usual secluded spots in the garden. He was nowhere to be found. He always waited for her at this time. Disappointment caused her to sit down hard on the bench where they often meet.

What if he didn't want to see her anymore? What if he'd grown bored of their visits? What would she do then? It was uncomfortable to admit how much she needed his company.

Baya shook her head. Don't be stupid. He's just busy … or something.

Baya headed for Vicaroy's tiny home on the far side of the garden. It rested against the tall rock wall that divided the palace from the rest of Una Sitka.

Azod, Vicaroy's caregiver, answered the door. "Mistress." He bowed slightly and spoke cautiously.

"Hello. Have you seen Vicaroy?" Baya asked.

Azod frowned. He opened the door wider to reveal Vicaroy washing dishes. "I'm headed out to get supplies."

"Bye," Baya and Vicaroy said in unison.

Vicaroy dried his hands with a towel. Baya was relieved to see the light dance in his eyes. As always, he was happy to see her. Her insecurities melted away.

"I'm glad you found me," Vicaroy said. "I had too much to do here today to meet you in the garden." He ran his hands through his short curly hair. "Sorry about that. Azod said the house is filthy. It's overdue for a good cleaning so I have to spend the day working inside." He shook his head. "I hate it."

Vicaroy moved a pile of clothes so Baya could sit. "Sorry the place is such a mess. We don't spend a lot of time in here. Azod and I prefer to be in the garden and neither of us are good housekeepers."

Without a woman around who expected a clean home and food on the table, they could be more relaxed with household chores. "I don't need to sit. I can help you. Besides, it seems like I sit all the time."

"You're willing to do house chores?"

"I help you in the garden sometimes. Why not here?"

"Okay, if you're sure. It's boring and not work for a woman. Especially one of your status."

Baya gave him a playful grin. "Well luckily I'm not a woman yet."

They both laughed.

Vicaroy handed her a well-worn rag. "You can dust while I finish cleaning the kitchen."

She moved to a cluttered shelf and began organizing the jars and wiping them down. "You know, I get the feeling that Azod doesn't like me."

"I don't think it's that. He doesn't even know you. Not like I do. He thinks that it's strange that we're such good friends."

"Why is that so strange?"

"Boys and girls aren't usually friends."

"And why is that?"

"We're too different. Girls usually get along with other girls better and it's the same with boys — I guess."

Baya's brow furrowed. "Then I wonder why we get along so well?"

"You're not like the other girls in this place."

"Are you implying that I'm like a boy?"

"No." He chuckled. "Well ... yeah. I guess you kind of are." He gestured to her scrubbing the shelf.

They both laughed. Then Vicaroy's expression turned serious. "Azod doesn't think I should spend time with you."

"Why?"

"He says that women are complicated and that they don't treat us well. He wants me to stay away from all girls until I'm much older and ... until one chooses me to be her theo."

"Then you would have to wait on her all the time and take care of her kids."

"Not the life I want." Vicaroy kicked the leg of a table in frustration. "Azod thinks that our friendship will only lead to trouble — for me."

"What kind of trouble? I would never do anything to hurt you."

"I know. That's what he doesn't understand. And as long as you want to see me then there's not much he can do about it."

"Right." Baya bit her lip. "It's not like he could tell a mistress what to do."

"I want to show you something. But you can't tell anyone."

"Of course." She never spoke to anyone about her time with Vicaroy. It wasn't like she had anyone else to talk to here, anyway.

Moving to the small fireplace he arranged a handful of straw into a pile.

"Do you need me to light that?" Baya held up her hand.

"No. I don't. That's the trick I want to show you." He picked up a small black stone, not unlike the black stones that made up so many of the buildings in Una Sitka, including the palace. Taking a larger gray stone in the other hand, Vicaroy held them both close to the straw. He struck the black stone against the gray one.

There was a spark of light and Baya's mouth fell open.

He blew on the straw. The gray smoke sprang to life as it turned into red flames. Eventually he placed some sticks on his small crackling fire.

"That's amazing! How did you do it?" She had never thought about how men living alone would start a fire. Vicaroy's household was rare. After all, men need women to take care of them.

"Not just any stones work. I accidentally discovered that if you strike this stone really hard," he held up the black stone, "it creates a spark."

"Wow. It's like magic."

"I almost burned a tree down when I first discovered it. It was a long time ago when I was playing in the garden. Azod told me not to tell anyone. He said that Shema would be angry if she knew I could start a fire."

Baya's eyes widened. "Shema would banish you. Or worse imprison you. The old scrolls told stories of men who could do such things, not from their own powers within but by using tricks like this. Ameris condemned them, calling them evil-deeds."

Yet, this didn't seem evil to Baya. There was something … natural about it. You simply hit two stones together and sparks appeared. Okay, so it was strange, but not evil.

"That's why you can't tell *anyone*." Vicaroy's eyes pleaded with Baya.

"No! I would never do that." Baya's eyes shone bright. "Can you show me again?"

CHAPTER 11

The mistresses that were Baya's age talked excitedly over one another. One girl fanned herself with a piece of parchment, even though it wasn't an overly hot day. Fay spoke to her friends, waving her arms about with more exaggeration than usual. Her audience giggled with anticipation. They, like Baya, couldn't wait for their first inflection lesson.

The wooden doors to the classroom creaked on their hinges as they opened. This caused the girls to fall silent. The Unawi entered the room but this time she wasn't alone. Her creepy pet was wrapped around her.

After the brief morning prayer ritual, Shema said, "Baya, come to the front of the class."

Baya dragged her feet as she made her way toward Shema. She dreaded having everyone's eyes on her.

"The ability to inflect allows us to read the minds of simple creatures." Shema gestured to the giant insect resting on her shoulder. "This is Doba. Some of you may have seen him in the Great Hall. He will be kind enough to help us with our lesson today." She scratched under his chin.

The insect made a clicking noise and leaned into her touch.

"Ameris was powerful enough to read people's minds, as if they were talking out loud. But I have never known anyone with such powers as Hers." Shema turned to Baya who had been trying not to fidget nervously while she waited for further instruction. "Look deeply into Doba's eyes. And don't be shy." She took Baya by the shoulders and pulled her uncomfortably close. "He is harmless."

Baya couldn't help but arch her back away from them. She didn't like her space invaded especially by such a large bug. Many girls in the class chuckled at Baya's discomfort.

"You can do this," Shema whispered.

With a quick awkward glance at Shema, Baya turned to stare into the large round eyes of the creature. All four of them bulged with expectation. Their solid blackness seemed empty.

"Now reach out —"

Baya jerked her head toward Shema in alarm. "You mean I have to touch it?"

"With your mind. Look him in the eyes and reach out with your powers, not your hand. It's similar to lighting a fire or creating smoke. Feel the power radiate outward from inside you and reach into Doba's mind."

Doba shifted anxiously on Shema's shoulder as if he were eager to "speak" to someone new.

Baya focused on hearing the creature. It took a couple heartbeats before she heard it, a voice, clear as day. She looked around to confirm that the other girls hadn't heard anything.

"That's it. Now tell us what he says," Shema prompted.

"He says ..." Baya no longer wanted to look away from the beady eyes. Instead she felt like she might fall into them. They no longer appeared empty but rather, infinite — bottomless.

She wanted to know what he was trying to tell her. There was a sense of importance to his words. She narrowed her eyes in concentration. The voice was faint and raspy. "He wants to find a mate. He worries that he is the only one left of his kind. He's kept in captivity primarily for these lessons and he wishes every day for —"

"That is quite enough, Baya. Very well done. You may take your seat." Shema scratched Doba's chin and whispered. "You're in a mood, now aren't you. You had better behave, Doba."

Baya stared wide-eyed at the creature. She didn't want to break the connection.

Doba made the clicking noise again and was completely distracted from his previous outburst. *Oh, that feels good! Please don't stop,* he said or thought — that's what Baya heard anyway.

But Shema did stop scratching his chin. "Who's next? Doba is quite intelligent, he will change his thoughts for each of you, so you can all practice reading them."

Baya wanted to take the creature in her arms, long scaly body and all, and steal him away. All he wanted was to be free to find a mate. Although Baya had no idea why that was so important. Maybe he was lonely and just wanted a friend — someone like him. Shema knew that the poor thing hated being stuck on her shoulder all the time and yet she didn't care.

Baya reluctantly took her seat and she scowled at Shema as the next girl tried to read Doba's thoughts. There must be a way to free him. She wondered if she could talk to him in return. What about other animals? Could she talk to them as well? Animals were not easy to come by on the island. Shema's pet was rare. The only creatures that remained were the ones humans ate. Maybe Baya didn't want to know what they were thinking, after all.

AT THIRTEEN, Baya had grown taller than most of the other girls but she still had no curves to her thin frame. At the morning meal mistresses were given an infusion, the women's brew. This was a tea that females drank every morning once they came of age. Baya was still served milk with her meal, the same as a couple of new eleven-year-olds.

The women's brew contained special herbs that prevented the Great Goddess from forming a new life inside a woman. Unawi were to drink this tea every morning until their reign ended. Their duty was to serve Ameris and the people. They could not afford to be distracted by children of their own.

Young mistresses could not risk having a child, as that disqualified them from being in the running for Unawi. So the girls were careful to drink the infusion each day.

Fay eyed Baya's milk. "I wonder when you'll finally be given the women's brew."

"Maybe when she's eighteen," another girl offered.

"Or maybe never. You might be shapeless and scrawny your whole life." Fay and her friends laughed.

Baya slammed her cup down. Her chair screeched across the stone floor as she stood to leave the refectory.

"Oh, come on Baya. Have a little fun. We're just messing with you," Fay called after her.

And they wonder why I don't want to be their friend, Baya thought.

* * *

THE MISTRESSES WERE NOT ONLY TAUGHT how to use and control their powers. As the future leaders of Pathins, they were also taught about the politics of the island. Shema looked weary as she explained to her students the troubles of the land.

"Overpopulation is the greatest problem that we face today," Shema began.

One of the younger girls raised her hand.

Shema nodded for her to speak.

"The island doesn't seem crowded to me. There's lots of wide-open land that doesn't have any people living on it."

"That is correct. The island is not completely covered with people. What is meant by overpopulation is that all fertile farmlands, vast as they may seem, are straining to produce enough food for the population that we do have." Shema sighed. "It takes a lot of land to sustain people."

Shema began to pace in front of the class. "This is a problem unique to this time. In the past, this vast island had always provided more than enough for us. Over the past couple of decades we have seen an increase in the number of baby boys who are thrown into the sea. Some argue that this is fitting, as that is where men came from." Shema shook her head in despair before continuing.

"Less fortunate families are finding it difficult to feed their daughters — let alone their boys. Boys are too much of a bane for a poor family, so they are given back to Ameris — to the sea from where they came."

Baya thought back to when Bek was a tiny baby in her arms. Boys were being killed! The thought made her breakfast rise from her stomach and catch in her throat. Aga always treated Bek as if he were a burden, even though she could easily afford to house and feed him.

What if Mother had been poor? Baya shivered at the thought. Her heart felt like a stone in her chest — an intruder inside her body. Killing babies was wrong, no matter if they were boys or girls. Ameris wouldn't give them to women if she wanted them dead.

Baya looked at Fay who appeared bored. Fay had stopped listening. She obviously didn't care about baby boys so she had let her mind wander.

"Excuse me Madam Unawi," Baya raised her hand.

Shema nodded, indicating she could speak.

"What's being done about overcrowding?"

"Every year overpopulation becomes more of a problem," Shema said. "More people go hungry and more babies die. So a couple of years back I passed a law that only the high priestesses are allowed to have children. I presented this law with a rather clever speech that Aga helped me compose. I stated that this new law was an honor for the women of Pathins, as they were to become like the Unawi — they too were to remain childless in service to the Goddess."

Baya had never seen Shema look so full of sorrow.

"Yet," Shema went on, "babies continued to be born. So the women's brew is put into every watering well across Pathins, except for the royal wells here, at the palace. If a priestess wishes to have a child then she is to drink only from my wells."

Shema tried, unsuccessfully, to smile. "As you all know, I myself and you mistresses are given our tea each morning to prevent pregnancy."

"So this worked?" Baya asked. "Putting the brew in the water has stopped women from having children."

"Yes ... Well, we thought this would solve the problem and in a way, I suppose it has. Women are no longer giving birth. However, the masses are not pleased — the desire to have a daughter is a strong one. Believe me I know..." Shema scowled at the floor. "For the first time in the long history of this island we are worried about women rebelling."

Baya's mind ran away with her thoughts. The land that Ameris had given them, the Holy Land of Plenty, was no longer enough.

CHAPTER 12

Vicaroy learned how to do many unconventional things. Beyond the miracle of being a boy who could start a fire, he made other discoveries as well. His love of the water drove him to invent a long narrow raft. He could only stand on it as he paddled around, never straying far from the beach.

Baya had played around on it but was not very good at keeping her balance. After falling in the water several times, she would give up and use it as a floatation device while she swam.

Vicaroy wanted to make something that Baya could ride in as well, so he eventually abandoned the crude raft and went to work building a canoe, which could easily hold four people.

Baya didn't think his idea of a larger boat would work. Then again — back in Ameris's day — they'd had ships that could carry many people and lots of cargo. It took several sails and many men with oars to move them. But the knowledge of how to build such a vessel had been lost for a thousand years. Vicaroy had to essentially reinvent his contraptions.

Baya and Vicaroy spent the majority of their free time in a secluded cove. The place was not easy to reach. First they had to head down the well-worn path from the palace to the popular beachfront below. When it was hot and sunny — which was common in Una Sitka — the long beach would usually be crowded. The mistresses and even the high priestesses would enjoy themselves in the water and soak up the sun whenever their busy lives permitted.

At the east end of the beach rose a small mountain. What most people didn't know was that there was a trail of sorts leading up and over the mountain. The trail could only be found if you knew precisely what you were looking for. It was a serious hike, so few people ventured there — they would much rather relax on the beach. But not Baya and Vicaroy.

A large rocky wall jutted out into the sea. This prevented people from swimming to the cove on the other side of the mountain. As boats were not allowed on the island, this made walking the only way to reach the cove. There was no clear or easy path through the mountain's thick foliage, which also kept people from wandering over.

Baya and Vicaroy covered the trailhead with leafy branches. He made wooden ladders held together with twine which they used to get over some of the steepest rock faces. When they left the cove they were careful to hide the ladders under shrubs.

When Vicaroy had first shown his hideaway to Baya, she had panted breathlessly as she climbed over the last rocky wall. She found herself overlooking a wondrous sight.

Below was a small crescent-moon-shaped beach surrounded by mountains. Water fell over steep rocks and settled into a glistening pool. This was to become their favorite swimming hole, as the fresh water was preferable to the salty seawater.

On the far side of the cove sat a large cave. They would spend their time here when it rained. And this was where Vicaroy created and hid his forbidden inventions. Like the cove, the cave was not easy to reach. It required a difficult climb up a rock face that was twice the height of Vicaroy. After Baya almost fell trying to climb to the cave, he built a ladder for her.

* * *

UNLIKE BAYA, who had precious little free time, Vicaroy spent every spare second at sea. But on her days off, she would always join him. The canoe allowed them to venture even farther from the land. Still, they didn't go too far out of the cove for fear of someone seeing the clandestine boat.

Baya often marveled at how Vicaroy's brain worked, as he also crafted other things. One day he covered Baya's eyes with his hands and guided her into the cave.

When he removed his hands, Baya blinked. Leaning against the rock wall was a long smooth piece of wood with a sharp stone secured tightly to one end with twine. It resembled a crude version of a spear from Ameris's scrolls.

Her brow creased. "What do you need with that?"

"For protection, I guess. And it's fun."

"Protection from what?"

Ever since the time of the first Unawi, Pathins had been peaceful. Weapons of any kind had been banned for centuries. Physical violence was rare and the perpetrators were imprisoned at once. If it was the even-more-rare case of a man hitting a woman, he would be locked away for life. Baya had never heard of such a case occurring, not in her lifetime anyway.

Not to mention, there were no predatory animals on the island. So what could Vicaroy possibly want with such a weapon? Sure, before Ameris created Pathins the world was violent. Beasts were a constant threat and there were even wars between humans.

The scrolls spoke of advanced weapons including long knives called swords. Any such weapons had long since been melted down into goblets or other useful metal objects. Thankfully, they had no need for such armaments.

"How is it fun?" Baya asked.

"Watch." Vicaroy grabbed the spear and headed out of the cave. He threw the weapon as hard as he could at a tree trunk. The spear narrowly missed the tree. "Target practice."

Baya laughed. "Well, you need the practice."

"I've made something even better." From the back of the cave he retrieved an object wrapped in a large cloth. He uncovered a bow and two arrows. They were the most basic design. The bow was a string fastened to either end of a tree branch. The arrows each consisted of a stick with a whittled tip. Feathers were fastened to the other end.

Like Vicaroy's water-going vessels, these too were forbidden on the island and viewed as the work of pure evil. Any inventions from men were seen as insignificant compared to the powers of women. However, the weapons were the most forbidden thing on the island — relics from a violent past, proof of man's destructive and barbaric nature.

"I hate to think of what would happen if we were caught with these," Baya said.

"No one will find them here." Vicaroy pulled the bow back and aimed an arrow at the tree. It missed by at least an arm's length. He shot the second one and it hit its mark yet bounced off the tree trunk, falling harmlessly to the ground.

"Isn't it supposed to stick into the tree?" Baya asked.

Vicaroy studied the bow. "I need to make the string tighter."

"How will that help?"

"It should add more force behind the arrow when I let it go. I couldn't get the bowstring any tighter by myself but with your help … I'll bend the branch as far back as I can then you refasten the string."

Baya didn't fully understand why the string needed to be tighter but she was glad to help. She strained to secure the string as he had instructed, while he forced the branch to bend as much as possible without it snapping in two.

Vicaroy tried again. It took several more attempts before he finally hit the tree again, and this time the arrow stuck.

"It worked! You were right." Baya pursed her lips in concentration. "You know, sometimes I think boys are smarter than girls."

He laughed. "Don't let anyone else hear you say that." He readied another arrow. "It's not that we're smarter. When it comes to studies and the like we don't stand a chance. Girls are way smarter."

"It's not men's fault that they're not allowed to be educated. If they were, boys would be as smart as girls. I've seen it with my brother."

Vicaroy frowned. "I don't know about that." He let the arrow fly. "I think it's just that we understand some basic things about how the world works, that's all."

Baya thought about it. "Hmm, maybe. Like a different type of intelligence. Let me try." Baya's arm shook as she struggled to pull the bowstring back.

Vicaroy helped her. "And we're also stronger," he whispered in her ear.

Baya let go of the string. It landed in the water. Vicaroy bent over with laughter and Baya found herself rolling on the ground laughing uncontrollably.

"You see? It's not as easy as it looks," Vicaroy said.

They practiced with the bow and spear for the rest of the day.

"You're right. It is fun," Baya said, as they hid the weapons in the cave. Baya was determined to grow strong enough to shoot the bow on her own and actually hit the intended mark.

They covered up any signs that they had been there and headed home for the night.

CHAPTER 13

Baya did grow stronger — not only her body but her powers as well. She and Vicaroy became quite skilled with the bow and spear. It was their way of rebelling against the world. Their illicit fun. This kept their friendship exciting and it was a great way to pass the time — boating, throwing spears and shooting a bow in their secret cove. Baya found ways to hone her powers during these times. She felt she at least owed her mother that much. Aga had never let up when it came to pushing Baya to do better.

If she made a bad shot or throw, she would focus on the arrow or the spear and lead it toward the target with her mind.

"Hey! That's cheating," Vicaroy would claim.

"At least I didn't move your arrow away from the target."

"You wouldn't dare."

Baya gave him a mischievous smile. Yet she never messed with his arrow. She wanted him to become skilled at using the bow. Despite his best efforts, Vicaroy was never able to beat her at target practice, not with her powers as a backup.

* * *

WHEN BAYA WAS fifteen it was time for Tash to join the Unawi's school. Fay was towering over Tash when Baya came into the mistresses' common room. Baya had been in the garden with Vicaroy for as long as possible, of course. She hardly ever returned until she absolutely had to, which was just before the palace doors were sealed shut for the night.

"Look what we have here, another one of Aga's daughters," Fay was saying.

Baya stood behind Tash. "Leave her alone, Fay."

Tash turned to look at Baya with wide eyes.

Baya figured that that was how scared she must have looked on her first day.

"If you two are truly sisters, how come you look so different?" Fay asked.

"Tash is Aga's child. I was there the day she was born." Baya glared at Fay.

"Then that must mean you're the one who's not Aga's real daughter. I mean, think about it, Baya. You're tall and you have dark skin. She's short, even for an eleven-year-old and where did her yellow hair come from? Tash is nothing like you and you saw her born so that can only mean one thing. You're adopted."

"We're both Aga's so give it up, Fay," Baya snapped.

Fay turned toward her room. "Fine. I'm just saying, you might want to ask Aga about who your real mother is." Fay disappeared into her room.

"Thanks for sticking up for me," Tash gushed.

Baya sighed and headed for her room as well. "Would someone please show Tash to her room?"

"Wait, Baya. Could that be true, you know, what that girl said?"

"No." Baya stopped walking. "That's just what Fay does, she tries to make you doubt everything. She plays mind games like that. Lesson number one, ignore everything that girl says."

"So we *are* sisters, right?"

"Yeah." Baya headed for her room.

Tash's shoulders slumped. As always, she had hoped for a warmer reunion with her big sister. Tash was sure that once it was only Baya and her in school together they would finally become close. After all, Bek and Tash had become closer when it was just the two of them at home.

A couple of the younger girls stepped forward, eager to show Tash to her new room.

* * *

BAYA WAS HARD AT WORK, practicing her transformation skills. They didn't learn this skill until they were sixteen but Aga had shown her the basics and told her to practice every night. It was one of the most difficult powers to use; often taking girls a year or two to master.

Baya focused with all her might on the wooden carving of a bird on her desk. She allowed only images of fish to flow into her mind. She frowned at the carving — it was still a bird, no fish in sight.

A knock came at Baya's door.

Baya knew who it was. No one ever disturbed her and the last thing she wanted was a clingy little sister hanging around all the time. "What?" Baya said to the closed door.

Tash's blond head peered into the room. "Can I come in?"

"I'm busy."

"What are you doing?"

"Practicing."

"Oh! Can I watch?"

"No."

"Come on Baya. We're family and this is our chance to spend time together. I mean, at least we have each other in this place."

Baya sighed. "No, Tash. We don't. You need to make friends your own age." She didn't want Tash to find out about her and Vicaroy's secrets. She also wasn't about to let Tash see that she couldn't transform a simple wooden figurine.

Something had to be done to keep this nuisance away. So Baya took Tash by the shoulders, spun her around and marched her out the door. She pointed down the hall to the girls' common room. "Go find someone else to talk to."

Baya disappeared back into her room — alone — the way she liked it.

* * *

IT DIDN'T TAKE LONG for Tash to give up on Baya. After a month, they all but ignored each other. Tash made friends easily. In fact, she grew quite popular. The girls loved the strange color of her hair and eyes. Her flawless pale skin was envied by all. The other girls wanted to be just like Tash. Whatever food Tash liked, the other girls would claim it was their favorite.

One day Baya noticed that all the younger girls at Tash's breakfast table wore their hair in two long braids hanging down their backs. Baya's jaw clenched as she realized that this was how Tash always wore her hair.

"Would you all jump into a firepit if Tash did?" Baya asked as she walked by the table.

"Probably," one of the girls said.

This was followed by numerous giggles.

Baya rolled her eyes.

CHAPTER 14

It was shortly before Baya's seventeenth birthday when Shema announced to the class, "This is my favorite lesson to teach. It is one of our best-kept secrets. There are full-grown women who have not mastered this skill." Light sparkled in her dark eyes.

This got Baya's attention and half the other mistresses sat up straighter in their seats. Baya was only a year or so away from graduation and her schooling had become more intense — and interesting, as far as she was concerned.

"Today I'm going to be teaching you about the ultimate form of transformation." Shema took a step back against the black stone wall and disappeared right before their eyes.

The class came alive with gasps and many looked around in confusion for any sign of Shema.

"It is called the Transformation of Self," Shema's voice came from the front of the classroom, where she had been standing. "This skill allows you to blend into your surroundings so perfectly that you become invisible."

"I've heard rumors of women who could do this but I didn't know it was true," a mistress sitting behind Baya murmured.

"Madam Unawi." One of the student's ventured. Her voice was shaky. "We can hear you but we can't see you."

"Then I'm doing it correctly. Now gather around. If you look closely, you may be able to see the outline of my form, or part of my body."

Baya was one of the first to make her way to the front of the classroom. Yet, there remained nothing where Shema had been standing. She narrowed her eyes — still nothing. To try a different light, Baya moved away from the windows. A brief shimmer caught her attention and Baya thought she could make out the outline of Shema's shapely curves. It wavered and as soon as Baya moved, Shema fully disappeared again.

Fay, who was closest to where the Unawi was, issued a piercing scream.

Shema materialized with her hand on Fay's arm. "Sorry to startle you but you were about to step on my toe."

Baya chuckled. Fay obviously hadn't seen the vague outline of the ruler.

"Take your seats," Shema said.

Fay glared at Baya as they headed for their benches.

"It is believed that this most difficult skill to master, was of great use to our ancestors." Shema continued with the lecture. "They simply made themselves blend into their surroundings whenever wild beasts drew near. It was most likely how women survived in the wild before Ameris saved us all by leading us to the safety of this island."

Baya's foot started its nervous tapping. She hadn't mastered the Transformation of Matter yet, let alone the toughest of all skills — now she was expected to be able to transform *herself*?

"Baya, please come to the front of the room."

Baya's stomach lurched and she stifled a moan. No, she thought. Why me?

The humiliation of still not being able to transform an ink quill into a bracelet after over a year of practice came flooding back. Aga had been utterly disappointed when most of the other girls could do it, yet Baya still struggled.

Fay crossed her arms and gave Baya an amused look as she passed by on her way to the Unawi.

Baya stood taller than the Unawi ... which made her want to lower her head and slouch so that Shema wouldn't have to look up at her. Baya frowned at her own thin frame. She still had none of the womanly curves that Shema had.

"This skill requires you to feel afraid." Shema didn't seem to mind that Baya towered over her.

Baya tilted her head to the side and her brow creased in confusion.

"Think of the last time you were afraid. I mean, truly in fear for your life."

That was easy, Baya thought. Only the night before she'd had one of her nightmares about being on a wide-open plain. Knee-high yellow grass swayed at her feet, it was all that could be seen for miles in any direction. A flash of bright colors in her peripheral vision was the only warning before pain shot through her shoulder and she was knocked to the ground. This sent a fresh wave of pain through her entire body. A mouth full of long sharp teeth loomed over her as she forced herself to wake.

"Okay, I got it," Baya said to Shema.

"Now keep that memory in your mind and step against the wall. It is easier if you have a close background to blend into. Once you get better at it you won't need to be against a wall. Your body will do it naturally, no matter where you stand."

Baya took a deep breath and placed her back against the cool stone wall.

"Close your eyes. Focus on that memory of when you were most afraid."

Baya nodded with her eyes shut tight. What if she couldn't do it? Baya's heart began to pound in her ears.

"You got this."

Could Shema read her mind? Baya shook her head to help regain her focus on feeling afraid.

"With all of your feminine strength, imagine yourself disappearing so that you can get away from whatever it is that scares you most."

Again, this was easy enough. Baya wanted nothing more than to get away from the salivating mouth full of huge yellow teeth that were about to rip her throat open.

Gasps came from the students.

Baya opened her eyes.

One of the students had gotten to her feet. "She did it."

Shema clapped. "Well done."

Other girls looked around the room as if they were looking for someone.

Baya raised her hands to examine them. They were gone! Her body was too. She felt for her stomach and it was there, to the touch ... but not the eye. Her heart raced even faster and her arms slowly came into view. She exhaled with relief at the sight of her body returning.

"How did you do that so easily?" one of the girls asked.

"Yes, indeed," Shema said. "How did you do it on your first try? It takes most girls a year to master the Transformation of Self. I dare say, it took me at least six months."

Baya's pounding heart slowed at the twinkle of pride in Shema's eyes. "I just ... imagined wanting to hide myself from a wild beast that was trying to eat me."

"Wow," one of the girls murmured.

"Outstanding work. Baya, perhaps you can help to instruct the next student."

Baya nodded.

The next girl was not able to make herself disappear, nor the next. In fact, only Fay was partially successful. She was able to make her arms and legs turn to a blackish tint, somewhat blending into the wall behind her.

Baya couldn't help but give Fay a smug look as she left the class.

CHAPTER 15

There was nothing special about this particular morning as Aga headed into work. She greeted Shema with the usual kiss to her cheek.

"I have great news." It looked like Shema was about to jump out of her own skin. "I received a calling from Ameris last night. It is time for Baya's tests."

Aga's face fell as she processed the information. "That can't be. Baya will not be eighteen for seven more months. I still have lots of time … time to finish preparing her."

"I'm afraid not, Ameris's message was clear. Baya is ready. She will begin the trials in one week."

Aga's heart pounded against her ribcage. She placed a hand over her forehead as it began to throb, hoping this might ease the painful sensation. "That's not enough time. I need more than that to work with her. She's too young. We have never tested a mistress before her eighteenth birthday."

"I know!" Shema beamed. "This can only mean one thing. Ameris is ready to name the next Unawi and that must be Baya. She is powerful and wise, there is no mistress better suited to become ruler. She is ready to take my place."

Aga tried not to scowl at Shema for being so jubilant about this. "And you are still young enough to retire to a quiet mountain villa and finally raise daughters of your own." For the first time in the many years she had served Shema, Aga questioned the Unawi's motives. Was this Ameris's will, or simply Shema's desire to finally have children?

"Yes, you know that is my dream."

Aga rubbed her forehead again.

"Aga, Dear, don't worry. Baya is as ready as any student to ever come through this school. She will do fine."

"Are you certain of this?"

"Yes. Ameris would not have been so adamant that it is time for her to move forward if she was not ready."

"Ameris told you that Baya will survive?"

"Of course." Shema lied. She trusted the Great Mother and hoped that she would not call a mistress early to the trials unless she would make it through the grueling tests … alive. Yet Ameris's motives could be difficult to understand. The Goddess often worked in mysterious ways. Shema's vision had only made it clear that it was time for Baya's trials. There had been no guarantee of Baya's survival.

"This can't be. Baya has not even mastered the Transformation of Matter."

Shema frowned. "What?" This came out sharper than she had intended. "But she did better than any student ever has with the most difficult task — Transformation of Self."

"I know, but when she tries to Transform things that are not herself she still struggles. It can take too long or she transforms things into unintended matter. Like the quill becomes a knife instead of a bracelet."

Shema pursed her lips and tapped them with her index finger. "I was not aware of this. Her performance in my classes is unparalleled." Shema bit her lip. "Perhaps I should work with her, she may respond better to my instruction."

Aga didn't refrain from her glare this time. "She is *my* daughter and I will make sure she is ready. I have no time to waste." Aga headed for the girls living quarters. "Would you be so kind as to have another priestess fill in for me at the morning protection rituals?" Aga didn't wait for an answer.

* * *

FAY HAD TAKEN the final tests recently and passed with great skill. She was expected to get her calling from the Great Goddess any day. Fay also took every opportunity to fill Baya with fear over the upcoming tests.

"I honestly thought they were trying to kill me," Fay would muse. She was not allowed to discuss any of the details about the series of trials. Not that she would have anyway. Fay was not about to give Baya any insights that might help her to get through them.

Aga rarely left Baya's side. Baya had no free time to hike to her and Vicaroy's secret cove. Aga pushed her to train every waking moment in preparation for the three tasks that awaited her. Baya had to beg to get one hour of free time. If she could convince her mother such a break would be beneficial, she would rush out of the palace and into the garden.

Vicaroy was sure to stay nearby so he wouldn't miss her in the evenings, on the off chance that she could get away.

Baya didn't mind this so much because it meant that her tedious schooling would be over soon and she would no longer be a mistress but a wi, a full-grown woman. And with this would come many more freedoms. She would have much more time to spend with Vicaroy. Baya could come and go as she pleased. She would not have to be inside the palace every night at curfew. This also meant that she could go home whenever she wanted. These were the thoughts that kept her going throughout this hellacious week.

Vicaroy stayed busy as well. He was hard at work on the construction of a new invention, his greatest one yet. He couldn't wait to show Baya.

They were both looking forward to a wonderful future together. Soon, nothing would stand in their way ... or so they thought.

CHAPTER 16

The day before Baya's trials were to start, Aga placed her hand on Baya's shoulders and squeezed — a little too hard. "Your entire life has been about preparing for three critical tests. They are designed to assess your mastery over your powers." Aga's eyes seem to pierce Baya. "You will be pushed to your limits. This is how you will prove that you are worthy of the Priesthood. Only mistresses who can survive the tests are deemed brave enough and wise enough to become rulers."

Somehow, Aga's penetrating stare grew even more intense. "When you are … in the trials, remember that all the Priestesses and Unawis of the past have succeeded. No matter what you may think, the tasks are not impossible. You are not yet eighteen but I'm confident that you're ready. In fact, Shema feels the same. You will make it through."

Baya's brow furrowed. This sounded serious, as in life or death. Her mother was throwing around words like, "survive" and "make it through." What was with the strong language? Of course, passing was important but Aga made it sound like Baya might *die* if she couldn't get through them. Surely she was being melodramatic or perhaps overprotective.

Fay's words crept into her thoughts, "They tried to kill me." A hollow dread formed in Baya's stomach.

Aga, like everyone else, wasn't allowed to give Baya any details about what she was to face. The tests had been the same for centuries and no one ever spoke about them in more than general terms.

* * *

BEING one of the oldest girls, Baya's room was now close to the common room. Aga woke her as the first sun rose. Even before Baya was awake enough to remember what day it was, she knew something was different, as her mother had never been to her room before.

"Are you ready to take the first step to becoming a woman?" Aga's tight-lipped expression showed her worry.

Baya's stomach lurched. "I don't know. Maybe being a mistress isn't so bad after all."

Aga gave a nervous chuckle.

This did nothing to help put Baya at ease.

Baya and Aga joined the other priestesses and the Unawi, who were waiting outside the girls living quarters. They would escort Baya to her first trial. She envied the other students who were still fast asleep.

An entire entourage, just for her, Baya thought, as the gravity of the situation hit her.

Their solemn expressions and complete silence caused Baya's hands to tremble. She wondered why they were all wearing long black robes. They looked like they were going to a funeral. Had someone died and the test been postponed? Surely they would have told her if someone had died. She swallowed hard.

Baya felt some relief when she saw that they were leading her out of the palace — to the garden. The garden was the safest place on the planet. But before they exited the base of the palace. Shema moved to the far end of the room. With a wave of her hand three rows of the thick stones in the floor fell away. They formed perfect stairs leading downward. The stones that were once the floor now formed the top of a much longer staircase.

Baya's heart sank. This place had a dungeon? She studied the dark passage. The bottom could not be seen.

Shema gestured for Baya to lead the way.

Baya stifled a whimper. She had never been below ground before. An intense feeling of being trapped took over before her foot touched the first stair. She fought against the sense of doom that increased with every stair she descended. It was only Fay and her lies, creeping into Baya's mind to scare her.

Don't listen to Fay and don't be a coward, Baya scolded herself.

The High Council followed behind Baya in single file. It soon grew too dark to see.

"Is there a torch or something?" Baya asked.

"It is your job to light the way." Shema's voice was serious.

Of course, Baya thought, as she created a fire ball in the palm of her hand. Even with the light all she could see were stairs in front of her, still no bottom.

They eventually led to a small room with a door on the far side and a metal hatch in the floor — nothing else. The walls were made of large tan stone blocks.

The small room was crowded once all the women reached the floor. Baya was instructed to stand next to the hatch. She couldn't take her eyes from the small round door. What could possibly be under this room?

With a wave of Shema's hand, the metal hatch opened upward.

Baya reluctantly looked into the hole in the floor. It was too dark to make out much. She thought she caught a glimpse of a shimmering liquid but she was not sure. It looked like a solid black hole.

The priestesses surrounded her and chanted in prayer. Baya felt like a sacrificial offering. She had been taught that live-sacrifices to Ameris no longer happened. She hoped that this was true.

When the prayers ended. Shema nodded to Aga.

Aga stepped forward. For a long moment Aga's eyes desperately searched Baya's face. "I'm sorry, Madam Unawi. I can't do it."

Shema nodded to another of the priestesses, Baya thought it was Fay's mother but she wasn't sure because as the woman stepped forward she shoved Baya into the abyss. Baya quickly turned her attention to where she was going and not on which one of the cloaked figures had pushed her.

Freezing, wet darkness devoured Baya.

CHAPTER 17

Baya was completely submerged under water. She could hear the faint muffled sound of the metal door slamming shut above her, stamping out what little light there had been. She raced for the surface but her head hit the roof with a painful thud. Her heart beat faster as she realized the hole was completely filled with water. She would not be able to come up for air. Her eyes were wide open but she could see nothing in the pure darkness. She began to feel her way around, swimming as quickly as possible.

There had to be a place where she could come up for air. Her outstretched hands found wall after wall rather quickly, no matter which direction she swam. She was in a very small space. Deep underground in a ... well that was completely filled with water.

Think! A panicked voice screamed in her head. First of all, she had to get out of the long tunic. She yanked it off her shoulders, quickly shedding its entangling weight before continuing to move around the well.

Her lungs demanded air.

Stop! Think! Mother had said that no matter what you may think, there was always a way out. But she couldn't see anything! ... See! She needed to see.

Baya closed her eyes — which did not change her view in the least — and focused on making a fire ball. Surely she would not be able to light a fire under water. As stupid as it seemed she decided that she had to try. What other option did she have?

But she was out of any other ideas. She had to try. To her amazement, when she opened her eyes, she could see! The fire ball, or what would have been a fire if she was not under water, formed a blue orb of light in her hand. She could make out the vague outline of the hatch above her. She swam straight for it. There was no handle.

Of course not, these tasks were meant to be difficult. She braced her feet against the walls and pushed her shoulder into the hatch. The effort made her lungs scream even louder for air. She closed her eyes again and tried to force the door open with her mind.

Nothing.

Baya knew that Shema must've sealed the door with her powers. There was no opening it until Shema deemed it so.

Baya knew she would drown before that happened. This was the test. Think! Her mind screamed at her while her lungs painfully demanded air. There has to be another way! With the light in her hand she swam. It didn't take long for her to discover the four walls of the small well. She was trapped in a rectangular box with impenetrable walls that she swore were closing in on her. Fear consumed her.

Don't be ridiculous, Baya scolded herself. Surely the well wasn't shrinking.

Holy Goddess, Fay was right! They were trying to kill her. She was going to die right here. Calm down! Baya argued with herself. Now was not the time to start listening to Fay. She got out of this … somehow. Don't panic! Think!

But the tank was void of anything but Baya, her discarded robe in a pile at the bottom of the well, and the water — there was no room to come up for air. There was no other way out.

Baya's heart skipped a beat when she saw it at the bottom of one corner. Bubbles came from a tiny hole in the rock. It must be some sort of ventilation used to aerate the well. Obviously, she couldn't fit through that tiny hole. She turned to swim away when it hit her.

Aerate! Bubbles! Air! She kicked hard as she moved toward the pockets of air.

With her first attempt to suck in some precious air from the hole she took in water. Baya could not cough under water so she had to suppress it and try to ignore the burning pain as water went into her lungs.

The stone walls had cracks in them wide enough for her fingers, which allowed her to barely grasp the rocks. At least she could hold herself in place. She put her mouth tightly over the hole this time. Pure, sweet air filled her lungs.

There was always a way, she thought, as relief flooded through her.

Baya could think more clearly now. She took another deep breath before swimming around hitting the stones in various places for some sort of way out. She hoped that one would give way and open a door or allow the water to drain from the well ... something. Anything.

No stones budged.

The next problem began to consume her. Her feet were numb with cold. She shivered as she gulped more air. That's when she realized, the test was not to get out. There was no way out. The test was to survive in here until Shema opened the hatch.

Baya took another long breath from the air hole. She focused on using her powers to raise her body temperature. Soon her feet felt warm and she no longer shivered. She held onto the crack in the rock, breathed as needed and waited. And waited. An eternity passed. Still she hung on, focusing only on breathing and keeping her body temperature up. More time passed. Her thoughts strayed to her favorite places ... working and talking and walking with Vicaroy in the gardens, or playing in their private cove.

She began to feel cold again. She couldn't let her mind stray to escape the horror. She had to stay focused!

Breathe, force heat into her body, breathe, heat, breathe, heat. Baya had to fully concentrate if she was going to survive. She couldn't allow her mind the luxury of drifting off to a better place. The problem was that this made it harder to keep the panic away.

The light in her hand faded as she tired. It was impossible to keep the glowing orb lit and keep herself warm for much longer. She let the light fade away. But in the complete darkness fear threatened to get the better of her. She was trapped. There was no way out.

Baya held the stone tight and breathed and kept her body from getting dangerously cold. More time passed until Baya grew weaker.

What if she couldn't keep this up long enough? What if she wasn't as good as Shema thought and the Unawi opened the hatch too late? The answer was obvious. Baya would be dead. Maybe Baya was wrong? Maybe the test wasn't simply to survive in the well but rather she was supposed to find the way out? Her heart began to race.

Should she waste her remaining energy swimming around or should she keep trying to withstand the freezing water? She had to conserve her energy and there was no way out. She'd already covered every inch of this small stone prison several times.

Stay focused and stay alive, Baya told herself. And if she was wrong, then ... she was dead.

Baya forced her heartbeat to slow. The thought of leaving the safety of the air hole was unbearable, so she held on to the stone as best she could. Her life depended on it. So she tried not to think about the throbbing pain in her hand as it strained to hold her in place.

Breathe, heat, breathe, heat, breathe, heat. She did her best to block out the terrifying thoughts as they popped into her head, completely against her will. She was driving herself mad, second-guessing herself.

Focus!

Her feet went cold again and then her hands. She was no longer able to keep herself warm. Soon she would not be able to hold on to the stone. Which meant she could no longer breathe. She shivered. This was it. This was the end. She would not make it to her eighteenth birthday — to freedom.

Baya let herself escape the underwater prison. Her thoughts were only of Vicaroy, Bek and Rus. She no longer feared for her own life. Her only thoughts were of how the people she cared about would miss her. They would mourn her premature death. She didn't want to cause them pain.

I'm sorry. I couldn't make it, were her last thoughts.

CHAPTER 18

When the hatch to the well had slammed shut Aga had hit her knees to pray ...

Please give my daughter the courage and intelligence to make it through this. You have graciously blessed me with this lovely and gifted girl, I beg you not to take her from me. Please let Baya survive. Please...

Aga remained on her knees rocking back and forth for some time.

It seemed like Baya was in there for much longer than other girls had been. But Aga had no other choice but to trust Shema's judgment. She would open the door after the allotted time was up — the correct amount of time. Yet Baya had been down there for so long.

Aga paced only a couple of steps back and forth in the cramped dungeon room. She simply had to keep moving, or she would lose her mind.

Shema waved her hand and the hatch swung open. She held a ball of fire over the hole to help guide Baya out.

Aga ran to the opening.

Nothing.

"Baya," she screamed. She shrugged off her long robes and readied herself to jump in when Baya's head broke the surface —

gasping. Aga pulled her from the water, wrapped her in a blanket and held her tight while she coughed and gasped and shivered uncontrollably. Aga raised her own body temperature to warm her daughter.

"You did it. You're alive." Aga whispered over and over.

* * *

BAYA STARED at the wall of her bedroom but didn't see it. She couldn't see or feel anything. A soft rap came at her door. Baya didn't speak or move or even flinch a muscle. Aga sat down gently beside her on the bed but said nothing.

Baya had to shake her head and blink several times to get her eyes to focus. The numbness that was protecting her slowly slipped away. Fear and anger took over. "How could you not warn me?"

"I couldn't. No one can speak of the trials."

"Why, because it's forbidden?" Baya spat.

"That is correct."

Baya glared at Aga for a moment then rolled over turning her back on her mother.

A long silence followed.

"I'm very proud of you," Aga ventured.

"How long was I in there?" Baya's voice was flat.

"Three hours."

"It felt like days."

"Yes. It did seem like days. I remember when I was pushed into that same well. Both times it seemed like the hatch was latched for an eternity. It was even harder when it was you trapped in there."

"Have mistresses died before?"

"I'm afraid so."

Baya bolted upright and stared at her mother in disbelief.

"If a girl is not performing well we let her go before the trials."

Baya remembered a couple of girls who had been kicked out of school the previous year. They hadn't been able to master their powers well enough. Thank the Goddess that they hadn't been thrown into that well. They would have died for sure. Baya shivered at the thought.

"However," Aga continued. "There have been times, although rare, that the Unawi has misread a student's abilities."

Baya looked at her mother with wide eyes.

"Not Shema, but previous Unawis. Thankfully we have not lost anyone for a long time. Nevertheless, mistresses have failed."

"Meaning … died." Baya swallowed hard and the numbness returned. It started in her hands and feet and slowly consumed her. She simply nodded as if this all made perfect sense. Life or death trials. Oops, we thought you were ready, sorry you're dead.

"Now do you see why we push students so hard? Why *I* pushed you even harder?"

Baya was suddenly grateful for her mother's relentless hounding. She would be dead right now if it weren't for her rigorous training. Baya threw her arms around her mother and this caused the tears to fall. This time, Aga didn't scold her for crying.

Her crying was cut short when a thought hit her. "Maybe Shema is wrong. I mean, about me being ready. When I try to transform matter it doesn't always work."

"You are ready. You have to be. Don't allow doubts to creep in." Yet there was worry in her mother's eyes.

Baya thought the tears were going to fall again but her stomach gave an angry growl.

"Yes. That is the other reason I came here. Baya you have to eat and eat well. You used a lot of energy today. More so than you ever have before. You used your powers to the fullest. You must fuel your body if you are going to make it through the next test."

Baya grabbed her hollow stomach as it growled again.

"Come. I will eat with you."

Baya craved Rus's cooking more than usual, or was it his comforting embrace that she really wanted? Either way, she was not allowed to leave the palace grounds until her trials were over.

"I can't tell you much more than to issue this warning … the tests don't get any easier. In fact, they get worse — much worse."

Baya swallowed hard. She opened her mouth but nothing came out. How, in the name of Ameris, could it possibly get any harder than being trapped in a freezing well?

"The test today only required that you use basic abilities, making light under water and controlling your body temperature. Most women possess these skills. Yet the first test is designed to push the limits of your endurance. The second trial is designed to test more advanced skills and the third requires mistresses to have mastery over the most difficult skills." Aga studied Baya's face which had gone from a lovely olive-bronze to a ghostly grey. "Don't worry, my dear, you will be fine. Besides now you know the secret."

"What secret?" Baya demanded.

"I can't spell it out for you but it doesn't matter because you already know. In here." Aga placed a hand over Baya's heart. "And in here." She gently tapped a finger on Baya's forehead.

What was that supposed to mean?

"Now, let's eat." They stood and Aga eyed Baya. "Today you proved that you're brave and smart and powerful, so act like it."

Something shifted inside Baya. She did have the right to be proud that she had made it through the first test. She straightened to her full height and squared her shoulders. She stood taller than Aga.

"That's my girl." Aga smiled.

CHAPTER 19

Baya led nine of the world's leaders into the secret dungeon once again. This time she was not as frightened. Perhaps she was more confident ... or more likely, she had simply gone numb.

When they entered the small room at the bottom of the stairs, Shema gestured for Baya to pass through the door on the far side. Baya skirted around the hatch in the floor, careful to stay as far away as possible.

The door Shema had indicated led to a stone passageway. At the edge of Baya's light was nothing but darkness. After twenty paces the walls disappeared. The women's movements echoed in the distance and Baya knew they were in a large open space. She exhaled with relief. At least it wasn't another confined space.

"Stop," Shema demanded.

Baya halted at once. She feared a precipitous cliff or some other unforeseen danger lay directly in front of her. The fire ball in her hand only shed a small sphere of light around her.

"Light the torches," Shema said.

Baya held her fire ball above her head and squinted. "I can't see them — or anything for that matter."

"You don't have to see them with your eyes. See them with your mind."

How? Baya thought. She closed her eyes and imagined that she was causing torches to catch fire. She heard the woosh of new flames flaring to life. When she opened her eyes, torches to either side of her jumped to life. As each torch was lit along the walls, more of the large room came into view. Baya's mouth fell open as she realized she was in an underground coliseum. It was smaller than the one the city used for festivals and the like. But the area was still impressive, especially since it was so far underground.

Baya guessed it was about two hundred paces long and one hundred paces wide. Surrounding her was a perfectly elliptical wall. It stood many times taller than a person. Starting from the top of the wall, rows of seats stair-stepped their way upward.

This place could seat hundreds of people. Baya was suddenly grateful that the trials were a secret. Thankfully there would not be a full stadium of people in attendance. She trembled at the thought of having to get through her second task with half the city watching. It was bad enough having the leaders of the world scrutinizing her.

In the center of the coliseum was a large brazier, which — once again — Baya was instructed to light. Two by two the priestesses filed up identical staircases that stood opposite each other. They moved gracefully into the stands around the arena. The priestesses spread out evenly around the grand oval; four on either side of Baya.

Shema drew a circle in the dirt around Baya's feet by moving her finger in the air. "As long as this circle is here, do not step outside of it." Shema moved to take her place high above the main entrance.

Once everyone was in position, the priestesses held out their arms and chanted. The metal brazier rose into the air. It remained suspended above the arena, providing even better light.

All the better for them to watch Baya's performance. The taste of bitterness filled her mouth. At least they hadn't been able to see her in the well. Now she had an audience — she was their morning entertainment. Baya clenched her fists. These trials were disgusting.

The critical eyes of the priestesses felt as if they were boring holes into Baya.

Baya's mouth fell open again, or perhaps she had never closed it, as the domed ceiling came into view from the brazier's light. Thick wood beams supported the stone roof. Carvings covered both the wood and the stone. She wanted to study them but there was no time.

Behind her came the sound of stone grinding against stone, followed by a loud crashing that shook the ground beneath her. She turned to find that she had been trapped in the arena. Shema had caused a large wall to rise, blocking the exit and the staircases on either side. Baya scanned the area. Of course there was no other way out.

Baya heard the sound of more stone grinding. She spun back around to investigate the source of the noise. A large rock slab slid upward in the far wall.

Out of the darkness emerged something that looked like it had come straight out of Ameris's scrolls. First she saw a long scaly snout with a mouth full of sharp teeth — teeth that were longer than Baya's fingers. Four black eyes were intently focused on her. Each side of its face contained two eyes, one right above the other. The eyes blinked at different times as they adjusted to the light. The beast's head gave way to a thick mane of feathers around its neck. Baya took a step back.

"Be very careful to stay inside the circle," Shema warned. "Exiting the circle is an automatic failure."

Baya had completely forgotten about the circle that had been drawn around her feet. She had to flail her arms to keep her balance and remain inside the circle.

She could have reminded me of that sooner, Baya thought.

The creature slowly, almost lazily, headed toward her. The large stone door slid shut behind it.

Now Baya could see the entire monster. It stood at least twice her height. Small scales covered its thick muscular body, save the neck, which was adorned with brightly colored feathers. Both the scales and the feathers changed hues as the beast moved. The firelight caused an array of pinks and oranges, blues and purples to flash with each step the monster took. The colorful beast was in stark contrast to the drab golden-brown stone walls of the arena.

Its powerful hind leg was meant for leaping and bounding forward. Most likely to help it catch its prey … wait! Baya was its prey. This thought snapped Baya from her previous state in which she had been completely enamored by the lovely creature. She had seen drawings of animals that resembled this beast but the scrolls were not in color. They didn't depict its true magnificence.

A rainbow of light shimmered from its powerful and graceful body. Its clawed feet fluffed up dirt as it made a wide circle, never taking its many eyes off Baya. The two front paws were slightly smaller than the one large back foot.

A whip-like tail slashed through the air. The sharp point on the tip looked like it could slice through flesh and bone as if they were little more than water.

If these creatures ever had a name, or at least a category like birds or fish, it had long since been lost. The scrolls referred to all predatory animals only as beasts. They had fish, birds and insects on the island but that was it. Baya had no idea that one of the beasts from the past remained on this island, albeit in captivity.

Baya shivered but held her ground and held the beast's stare as it made its way closer.

Shema must have to remove the circle at some point. Right? Or did she have to stand here and let the beast eat her?

Baya thought she heard it try to tell her something. But the high council raised their arms toward the domed ceiling and began to chant again. This distracted both Baya and the beast. The earth shook and Baya struggled to stay on her feet. The sound of loud cracking and snapping assaulted her ears.

Now what? she thought.

CHAPTER 20

A stone wall jetted out of the ground in front of Baya, flinging dirt through the air. Baya's teeth chattered and her vision blurred as the earth rattled. When the noise and shaking stopped, Baya looked at her feet. Shema's magic circle was gone.

Thank the Goddess! She was free to move. She peeked around the new wall in front of her. The arena floor had been transformed, it was no longer empty. There were stone structures scattered about. They ranged from short to tall and consisted of all sorts of different shapes.

Baya searched for the beast but couldn't see or hear him.

What do I do now? I can't just wait here — where the beast last saw me. He's most likely making his way toward me.

She darted for the nearest wall. With her back against the stone she slowly moved to look around the next corner. Nothing. Again she ran. She looked around the next wall and heard a crack as small pieces of stone rained down on her. The creature had sneaked up on her from the other side. He flung his long tail around getting ready to strike again.

In case Baya had any doubts before, this confirmed that the beast did indeed want to hurt her. It was time to disappear. She closed her eyes and focused on blending into the wall. She ran around the stone structure as the tail hit the wall where she had been.

The beast looked from side to side, searching for his prey that had vanished. Baya pressed herself against another wall. Glancing down she could only make out the vague outline of her body. She blended in perfectly with the stone around her.

She watched from around the corner as the beast sniffed the air. A curse escaped Baya's lips. It would still be able to find her with that long scaly snout. She bolted for the next rock wall, then watched him smell his way toward her.

Baya preferred to keep him in sight, but she had to keep moving. Speeding around the next wall, she came face to face with the beast, as he had bounded around the other side and caught her off guard. With one mighty leap his nose was close, pressing Baya against the wall. His mouth opened and the horrible stench of its breath washed over Baya. She watched saliva drip from its long yellow teeth. Her nightmare had come to life.

She opened her palms and released as much smoke as she could. The beast howled in protest and snorted. It rubbed its nose in the dirt to try to get the smoke out. Baya ran.

Maybe she could use some of the smaller stones as steps to get up higher where the beast couldn't reach her. This test must be like the first, in that she had to survive for an allotted amount of time. She prayed it wasn't three hours, like the first test. These trials were designed to test their endurance to the fullest. She needed to conserve as much energy as possible. There must be someplace where he couldn't get her — where she could rest.

Baya leapt up a couple of smaller stone walls as fast as she could; all the while, focusing on blending into her surroundings as much as possible. As she climbed higher, her pace slowed and each step was deliberate. It was a long way to the ground on either side.

The beast sniffed around until he caught her scent again.

He can't see me but he can still find me, Baya thought. At least it takes him longer when I'm up high.

The beast pointed his nose upward and inhaled deeply. Soon he was not far from her.

Baya hesitated when she reached the end of the wall. She was unsure if she could make the jump to the top of the next wall. She would have to land perfectly as the walls were only about as wide as her feet.

The beast could smell that he was getting close. His tail flicked wildly in all directions, in the hope of accidentally finding her.

He will kill me with that damn tail, she thought, as she leapt with all her might. Her feet barely missed the wall. She caught the wall with her arms draping over the top. Her body slammed into the stone. Lifting herself with her arms, she scrambled to the top. The beast must have heard her struggle and guessed her location, because Baya felt a sharp pain in her upper arm where the tail found its mark.

A painfilled scream escaped from her lips before she could stop it. She thought she heard her mother call her name. Yet, there was no time to think about that, as the force of the blow knocked her off balance and she was falling from the wall. She grabbed for the edge with her fingers, which barely latched on to keep her from falling to the floor. Her injured arm felt as if it were on fire.

Baya tried to pull herself back up on the wall but pain shot through her arm and it gave way, losing its grip. The hand on her good arm slid, her fingers could hardly hold her full weight. Stifling a scream, she forced her injured arm to grasp the wall again. Her feet slid against the wall when she tried to use them to crawl to the top.

She couldn't get any traction and she couldn't hold on for much longer. Her hands ached with the effort it took to keep herself from falling. She strained to look down. A fall from this height would at least break a leg. Then she couldn't escape the beast.

Frantically she glanced to either side. No beast in sight. Not far off was an outcropping in the wall. She slowly inched her hands along the ledge moving herself toward the step. With each inch she advanced, the pain in her arm flared and each flare burned more than the last. She bit her lip to keep from screaming. Sweat trickled down her spine.

As she reached the step, she heard the sound of large feet pounding toward her — growing louder and louder as they approached.

Thankfully she had been able to keep herself invisible. But the beast must've had an idea of where she was, even though it didn't know her exact location. It bound toward the wall where Baya hung. With all its power it slammed its front paws into the wall straining with his muscular back leg.

Loud cracking sounds befell her ears as the wall gave way. Baya had no choice but to ride the wall to the ground. Her body slammed into it as it toppled to the arena floor with her on top of it. All the air was ripped from her lungs at the impact. This caused her to materialize before the beast.

Before she could force air back into her chest, the monster was upon her.

CHAPTER 21

Baya gasped for air. The beast stared down at her with a mighty paw on either side of Baya. She saw something in the monster's eyes — a hint of intelligence. She wanted to try to communicate with him. She had no idea if she could but she wanted to try. It was difficult to decide which one of the four eyes to focus on.

"Make yourself blend in!" Baya heard someone scream, her mother probably.

Baya ignored the advice. The beast's hot breath brushed over her.

Just pick an eye and do it quickly before he mauls you to death, an impatient voice in her head warned.

"What do you want?" Baya asked the beast. She looked deep into one of its eyes.

The four dark eyes blinked at different times and the beast withdrew. Baya's arm throbbed as she slowly got to her feet.

"What do you want?" she asked again.

"What, in the name of Ameris, is she doing?" one of the priestesses said.

The beast blinked again and cocked its large head to the side.

A slight smile crossed Baya's lips. It was almost cute when it did that.

How can it be? I thought humans couldn't talk. A deep and unintelligent-sounding voice came into Baya's head.

"We can read the minds of simple creatures —"

A growl came from deep inside the beast and it lunged for Baya.

She held up her hands. "Please. Wait! I'm sorry."

The beast paused only inches from her. *Are you calling me simple?* It snorted.

She looked intently at him. "I mean, we can read animals minds. I didn't mean to insult you." She couldn't believe she was trying to reason with a beast. "What is it that you want?"

What do you mean? What do I want? The voice roared in Baya's mind. He had clearly never been asked this question before.

"Are you lonely? Is it a companion that you seek?"

No. His deep voice boomed, causing Baya to jump. *I'm not alone. There are others like me.*

"There are more of you?" Baya asked.

He snorted a yes.

Oh no, Baya thought. He already had companions. This may have been a terrible idea. What if she couldn't offer him anything that would help her to get out of this … alive? Maybe the only thing he wanted was to eat her.

"Is there … something I can do for you. Something that you would like more than … chasing after me?" Or eating me for your mid-day meal?

It's very boring in this place. Chasing humans is the only fun I get. And I don't get it often. The deep voice replied.

"You're bored being penned up all the time?"

It's bad. At least they let us out sometimes. But mostly it's just … boring.

"So you're tired of being locked up all the time?"

The beast flicked its tail and began to pace.

Perhaps this conversation was boring him. Think Baya! "Okay maybe we can work something out. You want to chase something?"

Yes! Yes I do. The beast's four dark eyes lit up.

"Alright." Baya looked around. She reached for a piece of broken stone from the fallen wall next to her.

The beast bared its teeth and a terrifying growl echoed through the coliseum.

"I'm not going to throw this *at* you. Please ... trust me."

She held the stone up and waved it back and forth. The beast followed it intently with all four eyes. She tossed it as far away as she could. The keen senses of the beast followed the movement with precision and he leapt into action. Its powerful back leg propelled him through the air many times faster than Baya could run. In no time he brought the rock back and dropped it at Baya's feet.

Chase. Again. The beast's deep voice came into Baya's head.

She tossed the saliva covered rock. When the beast bounded after it, Baya ventured to look up at some of the priestesses. They watched in open-mouthed disbelief.

The beast retrieved the stone and Baya tossed it as far as she could in a different direction. She tried to trick him but his keen eyes couldn't be fooled.

"This is not right." One of the priestesses protested. Baya thought it was May, Fay's mother. "She can't do that!"

Shema smiled. "Why not? The rules are clear. She simply has to survive in the arena with the monster. And it appears that she's doing a fine job."

With Baya's next throw the rock landed high up on one of the walls.

Oh, no. Will it upset him if he can't get it? Baya thought.

The beast paced at the base of the wall that held the stone — his stone. With a hard, sweeping flick of its tail, he hit his mark. The rock flew through the air. The beast's hind leg sent him straight up after it. He caught the rock in his mouth and landed gracefully.

Baya laughed. "That's amazing!"

The beast strutted toward her with obvious pride.

Baya laughed again as he dropped the rock at her feet. "I guess I will have to try harder to challenge you."

When the beast was finally tired, he lay down panting at Baya's feet. She was relieved. Her one good arm ached from throwing the rock so many times.

Cautiously, she ventured to run her hand across the beast's feathery neck. "Your feathers are lovely," Baya said.

Why thank you. The beast let out a low throaty chatter of pleasure. So Baya continued to run her hands through his feathers.

"You would blend in perfectly with the flowers in the garden." It seemed that once the connection had been made between her and the animal, she didn't have to be looking in his eyes to communicate with him. She also didn't have to speak out loud. He knew her thoughts and she knew his. It was from habit that Baya spoke out loud to him.

What's a ... garden?

Baya's heart grew heavy.

Why did my question make you sad? The beast asked.

"You can sense my feelings?"

Ahh ... I guess so. Before you were scared and then curious and now sad. Why?

Baya was surprised at this accurate description of her feelings since she had entered the arena. The creature was rather perceptive. "It's just that you belong in the wild — in wide-open spaces, where you can run and ..."

Sounds lovely. He purred. *You take me there?*

Baya shook her head in dismay. "I'm afraid not. Unless ... I become Unawi then ... maybe —"

Smoke from the priestesses began to fill the arena and the stone door on the far wall ground its way open once again.

The beast got to his feet. *Then become this Una-whatever and set me free.*

The beast knew his time was up. He also knew that there was no use in fighting. The powerful priestesses would force him back into his cage. He slowly lumbered toward the door from where he had come.

"Wait. Do you have a name?" Baya asked.

Mook.

"It was nice to meet you, Mook." Baya waved goodbye as smoke surrounded her. It didn't bother her. She could protect herself from it.

That was why it didn't bother her when she released it. Women were immune to it — but not animals or men.

He gave her a piercing stare and a slight nod as the stone wall slid shut.

The priestesses gathered around Baya.

"What happened?"

"That was remarkable."

"I've never seen the like."

These were some of the comments that rang in Baya's ears. Her mother had never looked more proud.

One of the priestesses tended to Baya's wounded arm — Baya winced when the woman touched it. She looked down to find a long swollen red welt across her upper arm. She hadn't ventured to examine it prior to this.

"How many of them do you have in captivity?" asked Baya.

"Currently we have four," Shema said. "We use the males in the arena and the females produce a steady line of them."

"We won't be able to use that one again. He's clearly too tame." May stood with her arms across her chest.

"Well he wasn't tame for Fay," Aga retorted.

"No. Fay had to use her skills. Not just play with it," May said.

"That's enough ladies," Shema said. "Baya demonstrated her powers." Then to Baya she added, "That was impressive. Well done."

Baya bowed slightly and Fay's mother stormed off.

For the first time it dawned on Baya why the leader was forbidden to have children. Aga and May couldn't see the truth when it came to their daughters. Their love blinded them. Not having children of her own helped to keep the ruler objective.

Baya, like Shema, shouldn't question Ameris's laws. They simply were facts — the way things had been for a millennium. It was comforting to realize that they did serve a purpose; there was a good reason why the Unawi had to drink her morning brew that kept her childless — so she could more easily see the truth and be a fair and just ruler.

Once ointment and a bandage covered Baya's upper arm, she and Aga headed to the dining hall.

"You might want to double your portions tonight," Aga said, "as tomorrow is the ultimate test of your powers and stamina."

"I ate double what I normally would last night. And I'll do the same today." Baya was starving.

"Then make it triple. You'll need the energy."

This gave Baya a clue about her final test. The most difficult power to master, and the one that took the most energy, was transformation. Baya recounted the first two tests in her mind. …

The first one had required her to be able to light a fire and control her body temperature. These were the most basic skills. Today's test had required her to emanate smoke and transform herself into her surroundings. These were more difficult skills. Each test required the mistresses to use harder and harder skills. Transforming herself to blend in was easier for her than changing other objects, which had been the toughest skill for Baya to master.

Aga had warned that the tests would get more difficult. Baya knew that her ability to transform matter would be tested to the fullest tomorrow. She still had not figured out what the "secret" was that her mother had mentioned the previous day.

So much for "already knowing it" as her mother had claimed.

Once Aga was satisfied that Baya had eaten enough, she left her daughter and headed home for the night. This meant that Baya was free to head to the gardens. She had not seen Vicaroy in days and was anxious to tell him about the trials. Last night she had been a mess, but tonight she was in much higher spirits. She had made it through another test and she had made a new friend, Mook. She wished Vicaroy could see him.

Even though she needed to be in bed early for her big day tomorrow, she couldn't resist the opportunity to get outside for a bit of fresh air. Of course, getting to see her best friend had a lot to do with why she didn't head straight to her room, as her mother would have wanted.

CHAPTER 22

From high up in the palace Fay watched out of the classroom window. Below, Baya and the garden boy strolled. Even from high above without being able to hear them it was clear that they were talking freely and laughing. That was a side to Baya that few people saw.

She's so … happy when she's with him, Fay thought. Everyone knows that Baya is close to the boy. No one really cares because it doesn't matter. But what's so special about *that* boy? Sure he's strong and has a face to die for. But there are many cute boys. Why is it that she chooses to spend all her time with that particular one? Why is she so different from the other girls?

Fay watched as the figures below reached for the same weed to pluck.

Imagine that, a mistress doing a man's work — pulling weeds, Fay scoffed.

The couple's hands touched. Vicaroy took Baya's hand in his. They seemed to forget about the weed as they looked into each other's eyes.

They're no longer childhood friends, running through the garden playing silly games, Fay thought. No, they're playing grown-up games now. They have fallen in love. How sweet.

Fay narrowed her eyes. She would show Baya that *that* boy was nothing special and that he was like all the other boys. He would jump at the chance to be with any girl. When I'm done with him, Baya will wish she had befriended me instead of always pushing me away and running off to see that boy.

Fay headed for the garden.

* * *

BAYA RAN into Vicaroy's arms. Their hug was brief.

"It's good to see you. I've been worried. How are the trials going?" he asked.

"They're awful, well mostly. The first test …" Baya put her hand to her throat.

"What's wrong? Are you choking?"

"No. My voice … quit working." Baya shook her head and tried again. "The first test …" Her gag reflex took over and once again her voice was lost. "I can't tell you. The priestesses must use their powers to keep people from talking about what the tests are like. That means mother couldn't have told me even if she had wanted to." Any remaining anger she felt toward her mother for not warning her about the tests faded. "We *literally* can't talk about the details of the tests."

"That's disappointing. I always wondered what the big deal was."

"It *is* very disappointing and they are a *very* big deal." Baya stamped her foot. "Oh. I wish I could tell you." Baya desperately wanted to process everything she had been through. She needed to get it all out. Talking to someone she trusted would be such a relief. Baya sighed. "But I can't."

"But they're pretty bad, huh?" he asked.

"If I didn't know better, I would say they're trying to kill me."

"Well, it can't get much worse than that."

Baya pulled her tunic down over her shoulder to reveal her bandaged arm.

"Are you okay?"

Baya nodded. "Only one test left. But I fear it may be the most difficult one yet."

"You can do it. I know you can."

"Thank you." She smiled. "What about you? What have you been up to?"

"I've had a lot of time to spend in our cove these past weeks. I've found stuff to keep me busy." He wanted to show her his latest invention and not simply tell her about it. So that would have to wait until after her trials. Then she would have more free time. "I can't wait until this is all over and you can spend more time with me."

Baya smiled. "Me too."

They strolled through the gardens, content with each other's company. When the last sun was about to set, Baya had to be getting inside. Vicaroy walked her to the palace doors. She didn't understand the shyness that overtook her sometimes when she was with Vicaroy. The way he would look at her made her tingle all over and she would have to look away. Things were different between them. "See you tomorrow," Baya said.

"Of course. After you pass your final test. I'll be waiting."

Fay swung the palace doors open. "Ah, perfect. You two were just saying goodbye. So you won't mind if I borrow him." It wasn't a question. Fay took Vicaroy by the arm and pulled him away.

Vicaroy's face paled.

Baya stared in disbelief for a moment too long. "Fay. What are you ..." but they were out of earshot.

Behind her a voice beckoned, "Mistress. If you will." One of the palace theos gestured for Baya to enter. "I must lock the doors for the night."

She looked back to where Vicaroy and Fay had disappeared into the dusk. Her heart felt like it was going to explode. A low growl escaped her lips.

"What are you up to, Fay?" she whispered through gritted teeth

"Please, allow me to do my job," the theo behind Baya prompted.

"I'm coming," Baya snapped.

* * *

"DON'T you have to be getting inside?" Vicaroy was frantic to find a way to get away from this woman.

"No," Fay said. "I passed my tests months ago. I'm no longer a student. I'm waiting for my calling, which will come any day now. I passed with top marks. I volunteer now — help out in the classroom and the like, until my calling comes, you know?"

Vicaroy nodded even though he didn't know.

"Anyway, I thought I would go to my family's home tonight. I would like someone to walk me home. You know? To keep me company." Fay smiled playfully.

Vicaroy gently slid his arm out of hers. "Oh … I … can't. Azod will worry if I'm not home soon."

"Why? You must be about eighteen. He won't worry too much. You're a man now and you have not been chosen as a theo, so you can do as you wish."

Vicaroy rubbed the back of his neck. Okay, then I wish not to be here with you, he thought but didn't have the strength to say.

"In fact …" She stepped closer. "I had plans for you to stay with me tonight."

He stepped away. His heart drummed in his ears. "I … I can't." How was he going to get out of this?

Fay narrowed her eyes. "Are you … refusing me?"

He swallowed hard. "Yes," he whispered.

"Yes, what?" Fay demanded.

"I'm refusing to do as you ask." A sudden calm came over him. "You don't even know my name."

"What does that matter?"

A sad smile crept across Vicaroy's lips. He longed for the love and caring that he always saw in Baya's eyes. Fay's dark eyes held none of that. He turned to walk away.

The nerve of him! Fay thought. Men must do as I say. I will not be rebuffed by a lowly ignorant garden boy. "Soon I will be a high priestess, if not the next Unawi. If you don't come with me tonight I will make you regret it for the rest of your life."

Vicaroy stopped, his back to her. He didn't doubt for a second that she could and would make his life utterly miserable, she already was. His shoulders sank — he was trapped. There must be some way to pacify Fay and not have to … be with her. He looked to the sky. It would hurt Baya. He couldn't do that. Regardless, he didn't want to be with Fay. There must be something he could do.

But nothing came to mind. He was stuck.

"That's right. Come with me. You know you really want to. All men are the same."

"You're wrong," Vicaroy whispered. He wasn't sure if she heard him. His eyes focused on the brightest star in the sky. He sent out a silent prayer, Please, help me, Great Goddess.

CHAPTER 23

Vicaroy heard the sound of far off footsteps. Someone was coming up the path. He resisted the urge to run toward them, to run away from *her* — Fay.

Azod came into view. "There you are, Vicaroy. I was wondering why you hadn't returned."

Vicaroy had never been happier to see him. "I was telling Madam Fay that I had to be on my way." He gave Azod a pleading look.

"I'm terribly sorry, Madam, but Vicaroy must be getting home. There's still much work to be done. You see we work in the garden all day and then we have to do our house chores at night."

This was a bit of an exaggeration but any excuse would do, Vicaroy thought.

Fay crossed her arms. "Spare me the sob story, gardener."

"If you would like someone to accompany you to your front door then I would be glad to assist," Azod said.

Fay glared at the two men in turn. "That won't be necessary." She gave Vicaroy a look that made it clear that she would not forget this and that this was far from over.

Vicaroy resisted the urge to shudder.

"Then we wish you a goodnight, Madam." Azod bowed slightly to Fay as he put a hand on Vicaroy's shoulder, urging him to move.

It didn't take any more coaxing than that to get Vicaroy to leave. It was all he could do not to sprint home to safety.

The gardeners walked in silence not daring to speak until they were inside the confines of their tiny home at the far end of the palace grounds.

"I told you to stay away from the mistresses." Azod struggled to keep his voice calm. "They are trouble and will only cause you pain. I have warned you many times. They only use us and throw us away when they are done. Yet here you go, putting yourself out there."

"You mean like my mother did to you?" This was not a malicious statement. It was a genuine question of concern.

"Yes!" Azod yelled. "I thought she loved me …" he lowered his head. "Until she ran off with another."

"They're not all bad, Azod. Baya is not like that."

"That's what I thought about your mother. You think Baya is wonderful and perfect. You had better listen carefully, she will be the death of you. I have told you time and again to avoid her at all costs. Avoid all women, they bring nothing but heartache. Let alone the daughter of the highest of the high priestesses — you are begging for trouble. Aga will never allow her daughter to choose someone like you."

Vicaroy sighed. He knew that what Azod said was true. "I couldn't stay away from Baya, even if I wanted to." His voice was barely a whisper. This had been a growing concern, as he knew he was not good enough to become her theo. The thought of her choosing another caused his blood to turn icy cold.

Azod threw his arms up in exasperation. "You're a foolish boy who doesn't understand how the world works."

* * *

FAY HARDLY SLEPT THAT NIGHT. She tossed and turned.

That boy will pay for rejecting me — outright defying me, she thought. Could it be that he really does love Baya? No! That's ridiculous. How dare he? Men who do not obey must be punished. We have to keep them in their place. They were put on this earth to serve us. We can't allow any defiance. If he gets away with this then what? He will keep pushing the limits until what? He no longer does what he is told. That is unacceptable.

* * *

MEANWHILE, Baya was not faring much better. When she closed her eyes she saw Fay and Vicaroy — his lips on hers. Her arms around his waist. Baya covered her face with her pillow, as if this might somehow block out the image. It didn't. In fact, it made it worse. She envisioned the two of them entwined, his naked black flesh against Fay's golden-brown skin.

Baya sat bolt upright in bed with a loud growl.

He would not do that to me, she thought. Then it hit her like a sack of stones. ... No. He wouldn't. So that means that Fay will demand that he be with her, against his will.

Her stomach turned. This was much worse than the thought of him enjoying being with Fay. No man should be forced to be with a woman.

"Poor Vicaroy," she whispered. This wasn't the first time she'd felt trapped in this place — helpless to do anything about her situation. With all this on her mind and no sleep in sight, how on earth was she going to make it through her final test tomorrow?

* * *

ON THE OTHER HAND, Vicaroy was tired from a long day of work and his near-miss with Fay.

Azod didn't understand, Baya was different. A feeling of relief washed over Vicaroy. He had prayed and he had been heard! The Great Ameris had saved him. All he had to do was ask for her help and she'd sent Azod to rescue him.

He gave his thanks to the Goddess and drifted off into a peaceful sleep.

* * *

THE NEXT MORNING, Fay was supposed to be helping with some of the younger girls. She had been appointed to fill in while the high priestesses and the Unawi attended to Baya's final trial.

Fay only half glanced at their writing as she spent most of her time gazing out the large windows to the garden below. She spotted the young garden boy a couple of times. He appeared to be going about his normal work. Why did seeing him cause all the muscles in her body to tighten?

She studied him as he helped the head gardener dig a large hole for a new tree. Sweat sparkled off the dark skin on his bare back and his muscles strained to drive the spade deeper into the earth. Fay wished that she had been able to enjoy him the night before. Fay had never paid this much attention to him before but he had grown into quite the specimen.

What does he see in Baya that he doesn't see in me? Fay wondered. That skinny girl doesn't have half the womanly curves that I do. Well, I'm going to make him wish that he'd chosen me. If he doesn't want me then I'll see to it that he can't have Baya. I will make it so they can't be together. Fay sighed. But how? I'll start by following him. There must be something I can use against those two.

"Pardon me, Madam Fay," a girl ventured to squeak. "It's time for our mid-day meal."

Fay glanced out the window again, this time at the sundial below. She turned to the class with an air of supremacy. "Hand in your scrolls. I will have my assistant review them and get them back to you tomorrow." This was a lie. There was no assistant. Fay would have to grade them all herself. It would be another long day.

The students floated their papers over to Fay.

In no time, a thick stack of work was piled on the desk in front of her.

I must get my calling soon. I can't fill in for Shema and the other instructors forever — doing their crappy chores. I'm destined for more than this.

As soon as everyone left the room, Fay glanced out the window. The garden boy was gone. The head gardener was filling in the last of the dirt around the newly planted tree. She searched the garden for the boy and spotted him as he stepped out of her line of sight. He was headed toward the main entrance. Fay dashed for the door.

Fay passed a handful of students in the hall. "Tell Shema that my stomach hurts and I had to retire early." She hurried down the stairs.

When Fay entered the garden, she saw Vicaroy as he was leaving the main gates of the palace. Being careful not to be spotted, she slowly followed, keeping her distance.

Vicaroy led Fay to the secret trailhead leading up and over the mountain. Fay changed her flesh and clothing so that it blended into a nearby tree trunk, while she watched him carefully place branches and palm leaves back over the trail.

Fay smiled maliciously. He's covering his tracks. I knew it! she thought. He does have something to hide. He's definitely up to no good if he doesn't want others to know where he is going. I'll find out what that is. It may be easier than I thought to make him pay for disobeying me.

CHAPTER 24

Baya was led past the well, which she tried to ignore ... or was it the memories of being trapped in there that she was pushing away? This time they did not light the torches in the arena. Baya held a ball of fire in front of her to light the way. As she approached the far end, she found that the stone wall where Mook had entered the coliseum the day before was wide open. Only darkness could be seen in the large entrance. The thought of seeing Mook filled Baya with excitement. But she had a feeling that her third test would not involve him.

I'm not that lucky, she thought.

Baya gave a questioning glance to Shema, who motioned for her to enter. Once inside, her fire ball provided enough light to see that the room was rather small. She turned at the sound of movement and a number of throaty growls. There were four cages built into the wall that this room shared with the coliseum. Inside each cage was a lovely rainbow-colored beast.

"Mook!" Baya called.

The beast raised its large head to Baya.

"This is where they keep you? In this tiny cage?" Baya looked around in disgust.

They let us out when we eat. The beast's deep voice rang in Baya's head.

"Out where?" she asked.

In the big room. He pointed with his nose toward the arena.

Baya's shoulders relaxed. At least he didn't have to spend all his time locked in a small cell.

One of the other beasts growled and tried to scratch at Baya through the metal bars. Mook roared and bared his teeth at his companion.

"Baya." Shema gestured for her to go through a doorway on the far side of the room.

Baya gave Mook one last longing look.

Don't forget about me, she heard him say.

"I won't." Baya whispered. "If I can make it past the final test."

"What's a Mook?" one of the priestesses asked.

Baya found herself in yet another small room.

"Baya."

She turned to find her mother in the doorway.

"We'll meet you on the other end."

Baya realized that it was a promise, of sorts, that she would see her mother again.

The stone door was shut and the sound of metal scraping against the door could be heard as it was locked.

No doubt Shema was sealing the door to keep Baya from opening it with her powers. And, once again, there were no instructions other than, "Use your skills to survive."

Baya surveyed the room. She didn't see any threats or dangers. The far wall was covered in a large tapestry. The tapestry contained a combination of letters and pictures. Baya had not seen this text before. There appeared to be nothing else in the room except golden-brown stone walls.

There was nothing else to do except read the tapestry. She moved toward it.

Thankfully she read quickly…

What do women love more than life
Yet fear more than mortal strife
What the poor have, the rich require
and what contented women desire
What the miser spends and the spendthrift saves
And all women carry to their graves

BAYA HAD BARELY READ the last line when a scraping sound echoed through the room. This was followed by the sound of fabric being torn apart. Sharp wooden spikes forced their way through the tapestry as they closed in on her. She took an instinctive step back.

The test must have been to solve the riddle before the spikes impaled her. She tried to make out the lines, memorizing them. She re-read the first couple of lines as the spikes ripped it to shreds. The cloth was soon in ribbons, rendering the riddle unreadable.

"Wait, what did the other lines say?"

She focused on the start of the riddle. Her first thought was what her mother said a couple days ago about it being even harder when it was Baya trapped in the well than when it had been her mother.

What we love more than life … our daughters! "The answer is daughters." She said out loud, to whom, she didn't know.

The spikes continued to creep forward.

Okay, that must not have been the correct answer. Think! The second line has largely the same meaning, skip it. Something about what the poor have and the rich … require. What in the name of Ameris does that mean? The poor don't have children. So the answer is obviously not children. What the rich want, this doesn't make sense! Think! The rich require …? "Status, power, prestige." She blurted out. The spikes crept closer. I don't know. Move on.

But the tapestry had been torn away. She couldn't re-read any of the other lines to study them further. The spikes were far too many to dodge. They pushed her back another step. She glanced at the wall behind her. She needed more time.

Baya would be impaled against the far wall in only a matter of seconds. She didn't bother with the door, there was no getting out that way. The trial would never be that easy.

The objective was clear: solve the riddle to get out.

What was the next line? She forced herself to focus. But the other lines were hard to recall. How was she supposed to solve this stupid riddle with so little time? If she couldn't think of the other lines then she was dead.

She closed her eyes tight. The words, "What we carry to our graves.," came to mind. What we love most and take with us when we die — our souls. That's it!

"Souls!" she yelled. Yet the spikes continued to move forward. "I can't do this. I need more time."

It sounded like her mother's voice in her head; "So use your powers to make more time."

Baya tried to focus on the riddle but all she saw were thick, sharp wooden spikes approaching. Her back was against the far wall and the spikes were only inches away. She focused all her attention on the wood that was about to penetrate her flesh. The wood gave way. It moaned and cracked as it bent away from her. The closest spikes broke in two under her transformation powers. Shards of wood rained down on her.

Baya exhaled with relief. Now she had more time to think. She kept her mind focused on the bent wood. If she let her guard down the spikes that she had not been powerful enough to fully break would snap back into place and impale her. The problem was that she found it impossible to focus on keeping the wood bent away from her and solve the riddle at the same time. It took all her effort to bend the wood.

Sweat broke out on Baya's forehead. Think, think, think! The far wall inched forward. The line of the riddle that confused her most popped into her head. "What the poor have."

Well not much, she thought.

"What the rich require."

The rich have everything. So they require nothing. What we take to our graves. That's it! And what we fear more than death. Nothing. The answer is ... nothing.

"Nothing!" she yelled. But her focus on the spikes wavered. They were bending back toward her.

Baya tried to concentrate on stopping the wall rather than transforming the wood. She issued an ear-piercing scream as the dirt floor below gave way. She slid out of control, through utter darkness. The sound of grinding stone and splintering wood could be heard from above.

CHAPTER 25

Baya was relieved to be out of that room and equally apprehensive about where she was going. The loudness of the room faded and soon all she heard was air flying past her as she slid into an abyss. The black hole she was falling through leveled somewhat, slowing her descent. She was spit out of the dark tunnel onto a hard surface. "Ouch," she said as she stood and brushed herself off.

Baya lit her fire ball and held it high overhead as she scanned her whereabouts. She was on a rock pedestal not much longer than she was tall. The room was larger than the one she had just come from. The floor was about three feet below her. It was covered in … something.

"What is that?" She got down on all fours and held the light low. It looked like coals. The ground was covered in … coal?

The floor caught fire. Heat accosted her face and she scrambled to her feet. "Yep. Definitely coals." She sighed. So almost being impaled was not enough, there was yet another test. Now she had to avoid being roasted.

With the light of the fire surrounding her, she could more easily see the far walls. They were black stone slabs, with shiny golden hues as the firelight danced off them. The only exception was one small door.

Of course, Baya thought. The objective must be to get to that door … through the fire.

Baya broke out in another sweat. This time it was not only from straining to use her powers but from the heat that came at her from all directions. Wave after wave of heat pounded against her body. She wiped her brow with her sleeve.

What if the only thing that awaited her through that far door was yet another test? How many could they possibly expect them to make it through?

"This is hopeless," she breathed.

Tired and no longer caring, Baya sat down. Flames licked the air all around the pedestal and the heat was unbearable.

Get up and fight for your life. Don't be weak! Baya yelled at herself.

But she could only make fire, not put it out. Maybe she should just lay there until they came for her. She could keep her body from overheating for quite some time. Couldn't she?

All she wanted to do was lay down and close her eyes. The heat made her drowsy and her sleepless night had caught up to her. The flames greedily consumed all the air around her.

Fay took Vicaroy last night just to distract her. She knew it would make her too tired to pass this test. It wasn't fair. She was too … tired. They would come for her … wouldn't they? Surely her mother would …

In the name of Ameris, get your ass up! Baya's inner fighter yelled. What we fear worse than death — nothing. Now get up!

She slowly got to her feet. There was more air up there and she took a deep breath.

Good. Now think! The last tests had to do with transformation.

"That's it," she whispered.

Women couldn't put out a fire this big with only their powers but they could take away the fire's source of fuel. Rus had always said that fire was a very hungry thing.

"I can transform the coals into ... what? Something not flammable. I got it! I can turn the coal into rocks."

Baya held out her arms, focusing on the floor in front of her but the fire flared angrily. She jumped back and covered her face with her arm.

"What happened?" she yelled in frustration. Stones shouldn't create more flames.

When the flare-up finally died down, she cautiously ventured to look over the edge, only to find the burnt remains of shoes. Baya's powers had failed her, instead of rocks she got ... footwear.

She was not ready for this. Why had they sent her into the trials early? Her Transformation of Matter powers were not reliable.

Despair threatened to consume Baya. Her vision blurred as she stared into the flames. In the flickering reds and yellows she saw Rus's face, followed by Bek's, then Aga's. Even Shema's shapely form appeared, or maybe it was Ameris. The last vision was of Vicaroy. His voice was almost audible, "You got this."

"They believe in me." She closed her eyes and raised her hands once again.

The fire died down instantly and there was some relief from the heat.

"It's working! And I wanted to give up."

Okay, the next problem. She could already feel herself weaken from the effort. It would be impossible to change all the coals into rocks. But she didn't need to. Baya only had to get to the door on the far side, making a path through the fire.

She slowly stepped down onto the newly formed rocks. The fire on either side of her felt like it would sear her flesh. Closing her eyes in concentration, she prayed that the coals didn't turn into shoes again. If they did the flames would consume her.

Thankfully, a wider, fire-free area formed around her. Focusing on the door she created a pathway of rocks, one step at a time. When the fire died down in front of her, she cautiously moved forward, slowly making her way toward the door.

By the time she reached the door, her clothes were drenched in sweat and her hands trembled with the effort of using her powers. Yet, it was better than being burnt alive. To her dismay she found that the door was locked. She leaned her forehead against it.

What if the only thing that awaited her on the other side of this door was another test.

"Oh, come on!" she yelled.

It's a simple locked door. Don't let that stop you. The agitated voice in her head was annoying. *Use your mind to transform the locking mechanism. And do it quick. You don't have enough energy to keep your body temperature down for much longer.*

The damn fighter inside would not let Baya give up, when that was all she wanted to do. The trials had been too much. Too traumatic. If this was what life was, then she didn't want it. Facing drowning, being eaten alive by a wild beast, being impaled, and now burning to death. What's next? What if the next test was worse … somehow? What was the point of fighting?

"Shut up!" Baya yelled at herself. "The point is, not dying! Now open this damn door!"

Maybe going insane was also a part of the tests.

With her head still against the door she closed her eyes and focused on unlocking the door with her mind. Heat relentlessly lashed at her back. At first nothing, then the faint sound of metal clanking could be heard.

She tried the handle again. It budged only a crack and stuck. "This can't be happening!" she yelled. Out of sheer panic she pulled again with what little strength she had left. The door came loose, flying open. This sent her tumbling backward. She landed hard on the rocks and one hand fell onto the flaming coals. She screamed as fire shot up her arm.

CHAPTER 26

Holding her burnt hand to her chest, Baya ran through the door and slammed it closed, shutting out the unbearable heat. She lit her light with her good hand, panting and fearful that there would be some new danger coming at her in the darkness. Her knees were weak and she wondered how much longer they would hold her. She didn't have the strength for any more trials. It felt like all her powers had been drained away … used up. Her legs trembled as she moved forward.

Before her lay nothing but stairs. They appeared to stretch far beyond the reach of her light. She didn't trust the emptiness, certain that every wobbly step she took would lead her into yet another danger. Any moment something unexpected would jump out at her. She cautiously headed up and up. As she continued to climb her light grew weaker. She had never used her powers to this extent. They were fading away. Soon she would have nothing left, not even a light to see by. Her legs would not be able to carry her much longer.

She must have been heading out of the underground dungeon. Maybe, just maybe, she thought, these stairs lead to safety. They simply have to — before it's too late.

The stairs finally ended and a door came into view. Baya's hand hesitated on the handle. What if it leads to another test? Dread and doubt consumed her. Perhaps she shouldn't have gotten her hopes up.

The handle turned easily and the door opened wide. Light surrounded her, stinging her eyes. She shaded her face with her good arm and blinked. Numerous blurry figures stood in front of her.

"Baya!" Her mother's arms were around her. "You made it out already. That must be a record."

Was she in the garden?

Yes, this was the Garden! She was safe.

"What do you mean, that was fast?" Baya spat. "It felt like an eternity." The knowledge that she was outside under a clear purple sky slowly sank in and she let herself go limp in her mother's embrace. As soon as she did, it felt as if her hand was back in the flames. It throbbed angrily, demanding her attention. She cradled her hand to her chest. "Please tell me there are no more tests."

"No more … ever. You made it through them all. You're done." Aga explained. Her attention turned to Baya's bright red hand. "You're injured. Where's the healer?"

Baya had made it out. No more tests. No more danger. She was safe. The suffocating underground dungeon was behind her — forever. The trials were over and she had passed.

The priestess who had bandaged Baya's arm the day before examined her red palm. It looked like there were air bubbles under her skin. Baya hissed and clenched her jaw as the woman rubbed an ointment over her palm. She used her powers to cool a wet rag and wrapped it around Baya's hand.

Baya sighed at the instant relief. "Thank you."

"Well. At least Fay made it through the trials without any injuries," May said. "While Baya somehow managed to sustain two."

"Baya made it through the third trial in far better time than Fay," Aga snapped.

"It's not a timed test," May retorted.

"Fay almost didn't make it past the hopeless spell. She all but gave up entirely. She would have burned to death."

"Enough." Shema sighed. "Both mistresses proved themselves to be powerful and strong."

Baya glared at her mother. "There was a hopeless spell cast on that last room?" Her cheeks burned with anger. "As if getting past the spikes and the riddle wasn't enough. As if the threat of being burned alive wasn't enough. Then you added a hopeless spell?"

The abject desperation she had felt in the fiery room, the unrelenting doubt, had been a spell to make her feel that way. That was unnecessary and excessive. Maybe they were truly trying to kill the mistresses. Baya kept her eyes narrowed on her mother. Never again.

"It only makes you stronger, my dear, as all the trials are designed to do."

"And if I hadn't been strong enough?"

Aga didn't speak the words but Baya knew the answer. Then she would have been better off dead as she couldn't become a priestess, let alone the next Unawi.

"All that matters is that you *were* strong enough," Aga whispered.

Shema stepped in front of Baya. "Kneel before me."

Baya was glad to give her weak legs a break. However, after she knelt all she wanted to do was lay down in the grass and sleep. She had no more energy to argue with her mother.

The priestesses formed a circle around Baya and bowed their heads in respect.

"Baya," Shema began. "Over these past three days, you were able to overcome great obstacles. You demonstrated that you can control your fear and persevere despite the odds being weighted heavily against you. You have proven mastery over your feminine gifts."

Shema placed her hands on Baya's head. "It also takes a great deal of intelligence to pass these trials. You have succeeded. That means you are no longer a mistress, you are not only a grown woman but you have proven yourself to be a true leader. You are worthy of serving on the high council, should you receive a calling from the Great Ameris."

"Now let us pray," Aga said. "Thank you Mighty Goddess for

guiding Baya through her trials. Thank you for returning her to us safely …"

Safe. She was safe. Baya's thoughts drifted from her mother's prayer. She was sleepy and her body was shaky and ached all over. It was all she could do to remain kneeling.

After the prayer Shema resealed the door where Baya had exited the dungeon. It blended in perfectly with the black stone palace around it.

Baya numbly followed her mother into the palace.

"You must eat and bathe and rest. In that order," Aga said.

Baya furrowed her brow as she tried to think what the secret to making it through the trials had been. So many skills were required and that stupid riddle. What if I hadn't been able to figure it out. She shivered at the thought. "Mom."

Aga smiled and put an arm around Baya's waist as they walked. This served two purposes, to help support her daughter's weight and to comfort her. "You never call me Mom. I like it."

"What's the secret that you mentioned after the first trial?"

"You haven't figured it out yet?"

"No." Baya felt rather stupid but her weariness kept her from caring too much — about anything.

"The secret is to be able to think beyond your fears. As Shema said, we must prove that we can control fear itself and not let it consume us."

"Oh. That makes sense." Baya's voice was flat. Like the riddle, it was obvious once you knew the answer. Not letting panic take over was the common skill needed in order to get through all the tests. She had almost let it consume her in the end. This thought sent another shiver down her spine.

Baya ate enough to feed three people, then almost fell asleep in the tub. She was asleep before her head was on the pillow. And yet it was barely mid-day. Aga tucked her in and issued a prayer of her own. She fervently thanked the Goddess that her daughter was alive.

CHAPTER 27

Fay made her way up the steep mountainside, being careful to stay a safe distance away from the garden boy, as she followed him. She stumbled over the rugged path and complained to herself. The barbaric trail was about to get the best of her and she contemplated giving up and heading back down the slope. But then she saw it — a lovely cove far below. As she reached the top, Fay's chest heaved.

She tried to suck in as much air as possible and take in the lovely view all at once. It was almost worth the effort it took to get there, but not quite. Fay rested on a tree stump and scanned the cove for the boy. She spotted him as he emerged from the trees below, and she forced her shaky legs to climb down after him.

When Fay reached the tree line at the bottom of the mountain she changed herself once again to blend in with a nearby tree. She couldn't see Baya's boyfriend anywhere. Her heart fell as she realized that he must have headed up the mountain on the far side of the cove.

Forget it, I'm not going up there and I can't stand here all afternoon for no reason, she thought.

Fay was about to head back when her eyes briefly scanned the sea.

She did a double take. He was sitting on the water! How, in the name of Ameris, was he able to do that?

It was the last place she would have thought to look for him. She squinted to better make out what she saw on the water. She had never seen anything that far out at sea before. Yet, it was clearly a man and he appeared to be rowing a boat.

Where had he found such a thing? Fay smiled with malice. This was exactly what she was looking for. Shema would want to hear about this.

She headed back up the mountain at once, and struggled down the other side, cursing the trail the entire way. In fact, it was barely traversable in many places. As branches and bushes scraped her arms and pulled at her hair when she passed, she told herself over and over that the trip had been worth it. The boy would pay dearly for rejecting her and of course this meant that Baya too would suffer. Fay should be able to take them both down with this information.

The mistresses would have been dismissed for the day and the council would be meeting in the Great Hall for the day's closing prayers. Fay barged into the Great Hall. Aga and many of the other priestesses lounged about talking freely. Fay approached quickly. The smug and contented look on Aga's face told Fay that Baya must have passed her final test this morning. She was most likely sound asleep right now. That's what Fay had done after making it through the dreadful tests.

"Fay, I thought you were not feeling well," Shema said. She had been speaking with Aga as she sat on her divan.

"Yes, my … head is ... much better." Fay was still winded from her strenuous hike, followed by hurrying up the handful of stairways to Shema's Great Hall.

"The girls said your *stomach* hurt." Aga narrowed her eyes at Fay.

"Yes. … My stomach is feeling better as well. Thank you for asking." Fay quickly tried to cover up her botched lie.

Aga crossed her arms in front of her chest.

"Please, Madam Unawi. I have important news. May I address the council?"

Shema nodded and gestured for her to continue.

"Thank you." Fay bowed slightly. "It's the garden boy."

Aga's eyes widened with interest. She was no fool. She knew her daughter was close to the boy — too close. "What about him?"

Shema lay back, relaxing into her divan, losing interest at once. The petty troubles surrounding a lowly garden boy did not concern her. This was about young love, which always included jealousy. She had no time for such trifles. After all, a garden boy could not cause much trouble.

"He's …" Fay paused for effect. "He's made himself a *boat*."

Aga's mouth fell open.

Shema snapped upright. "What?" she demanded.

"It's true. I saw him, way out at sea rowing a wooden boat."

"That's impossible. Boats are forbidden," one of the priestesses offered.

"Do you doubt the word of my daughter?" May interjected.

"How does he manage to keep it hidden?" Shema's thoughts whirled. How dare he go against the Great Goddess's laws, against me!

Ameris's laws existed only to protect people. It always amazed Shema when someone was ignorant enough to break them. Boats could take people beyond the protection of this island.

Shema stood and paced in front of her divan. The outside world was deadly. Therefore, boats had always been strictly prohibited. This was perfectly logical. Ameris had destroyed all of them and outlawed the creation of any new ones. Why were these basic concepts so hard for some to understand?

Shema took a deep breath, doing her best to regain composure. "Where is this contraption?"

"In a cove tucked away over the mountain to the east of the beach. It's not easy to reach. This is where he and Baya spend their free time. I'm sure of it. She must know about the boat as well."

"Are you saying that my daughter somehow had a part in this illicit behavior?" Aga's jaw clenched tight.

Fay opened her mouth but was cut off.

"What proof do you have regarding her?" Aga snapped.

Fay's shoulders sagged. "I don't, Madam Priestess."

"Then be *very* careful about making such strong accusations."

Of course Baya knows about the boat, Fay thought. Baya could not have spent every free moment with the boy and not have known about it. Can Aga be so blind? Apparently she could when it came to her own flesh and blood.

Yet, Fay understood her limits in the hierarchy. It would do no good to push the matter further. If only Baya had been with him, she could have taken them both down.

Shema sent four of her strongest theos and one of the younger priestesses to retrieve the boy. Fay was to lead the way.

Fay's shoulders slumped even farther at the thought of climbing that mountain again. Maybe she could make one of the theos carry her.

"Bring the offender to me at once," Shema said, as she finished giving her orders.

"Yes, Madame Unawi. And what of the boat?" the young priestess asked.

"Destroy it."

With a nod from the priestess, the entourage was on their way to find Vicaroy.

CHAPTER 28

"If this is true and the boy has managed to build a boat then what will you do?" Aga asked.

"No one has attempted such a feat in ages, certainly not since I have been ruler." Shema paced atop the platform that held her divan. Her theos watched her intently. "Such a crime requires a severe punishment."

Aga's lips formed a tight smile.

"Not imprisonment until death," Shema continued. "That is reserved for only the rarest of crimes — violent crimes. This is not violent, still some time in prison perhaps?"

"Might I suggest banishment?" Prison is not far enough away from Baya, Aga thought. She wanted this criminal out of her daughter's life. She had never liked it that Baya was so fond of the boy. But he made her happy and he was not a problem — until now. He could not be allowed to ruin Baya's bright future with scandalous rumors of forbidden activities.

Aga bit on her finger in deep thought. If the boy were imprisoned Baya would still be able to visit him. And, when his sentence was up he would be free and, no doubt, causing trouble again. No. The threat must be eliminated — for good. Not to mention the boy was not worthy of Aga's daughter. He was an unnecessary distraction for Baya. She would be better off without him.

Shema had been thoughtful as well. "Banishment seems a bit harsh. How will he make his way in the North?"

"That is his problem. How he will survive is not your concern. It's something he should have thought about before he ran off and built a boat. An example must be made of him before others start to think that it's okay to break Ameris's holy laws."

Shema massaged her forehead with her fingers. Every day she prayed for a calling from Ameris to appoint a new Unawi. It was tiring to have to make important decisions — decisions that greatly impacted people's lives. "As always, I am grateful for your guidance, Aga. I don't know what I would do without you. It is no secret that all I want is a life with children of my own before I am too old. I wish someone else could decide what should be done with the boy."

"I am always here to assist you, Madam Unawi."

Shema studied Aga for a moment. At one time, all Aga wanted was to become the ruler and all Shema wanted was Aga's life — to be blessed with lovely daughters. Shema shook her head. People always wanted what they couldn't have.

It seemed like eons passed before the entourage returned with Vicaroy, his hands bound behind his back and his eyes cast down to the floor.

* * *

"IT'S TRUE, Madam Unawi. We found the boy as he was pulling a small boat, like a canoe, onto the beach in a hidden cove, just over the mountain," the young priestess dutifully reported.

As if to further make the point one of Shema's theos threw an oar down in front of Vicaroy.

Vicaroy didn't dare to lift his gaze.

"I turned the boat to ash with my own hands," the priestess declared with pride. "No one will be able to use it again."

Shema nodded her approval, her thoughts whirling. A canoe was hardly a seaworthy vessel. He was simply playing around on the water. He most likely was not trying to leave the island. Still, boats are forbidden.

Aga could see that the Unawi was wavering. "Be stern, Madam Unawi. We must make an example out of him."

"What do you have to say for yourself?" Shema asked.

Vicaroy remained silent. He was grateful that they hadn't bothered to explore any farther. If they had found the cave and his weapons, or his latest invention — that would mean life in prison. Weapons were viewed as man's most evil creation. They would brand him as a violent person, even if he never hurt anyone. He would be as guilty as if he had actually harmed someone.

The imaginary verdict rang through his ears, *He intended to do harm with the weapons*. He didn't want to say anything to incriminate himself for his even greater crimes or to get Baya in trouble along with him.

"Who else knows of your boat."

Vicaroy raised his head and took a deep breath. He looked Shema in the eyes. "No one. I built it and I alone used it. It's … relaxing ..."

He's lying! Fay wanted to shout. Of course, he would say anything to protect Baya. She thought about calling him out on this but one glance toward Aga and she thought better of it.

"I hereby banish you from all of the South. You are never to set foot near Una Sitka again. You have one day to gather your belongings and be on your way." Shema's verdict was final.

Aga's shoulders relaxed and a tight smile crossed her lips.

Fay had hoped for more, but her mission of revenge had still been accomplished. The boy was exiled and Baya would have to live the rest of her life without him. Things were working out perfectly.

CHAPTER 29

Baya didn't have time to enjoy her new freedom or even think about celebrating the fact that she was alive, as Fay was waiting for her when she finally emerged from her room.

"Your garden boy has gone and gotten himself in trouble." Fay's smile was like the sun on a cold winter day. It was bright but there was very little warmth in it. "Big trouble, I'm afraid."

Baya's heart skipped. She blinked at Fay for a moment, still groggy from her nap. She ran for the door, not wanting to hear any more from Fay. She had to find Vicaroy.

Her only thought as she ran to Vicaroy's shack was that he was in danger. When Azod opened the door Baya blurted, "Where's Vicaroy?"

Azod's frown deepened. "You probably know better than I do."

He's in our secret cove, of course. "What happened? I was told he is in trouble."

"He's been permanently relieved from his duties to the Unawi. In fact, he will never work as a gardener again, his reputation will be ruined forever."

"Why would Shema do this? Vicaroy is the best and hardest working gardener around ... well next to you, of course."

"Then it must've had something to do with you."

"Me? I would never do this —"

"The daughter of the highest of the high priestesses was getting too close to the gardener's assistant."

It hit Baya like a blow to her head. She stumbled a step back and placed her hand to her forehead. It was becoming clear — Aga's disapproval of her friendship with Vicaroy and her advising Shema to get rid of the pesky problem — banishing him from the grounds. "He did nothing wrong."

"No, he didn't but that's our lot in life," Azod spat. "They've accused him of having a boat. But Vicaroy would never do such a thing."

Baya's stomach turned into a heavy knot. Her large lunch threatened to come up. They found the boat. That would be more than enough cause for her mother to convince Shema to send Vicaroy away. "What will … happen now?" Baya choked the words out.

"A boy like Vicaroy doesn't have many options and none of them are good."

Baya's heart pounded against her ribcage even before she began to run.

"Leave him alone. You've done enough damage already," Azod called after Baya.

Baya scarcely heard him and she hardly slowed her pace until she reached the top of the mountain. Her legs were on fire from the fast-paced climb and the loud drumming of her heart was all she could hear. She thought it might come right out of her chest.

Vicaroy could be seen far below, sitting on the rock outcropping in front of their cave. He sat with his elbows resting over his knees staring out at the sea. He had not moved an inch in the time it took her to reach him.

Baya slowly sat down next to him.

Vicaroy didn't look at her. "So you heard?"

She nodded. "Is this my fault?"

Vicaroy chuckled. "You didn't banish me. You were not the one who declared that I have to leave the South and never return. And that

I would never be able to find work anywhere near Una Sitka ever again."

"What?" Baya's mouth fell open. This was worse than she had thought. He was not simply kicked out of the palace gardens but … *banished.*

"It appears that Shema, or perhaps more accurately, your mother, doesn't want me anywhere near you."

"You see? This *is* my fault." Tears filled her eyes. "What will you do?"

"I'm sure Shema's shaming me as a sinner, a sacred-law-breaker, will quickly spread over most of the island. I have to move to the North where they don't know my face. I will have to change my name if I ever hope to work as a gardener again."

Baya wiped a tear away. "How did they manage to find the boat?"

"I don't know. Someone must've followed me here."

She narrowed her eyes. "Fay."

"It doesn't matter."

But it mattered to Baya. "Why would Fay do this?" Baya had almost forgotten about Fay taking Vicaroy away the previous evening. "What happened between you two last night?"

"Nothing." Vicaroy told her the story.

Baya smiled. "I'm relieved that you got away from her."

"You think *you're* relieved. I've never been more grateful. She's a wretched person."

"True — and I know her. She would be furious with you for refusing her. She must've followed you here and seen you with the boat. Of course, and then she ran straight to Shema."

Vicaroy nodded. "I suppose. It doesn't matter. The damage is done."

"Of course it was Fay." Baya could not let it go, as Vicaroy seemed willing to do. "One time, Fay hid a dead bird inside a girl's mattress because she had heard a rumor that the girl had said something bad about her. The bird was not found until it reeked so bad the girl could no longer stand to sleep in her room. It took weeks for the smell to disappear. That was when Fay was only twelve. She's playing grown-up games now."

Vicaroy shrugged. He would not waste another second thinking about that evil woman. He had bigger concerns and there was nothing he could do against a powerful woman like Fay. "Baya, I have to leave tomorrow."

"That soon! That doesn't give us much time to figure out what to do."

"Shema generously gave me one day to gather my things and get out of town."

Baya shook her head in dismay. "I'm finally free to spend more time with you. My education is done. I'm no longer a mistress and now this. … One of the only things that kept me going this past month was getting to be with you and my family more." Tears streamed down her cheeks.

Vicaroy gently took her bandaged hand. "I take it the tests didn't get any easier."

Baya shook her head. "No. But I'm alive and it's over."

"Thank the Great Goddess for that."

"That's enough about me. What will you do, Vicaroy?"

Baya looked at him with such dismay that he thought his heart would break in two. Her dark eyes with the burst of green and gold at the center had always made her irresistible. It killed him to see them so full of pain. "I'm not the son of a high priestess, so it's unlikely that I will be chosen by a woman who could support me. I have to work outside the home … somehow."

Baya narrowed her eyes. What did he mean — he needed to become someone's theo in order to survive outside the palace? She didn't fully understand why this bothered her — really bothered her. "Surely there's some other work you could do. Perhaps you could change your name and …"

"And What? Change my profession? I only know how to garden."

Baya searched for an answer. "There must be some other option, some way for you to stay." Nothing came to mind.

"The only way I would not have to leave is …"

"What is it?" Baya looked at him with wide hopeful eyes.

"Well, I'd have to go underground, out of Shema's sight completely."

Baya shook her head, not comprehending.

"I could join the theater."

"Don't be ridiculous. The Unawi forbids it and all *theaters* have long since been shut down."

"You live in a pretend world — safely tucked away in a palace. That's okay though. I often shut out the world beyond the gardens. Living here made it easy to believe that all of Pathins was as lovely and pure as the royal grounds."

He opened his hand to reveal a small rock. He threw it as far as he could. "Well, never again. I'm in the real world now. Just because something is banned doesn't mean that it doesn't exist, like our boat. Shema's men found one such establishment just eight years ago, remember?"

Baya nodded. She vaguely remembered hearing news of a functioning theater.

"Sure, Shema had it shut down but that in no way stopped it. It sent the theater ring deeper underground — to a new location."

Vicaroy knew more about life on the streets than she did, so she would give him this much. "But that can't be your only option if you stay here." The theater was a cover for the practice of prostitution. It had always been deemed unholy by the Unawi.

The *theater* usually consisted of a play, or sometimes men would dance, and then after the performance women would bid on the men they wanted. Baya had learned about this in her history lessons. She thought that the women who were low enough to do this were the worst of sinners. Only sick and desperate women would pay men to be with them. She had thought it was a very old practice that had died out centuries ago — or perhaps that was just what Shema had told her. Apparently, it still existed and always would find a way as long as there was a demand for such atrocities.

Vicaroy interrupted her thoughts. "A man, especially a young and handsome one, can make a good living this way. So I've heard."

CHAPTER 30

Baya jumped to her feet. "You can't be serious about this!" Her fingers curled into fists. This shot pain up her arm from her burned hand. She didn't care. "No! I won't let that happen. You can't ..." Baya panted, suddenly short of breath.

Vicaroy stood. He placed his hands on Baya's shoulders. To her surprise he was smiling.

"That's the reaction I was hoping for," he said.

She exhaled so deeply it pushed her lips out. "So you won't join the theater?"

"Azod thinks it's my best option."

Baya growled, actually growled at him.

Vicaroy laughed. "I think, I would try my chances with a new name in the North before I would resort to ... prostitution."

Baya's heart sank. "You have to leave? Or become a ..." she couldn't make herself say it. Prostitution was akin to the worst curse word in the world, especially with Vicaroy's name associated with it. He had come close to being forced to be with Fay. She couldn't bear the thought of him having to entertain sick old women. The tears were back. She lowered her head and covered her eyes with her hands. She shouldn't cry, women were stronger than this. Yet, the tears continued to fall.

"There's one other option."

Baya jerked her head up. "What?"

He was in deep thought, looking out at the sea.

"What?" she demanded.

He took her good hand in his and looked into her eyes. "Run away with me."

Baya's jaw dropped. She tried to speak but couldn't. There were too many questions all at once — far too much to process. So nothing came out.

"I've been thinking. Here's what I've got so far; we set sail —"

"Set sail!" Baya blurted.

"Yes —"

"Wait! You mean ..." She looked out over the seemingly endless ocean. There was nothing but water, an expansive nothingness. "You want us to leave Pathins?"

"What did you think I meant?"

"That you wanted me to go to the North with you."

"I thought about it but that would never work. Even if you could find a way to support us, your mother would post scrolls on every tree all over the island, with your face on each one. We could never outrun her — you're too well known."

Baya swayed. She sat down in case her legs decided to stop working altogether. She placed her hands on the hard rock underneath her. She needed to know that something so unchangeable and strong was supporting her.

Vicaroy sat down as well. He remained silent, giving her time to think.

"So those are our only options? We head out into the wild where no other humans can be found or you leave me and try to make your way in the North."

Her insides churned when she said the second option out loud. It was unbearable to think of life without him. They would never see each other again. He would eventually become someone's theo. She grit her teeth. Yet the thought of leaving Pathins was somehow not as bad — why? Because she would be with him. But —

"Yes, my options are limited, but just imagine what it would be like to see the world?"

The light of excitement shone in his eyes. It was a light that Baya hadn't seen in a while. "You have spent a lot of time thinking about this, haven't you?" she said.

"Of course, when I was a kid I used to dream about exploring the world. That's how I ventured far enough to find this place. I have only ever felt at home in the garden and when I head out to sea in my canoe. If I can no longer garden in the palace then ... what better place for me than the sea?"

"Well, I for one don't need to imagine what the world's like out there. I've seen it in Ameris's scrolls. We wouldn't last a day — if we could even find land."

"You don't really believe all that about the big scary world out there, do you?" he asked.

"Why wouldn't I? It's written in the ancient scrolls." She blinked at him in disbelief. "Don't you believe in Ameris's text?"

"I don't know. It could be true but the only way to find out for sure is to go there — to see for ourselves. Look, if there are truly deadly animals out there, we can protect ourselves. I have my weapons and you have your powers. Together we can do this. We can survive out there. I know it."

Mook popped into Baya's mind. She'd survived in the arena with him. The world would be dangerous but maybe he was right and they could make their way. "I can't even begin to see how we could manage this and ... Shema is too old to be the ruler for much longer. Everyone is certain that the next Unawi will be called upon to serve and I've just completed my studies. I'm ready —"

"To become Unawi." Vicaroy completed her sentence. "It's perfect timing. You've passed your tests and are poised to become the next ruler." He shook his head. "How can I possibly ask you to leave all that?" He pulled his legs in tight and lowered his head to his knees.

Baya took a deep breath. That was final. She had to stay. Her future was here.

He looked at her and set his jaw with determination. "Baya, you don't want to become Unawi. The pressures of ruling will wear you down. You want to have children … someday and … you've only worked so hard at your education because your mother wants you to. Forget about her. What do *you* want?"

The question took her by surprise. She had never thought about what *she* wanted. "Life is what it is. As Aga's firstborn, I have to be the best. Nothing less will do. There's nothing I can do about my life …" or was there? Could she possibly make her own choices? Part of her answered with an, Of course not! This was the side that longed to please her mother. Yet there was another side and it said, It's about damn time you make a decision for yourself.

Vicaroy gazed at her in silence, allowing her to struggle with her thoughts.

"I know that I don't want to die at sea or be eaten by some giant wild beast," Baya finally said. What if Tash were to become the next Unawi. She envisioned Aga gushing over her perfect daughter, forgetting about Baya entirely. "And I can't let Tash … win." She inhaled sharply as the next thought hit her, "Or worse, Fay." Baya shivered.

Vicaroy raised an eyebrow at her.

Baya looked away. She knew it was wrong to be jealous of her sister, but she was.

"What I'm about to do is the most selfish thing I've ever done," he said.

Baya was going to ask what he was talking about when Vicaroy wrapped his arm around her waist and pulled her to him. He placed his lips squarely on hers. She tried to pull back in surprise but he held her close.

Baya's head felt light as he continued to kiss her. The sensation that spread through her body was strange and wonderful. His kisses grew more intense, hungry. He ran his tongue along her lower lip before consuming her with another kiss.

A deep tingling feeling settled in her lower abdomen. She wasn't sure if she wanted to push him away to make the unfamiliar sensation stop or if she wanted to push him to the ground and crawl on top of him.

When he pulled away, Baya had to take a couple deep breaths. She shook her head to gather her thoughts. "Why…" she stuttered, "was that selfish? And why haven't you done that before?"

"It's rude for a man to be so forward. I'm sure it happens but it's the woman's job to make the first move. I've been waiting for a long time for you to kiss me but I'm out of time … I had to."

"Well, rude or not, I'm glad you did. It was … nice." This was a stupid thing to say as it was a complete understatement but it was the only word that came to her foggy mind.

"So many times, I've wanted to do that. It was selfish to kiss you because I'm trying to convince you that I'm what you want. You want more of that." He placed his palm gently on her neck and ran his thumb along her lower lip. "You don't want to become the ruler and have to deal with all the world's problems. I'm offering you something … different, something better."

Baya could only watch his lips. It was all she could do not to press her mouth to his. She forced herself to look away. Rubbing the back of her neck she thought, pull yourself together. "Alright, I'm listening. Tell me about this plan of yours."

Vicaroy smiled and his honey-colored eyes danced. "I've been working on a new boat, one much bigger than my canoe."

"Okay, that solves the problem of how we will get off the island." Baya's thoughts came quickly. "However, neither one of us knows how to sail. And if we did, where would we sail to? And if we did know where we were going, we have no idea how long it would take to reach land. So we couldn't possibly know how many provisions we would need to somehow carry with us." The reality of the situation fully hit Baya and her good hand clenched and unclenched several times before she jumped to her feet. "And I can't leave Rus and Bek and … my mom. Plus, we would be alone, no other humans."

Baya looked around, suddenly aware that the suns were getting close to setting. "I have to get back before the doors are locked for the night." Baya's eyes widened with realization. "Where will you sleep?"

"Well, I'm banished from the palace grounds so I brought my bedding from home." He pointed to the large cave behind them.

Baya put her hands over her face as she burst into tears. Vicaroy had to sleep in a cave, like some animal from the old scrolls. It was all too much. She ran.

"Baya. Wait!"

She glanced back briefly and the look on Vicaroy's face made everything worse, even though she didn't think that was possible. She'd never seen such dismay, such desperation before. "I can't! I can't do any of this." She didn't stop until she reached the palace doors, drenched in sweat and tears.

CHAPTER 31

Baya burst into the mistress's common room.

"Oh, there you are." Fay mocked. "I wondered where you disappeared to."

Something snapped in Baya as she rounded on Fay. "Why do you care where I go or what I do? You had better not have had anything to do with this."

Fay crossed her arms and smiled her smug, self-satisfied smile. "Why, Baya. I don't know what you're talking about."

"You had better not. I swear Fay, you and your games will catch up with you someday."

Fay inhaled dramatically and placed her fingers gently against her chest.

"Don't fake innocence with me. You had better pray that I don't become Unawi." Baya stormed out of the room.

She couldn't get comfortable in her bed. When she closed her eyes she saw Vicaroy sleeping alone on the cave floor. She finally drifted off but her mind was full of thrashing winds and rain at sea. The sheets of rain turned into large claws as they nearly missed ripping her flesh to shreds. When the first sun was on the rise her dreams calmed as Vicaroy wrapped his arms around her and placed his lips to hers.

* * *

BAYA SAT STRAIGHT UP in bed, shaking the dream out of her head. It had been of Vicaroy playing with two small children — her children. They squealed with delight as he chased them through tall grass.

She stood, and splashed her face with water from the washbasin. She peered intently at herself in the mirror. "I love him and I can't lose him," she whispered.

A smile crept across her face. "I do love him and I'm going with him, no matter what." Then she frowned. Her hair was a mess from the restless night. She quickly brushed it and put on her casual clothes, a pair of breeches and a tunic, before heading out with determination.

As she exited the common room she nodded to Fay. "Good morning." Have fun with your games, she thought.

Fay looked at Baya with wide eyes, surprised at Baya's high spirits. Then her face fell into a scowl.

Baya marched right up to Vicaroy. He sat staring out at the sea in the exact same spot as the day before. She wondered if he had moved at all. She tucked her tunic under her as she sat down gracefully next to him. With the slightest smile she said, "So, when do we set sail?"

He looked away and his shoulders slumped.

This was not the reaction Baya had hoped for. "What's wrong? I thought you wanted to leave the island."

"It was ... terrible of me to kiss you like that. I never should've. I couldn't sleep last night —"

"Neither could I, but maybe for you it was because you were on a cave floor."

"No. That's not it. You have everything here. And I can't take that from you just because I have nothing. You deserve a comfortable life ... in a palace. You were born to become Unawi and you deserve all the best. I can't give that to you. I can't be selfish enough to take all that from you."

Baya smiled at the sea. "Even if it's a life I don't want? One I've never wanted?" She was surprised at the absolute calm that she felt. Her mind was made up and she was utterly content. "You're all I've ever needed."

He shook his head and stood. She took his hand to stop him from leaving. "Vicaroy, I want to be with you." She got to her feet.

Vicaroy studied her. He looked deep into her eyes and finally wrapped his arms around her, pressing her body against his. "There won't be any palaces or manicured gardens where we're going."

Baya exhaled with relief. She had hoped for another kiss but there would be plenty of time for that. Besides they had a lot of planning to do. It was overwhelming to think about where to start. Nobody had left the island … ever.

Vicaroy's arms tightened around her shoulders and he took a deep breath, as if inhaling her scent.

Something felt wrong. She pulled away in order to look at him. His eyes shone with emotion. "What's troubling you?"

"Nothing." His response was entirely too quick. He cleared his throat. "I guess we'd better start by having a look at the new boat."

A ghost of a smile tugged at the corners of his mouth and Baya relaxed.

Vicaroy took her hand and led her into the cave. "A boat much bigger than the canoe will be needed to withstand the open ocean. Come, I've been dying to show you."

Inside the cave was a massive lumpy form hidden under blankets. He removed the covers and her mouth fell open. The boat was huge. It stood as tall as Baya. It had two distinct halves. The back end was open and wider, with two long benches running along either side. They ended with another shorter bench.

"This is the back of the boat." Vicaroy pointed to the smallest bench. "We'll steer the boat from back here."

Baya managed to nod.

A covered compartment made up the front half of the boat, which tapered to a point at its nose.

"How were you able to make this?" Baya said.

"I've been working on it for a while. You've been so busy with school and this was a way to pass the time. Actually, I've been collecting the wood for about a year, it came together rather quickly, once I started building it. Finding the perfect driftwood was the hard part."

"Wow." Baya ran her hand along the side of the boat. It felt sturdy.

"After I built my canoe I wanted to try to build a boat like the ones carved on the palace doors."

"Like the ones from the time of Ameris," Baya whispered.

"What do you think?"

"It … It's amazing. It could hold ten people."

"Fifteen actually. It will be enough to carry a couple of people and their supplies off this island."

"This might actually work." Baya looked at him with wide eyes. "You've been planning this all along. You always wanted to leave the island."

"Not at first. I wanted to see if I could build something this big and see if it would still float. I wanted to take it out at night and learn to sail, yet I never thought about truly leaving the garden or Azod and, of course, I couldn't leave you."

He looked away sheepishly. "Sometimes I wondered about what it would be like to leave but I never actually thought I would — until everything changed yesterday." He frowned. "My old life is gone … for good. And this is the life I want now, to find out what is out there."

"And yet a part of you must have suspected this day would come and you wanted to be prepared," Baya said.

Vicaroy shrugged. "I don't know, maybe. But really, I started making this boat for something to do, nothing more."

Baya nodded. She believed him. "Can I ask you something?" She didn't wait for a response. "You knew that getting close to me could cost you dearly and yet you still befriended me?"

"Azod always warned me about the mistresses. He says women are trouble but I couldn't have stayed away if I'd wanted to. I ..." he paused then changed what he was about to say. "I've always been ... drawn to you. I mean, you're my best friend."

"Yeah." Baya bit her lower lip and looked away. He had lost everything because of her and yet he didn't regret becoming her friend.

CHAPTER 32

Shema was carried out of the palace gates on her sedan chair. The four theos who upheld the sedan didn't appear to strain in the least. They carried her smoothly across the town square and up to the platform that overlooked the immense coliseum. This was where all important town celebrations occurred and where Shema would address her subjects.

The Unawi's presence in public always sent a ripple through the city. If it was not a major holiday, then it meant she had an important announcement. And today was not a holiday. So the citizens of Una Sitka gathered quickly — always hungry for news.

The ruler sat elegantly atop a high throne that overlooked the coliseum floor far below. She waited patiently for the masses to fill the thousands of seats stretching out in an oval shape around her. When it appeared that most of the city had gathered, she rose to address them in the loudest voice she could muster. "Thank you all for coming. You are here to witness the banishment of one of my very own palace workers."

On cue, Vicaroy was marched out onto the coliseum floor surrounded by four of Shema's theos. Gasps and whispers spread through the crowd. He was forced to stand facing the direction of the Unawi, even though she was high above. He kept his chin down.

"I'm sure you are all curious what this boy did to deserve banishment. He made and was using a ..." Shema paused to build suspense. "A boat."

More gasps were heard from those closest to Shema and the noise of the crowd spread as her words were passed across the stadium by her top priestesses. She held up Vicaroy's oar as evidence of his betrayal.

"Vicaroy!" She boomed. "Do you admit to the people of Una Sitka that you committed this crime?"

Without hesitation Vicaroy nodded that he did. He wanted to get the humiliation over with as soon as possible. He'd been caught with the boat and Shema continued to hold his oar out in front of her as a symbol of his guilt for all to see. No one would believe him over the high priestess who had found him. His punishment would only be worse if he denied it.

More gasps and even shouts from religious zealots could be heard. "How dare you defy the Great Goddess?" one man yelled above the roar of the crowd.

"You will bring Her wrath down upon us," another shouted.

Shema held her arm out and it took some time before the people quieted down.

"Let me take this moment to remind all of you about the dangers that lie beyond Pathins," the Unawi began. "The Almighty Goddess gave us this fruitful island and She guides us with Her laws that were clearly laid out for us. She did this because She loves us. She wants to keep us safe. This land and Her sacred scrolls are proof of this."

Shema slowly lowered her arm. "The creation of boats is forbidden. This is for our own protection. The High Council and I work hard every day to continue to protect the Goddess's island paradise. We must live by Ameris's laws if we wish to remain safe. The punishments for breaking Her laws are severe."

The ruler paused so that her words could be passed through the crowd before continuing, "If people defy Ameris then She will lower the powerful walls of protection that surround this wonderful and peaceful land. Womenkind would become hunted once again. All would perish. We are to remain here where we are free."

The Unawi smiled as if she were looking down upon children. "There is no need to leave this Divine Island that Ameris so graciously provided for us. Any attempt to do so is a grave violation that brings about consequences."

Shema dramatically threw her arms out, holding the oar over her head. The crowd roared their approval. Shema had always been able to move the masses with her impassioned speeches, which Aga helped write.

Vicaroy was marched out of the square. Once on the main street a crowd gathered behind Vicaroy as the four theos escorted him far out of town. He tried to ignore the murmuring of the crowd but the occasional shouts were impossible to tune out. The most religiously devout amongst them were furious that he would dare to put Pathins in such danger.

Baya followed, keeping her distance behind the crowd. She had watched the public spectacle from her mother's side, as Aga had demanded. Otherwise Baya would not have gone. The last thing she wanted was to see the man she loved publicly shamed.

There were no tears to hold back from her mother. Baya only felt a growing anger for a society that would treat Vicaroy like this. He was a loving and caring person — one of the few truly good people that she knew — and yet this community would cast him out like dirt.

Fay should be the one in his place, Baya thought.

Once the crowd reached the outskirts of the city most stopped following the criminal procession. Vicaroy paused to scan the remaining faces for Baya. Their eyes met briefly and she gave him a knowing nod, her face expressionless. He gave a slight tilt of the head in return.

She turned on her heel and headed back into the city.

The theos were to escort him even farther North — far out of the city.

Vicaroy was glad to see Baya had come all this way. She was the only one who had not forsaken him.

Azod had refused to partake in the public spectacle. He had said his goodbyes just outside the palace walls. Vicaroy had been instructed to return to the palace gates that morning. Azod was allowed to give him any possessions he deemed necessary. The theos took Vicaroy away and Azod returned to his home to weep for the boy he had raised, the son of the woman he had once loved.

The theos stayed with him longer than Vicaroy had expected. It was not until they were at the base of the mountain range that they unceremoniously turned and headed back toward the city. Vicaroy traveled north a bit farther until he was sure that they were gone and that no crazed zealots were still following him.

The mountains that loomed ahead were many times taller than the ones that surrounded their cove. He had always wondered what it was like in the North. It was colder than Una Sitka, so he'd heard. He shivered at the thought of the long trek up and over the huge mountains with only the pack on his back.

Thankfully, he wouldn't be going that way.

Instead of continuing north he darted off the trail and headed east. Being farther out of town than he had ever been before he didn't know how long it would take him to reach the cove. He had to stay off the main road, or any road, for that matter. He had to make his own path through the forest back to the cove. He prayed that he could get back before dark or it would be impossible to find his way.

CHAPTER 33

Once again Vicaroy's prayers had been answered as he had been able to make his way back to the cove.

The preparations for their journey began at once. Baya joined Vicaroy most afternoons as soon as she could slip away from her interim duties in the palace. There wasn't much for her to do in the palace since she had officially completed her education. Fay already did most of the grunt work, which she quickly tried to push off onto Baya.

Not on your life, Baya thought, as she conjured the sweetest smile she could muster. "I would *never* take any of your important duties away from you, Fay."

It was required that Baya join the priestesses for the morning protection rituals, as she was to learn how to carry on these traditions. Directly afterward, she'd head to the library to scour through the old scrolls.

Baya was familiar with many of them but this time she was looking at them with a different purpose. She looked for clues about the world beyond Pathins, anything she might have passed over as unimportant before — specifically, things that were not covered in her formal education. For example, a map of the world would have been incredibly helpful. Yet the geography section only contained maps of Pathins.

Beyond the common warnings about the "big bad world" that awaited beyond Pathins she didn't find much of use. Baya re-read the stories of the city where Ameris lived before she brought her people to Pathins.

When Ameris first came to this world She'd made Her home in a city called Merth. All accounts had been adamant that there were no survivors left behind, when Ameris and Her followers set out for the Holy Land of Plenty, Pathins.

A number of years of drought had caused crops to fail. People began to go hungry as well as animals that relied on foliage. When these animals died off, the predators that fed on such prey became more of a threat to the human population. It was a time of great famine and deadly attacks from wild beasts. The mistresses were taught that all who didn't follow Ameris to the new land had perished.

Buried in the back of a shelf underneath a pile of scrolls, Baya uncovered one that had not been unrolled in a very long time. She thought the parchment might break apart in her hands. Very carefully she unrolled it and quickly became immersed in its material.

Baya hardly moved until she had read it in full. It told of an uprising by a group of people who didn't believe that Ameris knew of such a perfect land. They thought Her talk of the island of Pathins was a ruse — some sort of trick — a land that never got too hot or too cold, a place where all the predators could be banished forever, a place that would never suffer a drought. According to some this was too good to be true.

These faithless people opted to remain behind. Ameris believed that She and Her followers were better off without these non-believers. Yet this was just one account, which seemed to contradict what Baya had read before. She had been taught that Ameris loved all humans and had come down from the heavens to save them all in their time of great need.

She never would have left anyone behind. Or would She? Baya wondered ...

Whether or not there had been survivors was impossible to discern. Even if there were humans who had stayed in Merth there was no indication that they could have survived the drought and animal attacks. There also was no record of a way to find the ancient society of Merth, no maps, no clues.

After days of searching the scrolls, Baya was losing hope. Any maps of the world must have been lost or — more likely — purposefully destroyed hundreds of years ago.

Her relentless searching led her to the bottom shelf in the back of the vast royal library. Under a couple of decades of dust was a pile of scrolls that caught her eye. She brushed cobwebs aside to read some of the titles. Her heart leapt. Maps! Hopefully they weren't more maps of Pathins. That was the last thing she needed.

The first one was indeed of Pathins, but it was much older and more rudimentary than the ones in the main areas of the library. Many of the more modern cities were not marked and the shape of the island was not as well defined as on the newer maps. It must've been one of the first maps of the island. She quickly unrolled the next one and sighed. "Pathins." Another — Una Sitka. Another — Pathins, again. She tossed them behind her, no longer caring about damaging these useless texts.

Another and another — smaller cities around the island. She was expecting more of the same and almost tossed it over her shoulder when the word "Merth" caught her eye at the top of the page. She jumped to her feet and let out a victory yelp.

She quickly glanced around to make sure no one was nearby before delving into the map. It contained an outline of a city and not much else — no indication as to where that city might be located. So she quickly snatched another scroll and unrolled it, being more careful this time. Her lips parted as she read the title, *The World as We Know It*.

Baya glanced at the large map briefly but was curious about the remaining parchments. The next was a text she had never read before followed by a couple more maps of the world. She scooped all pertinent texts up into her arms and headed out.

Baya was filled with excitement as she headed for the alcove. She was even more careful than usual about being followed. She made herself and all she carried blend into the forest long before she reached the hidden trailhead.

These weren't forbidden texts, per se, she mused as she hiked up the steep hill. They had simply been forgotten. They'd been filed away and, without a need for this information, they'd been cast aside as useless.

The information about the world beyond Pathins hadn't been relevant for a millennium ... unless someone was crazy enough to leave this paradise island. That's how confident the leaders of Pathins were. These maps were preserved for history, yet why would anyone be interested in them? Well, Baya, for one, was very interested.

CHAPTER 34

Baya unrolled a large scroll on the bow of the boat. It was a chart of the night sky. "With my knowledge of the stars, I will be able to guide us. This scroll here," Baya held up another parchment. "Describes vast lands to the East. Of course, they don't say how far East."

"So, we sail East." Vicaroy rubbed the back of his neck and shifted uncomfortably.

"You okay?"

"Yep. Hey, will you teach me how to read the stars?"

Baya frowned. He was a terrible liar — something was clearly wrong. "Sure. There'll be plenty of time while we sail for me to show you."

"I need to know now."

Baya narrowed her eyes. "Why? We have more pressing things to think about and I imagine it will be quite boring for days on end at sea."

"Please — teach me now."

Baya shook her head. "Okay." There was still much to do to prepare for their journey and time was running out. Yet it was not worth fighting over, so she began a brief summary.

"You see this star here." She pointed at the map. "It's called the immotile star. Unlike most of the other stars, this one is special. It remains in the same place throughout the night. It always hangs in the Eastern sky surrounded by the constellation of Ameris."

She outlined the shapely figure of a woman in the stars on the map. "It's the holiest of constellations. That's why it's thought to bring good luck to girls who are born when Ameris stands upright in the night's sky."

Vicaroy nodded. He had heard people say things like, "Ameris stands tonight, so we have luck on our side." He had not fully understood what that meant until now. "And we follow this star Eastward?"

Baya smiled. He was a fast learner. "That's right. And the largest sun will guide us by day."

Vicaroy studied the map intently. "Perhaps I — I mean *we* should leave when Ameris's constellation is upright."

"You're not usually so superstitious." Baya studied the map. "Although, we could use all the luck we can get. Ameris is lying flat now. She will have to rotate two-hundred and seventy degrees before she stands again."

Baya rotated her fingers along the map indicating the path of Ameris's constellation. She closed her eyes and did some quick mental calculations. "The constellation won't stand upright again for over one-hundred days."

Vicaroy frowned. "We don't have that long. Someone will find me and the boat will be destroyed. I will be imprisoned for life if Shema finds my weapons. I'm not even supposed to be near the city, remember, let alone making a real boat to leave the island."

"Right." Baya's stomach clenched at the thought of Vicaroy being caught. "We have to leave as soon as possible."

"One week. We must have the boat ready and stocked with supplies within one week," he said.

* * *

BAYA GATHERED supplies over the next handful of days, taking only what food, fabrics, water containers and the like that could easily be carried. She hoped they would not be missed from the vast royal supplies.

Vicaroy was busy braiding ropes and sewing sails. He spent most of his time hidden in the cave in case someone happened into the cove — again.

When their work slowed at the end of the day, Baya hoped that she would get another chance at a kiss. But Vicaroy stayed well away — busily out of reach at all times.

What is wrong with him? she wondered.

* * *

THE NEXT PROBLEM was getting the large vessel out of the cave. They could easily carry the canoe, but not Vicaroy's latest invention. Vicaroy looked down the cliff to the water. She could hardly lift one end. There was no way they could carry it over the cliff.

"We need a ramp to slide it into the water ... somehow." Baya's face was tight with concentration.

"That's it! We need two logs that reach from the cave opening down to the water."

Vicaroy secured two long poles less than the width of the boat apart from each other. Baya focused on lifting the front of the boat with her mind while Vicaroy shoved from behind. The boat slid down the poles. With outreached arms Baya used her powers to help guide it down the logs and into the water.

"We did it," Baya yelled.

Vicaroy took Baya in his arms and swung her around. When he looked back toward the water, the boat was heading out to sea. He raced down the ladder and plunged into the water. By the time he reached the vessel and dragged it back to shore he was soaked and panting.

"At least it floats." Baya yelled after him.

"Did you doubt my abilities?"

Baya laughed. "No. Never. I couldn't have built something like this."

After tying the boat off to a rock, Vicaroy waded into the water and swung himself into the boat. He inspected it carefully for any signs of leaks. He found none — his craftsmanship was good.

They loaded it with as many supplies as they dared.

"It's still sitting high in the water," Vicaroy said. "It should be able to carry us and our supplies with ease. It's as ready as it will ever be."

They looked at each other with wide eyes. The sudden reality of what they were about to do fully consumed them. It was as if a million tiny bugs scurried about in Baya's stomach as adrenaline flooded her body.

"Are we actually going to do this?" She studied the shoreline of the cove and surrounding mountains. This was her favorite place. It was quiet and safe — peaceful. "Are we crazy for wanting to leave?"

"Definitely." Vicaroy pulled her close and inhaled her scent. "You can stay, you know?" He wasn't sure if he wanted her to agree or not. He wanted her to care about him enough to leave with him but then again if she backed out on her own he wouldn't have to sneak away tonight. He could leave with a clear conscience.

Baya looked into his eyes. "I'm ready."

He nodded but couldn't hold her gaze — the guilt was overwhelming. "Tomorrow morning then. It's getting late."

Baya glanced toward the suns. One was still quite high in the sky. What's wrong with him? Maybe he was just nervous about the voyage? Of course that was it. This was the scariest and stupidest thing anyone could possibly do. That must be why he hadn't kissed her again. He's focused. That was okay, they would soon have plenty of time together.

"Well, I should spend some time with Bek and Rus. You know, to say goodbye, without actually telling them what I'm up to." Baya exhaled heavily. "It won't be easy."

"Maybe you should stay."

"Don't be ridiculous. I told you, this is what I want. I don't want a life of politics and petty games."

Vicaroy nodded solemnly and pulled on the rope that tied the boat to the shore, forcing the bow into the sandy shore. He helped Baya out.

"See you at first light." Baya was surprisingly more excited than nervous or sad.

Vicaroy only stared off into the distance. He didn't want to let go of her waist after setting her on the beach.

"What's wrong?" She gently rubbed his shoulder to try to get him to look at her.

He wanted to tell her so many things; like how hard it would be without her, how much he would miss her. That he loved her. …

Baya misread his sorrowful expression. "We'll be fine. With my powers and your strength and weapons we will survive out there. We'll find land and … make a new life for ourselves, one without Shema's rules. In fact, we'll get to make our own rules."

Vicaroy forced a smile. "That sounds … perfect." He paused for a long moment, then spoke quickly. "Of course we'll make it. See you at first light."

Baya moved to leave but he swiftly took her by the waist and pressed his lips to hers. She enjoyed the sensation that spread through her body and settled in her belly. Thankfully he was brave enough to take the initiative again. She slowly wrapped her arms around his neck.

"Good night." Baya whispered, when she pulled away.

With a brief wave, Vicaroy watched her walk away. He stared after her for a long time, even when she was out of sight. He fought the urge to run after her. Shaking his head to clear it, he went to the cave to make sure nothing had been left behind.

Vicaroy debated leaving Baya's bag of clothes on the beach. But they did smell like her, so he opted to keep them — something to have of hers. He sat on the beach for a moment, this time staring at the mountains around the cove. He'd have plenty of time to watch the sea. Actually, before this was over he would be sick of the water. However, he would never set his sights on these mountains again … or the cove … or Baya.…

When the last sun was on the horizon, Vicaroy untied the rope that had stayed the boat, wading into the cool water as he pushed it out to sea. He paused at the sound of rustling bushes behind him. Narrowing his eyes, he studied the tree line, but couldn't see anything. He must've been imagining things. So he swung himself into the boat and rowed away from shore.

CHAPTER 35

Fay ran as fast as she could toward the palace.

That is just like a man, sneaky and conniving, Fay thought. Vicaroy can't leave without Baya. She has to go.

This was the perfect way to get Baya out of her way. With her gone there would be no one better suited to become Unawi than Fay.

"Baya!" Fay yelled.

Baya was headed up the path to the palace on her way to see Bek and Rus for the last time. She frowned when she saw Fay running toward her from the beach.

Fay's brow sparkled with sweat and she gasped for air.

"What are you doing out here?" Baya asked.

"Never mind that. He's leaving!"

"Who's leaving? What are you talking about?"

"The garden boy — well, the *former* garden boy." Fay panted as she pointed to the sea.

From this vantage point Baya could spot a tiny speck making its way through the waves far below. "No," she whispered. "He wouldn't!"

It didn't take Fay long to catch her breath and find her sarcasm. "I guess he doesn't really love you after all."

Baya bolted down the path.

Fay gave a self-satisfied smile. "I'll tell your mother goodbye for you."

"Screw you," Baya yelled over her shoulder.

When Baya reached the water's edge directly South of the palace, she lifted her long tunic over her head in one quick motion, hardly pausing as she plunged into the blue water. She swam as hard as she could for the distant speck out at sea. The water grew cooler as she left the land behind. Her arms and legs grew heavy. She forced herself to keep going.

Don't stop. You can't stop, she kept telling herself over and over as she tried to ignore her aching limbs.

Baya swam much farther than she ever had before, when it hit her, what was she thinking? She couldn't make it that far out to sea. She paused and treaded water. The shore was now farther away than Vicaroy.

She had no choice, so she pushed on, forcing her arms to stroke and her legs to kick, again and again.

Not only did the water get cooler but the waves grew stronger. When the sea became too rough she could no longer make it over the tall waves. She stopped swimming and treaded water. Her eyes widened with fear and a scream escaped as she watched a powerful wave roll over her head, forcing her under. Baya fought to make it to the surface. She was able to gulp in some air before the next wave swept over her. Panic rose as the memories of being trapped in a dark well consumed her.

She couldn't breathe. Fighting for the surface, her head broke the water. She gasped for air only to have a wave smash down over her. Her throat and lungs burned as salty water rushed into them.

No. No! I'm stuck in water that I can't escape. Not again, please no, Goddess, help me. Baya's thoughts terrorized her.

The eerie bubbly silence of being submerged under water was all she could hear. She floated helplessly in the vast blue abyss.

This was it. She had been able to survive the royal tests, yet this was how she would die.

No. It can't be, not like this. I can't give up. I have survived worse. I can do this, she thought.

She forced her tired legs to propel her to the surface.

There was a sharp pain in Baya's armpits as she was forcefully lifted out of the water. Vicaroy pulled her into the boat. Her body crumpled in a pile as she heaved seawater out of her lungs. It was even more painful coming out than going in. When the heaving stopped and no more water came out she lay still gasping for air.

Vicaroy rubbed her shoulder, not knowing what else to do. He was overwhelmed with relief that she was alive and by some miracle she was actually in the boat — with him.

When Baya finally stood she had to brace herself with her legs wide apart as the boat rolled over one large wave after another. Vicaroy handed her a cloth to dry off. She jerked it out of his hand.

Vicaroy couldn't stop staring at her as she attempted to dry her arms and legs. She was breathing hard and barely covered by her undergarment which clung to her lean wet body. He was not sure if he had ever been happier in his life. Yet, he wasn't stupid, he knew very well what was coming.

He looked away and braced for the storm that would soon be Baya. Vicaroy thought he would have been long gone before she found out he had left without her. In no way had he prepared for her reaction. He tensed before she began to yell.

"You were going to leave me?" It hurt Baya's sore throat all the more but she didn't care.

He sat on the rowing bench in the back of the boat and kept his head down, as every man did when faced with a furious woman.

"Curse the Goddess!" Baya was glad her mother couldn't hear her use Ameris's name in vain. "Look at me, Vicaroy!"

He slowly raised his head and was again taken by her near-nakedness. He quickly moved to fetch a tunic from the supplies.

"I don't need you to wait on me. I need you to answer me, dammit!"

Out of habit he lowered his eyes again. The overload of emotion —

from her, and his guilt, and her sensual body — it was too much. He had no words.

"Fine! If you ..." her voice broke, "If you don't want me to go with you then ... take me back."

Silence.

"Damn you! Look at me." A traitorous tear ran down her cheek and the anger was gone, replaced by pain — overwhelming pain.

"I'll do whatever you want me to do."

"No! I will not force you to be with me. If you don't want me with you then ..." she couldn't bring herself to finish the sentence. She had no idea what she'd do without him.

He lifted his head and forced himself to look her in the eyes and ignore her dripping exposed body. "I want you with me more than ..." completely against his will his eyes wandered to her chest, still heaving and wet. "Please put a tunic on — a long, dry one."

Now her heart broke completely in two. He couldn't stand the sight of her. She glared at him for a moment and turned to the cabin. She threw open the knapsack full of clothes. The small cabin was littered with fabrics when she came out dressed as she usually would be.

No tears. She was determined to be strong.

Vicaroy gave her a warm smile.

Baya wanted to throw a ball of fire at his face. Instead, she glanced toward the shrinking city lights in the distance.

Vicaroy struggled to find the words to explain. He wanted to tell her everything. Yet he was no good at expressing himself. He didn't fully understand all he felt and he couldn't find the right words. Even though he frantically searched his mind — in the end it betrayed him.

Baya tapped her foot impatiently and when she got nothing, she said, "Take me back." Baya fought against the knot in her already aching throat. It threatened to send tears spilling out of her eyes.

"Baya ... please ..." was all he could get out.

She looked into his golden eyes. "I shouldn't have swum out here. I should have let you go alone, like you wanted."

"Baya —"

"Just take me back!" She wanted to be away from him so she could let the tears fall — without him knowing how much he'd hurt her.

Vicaroy reached for the oars. He would always do as she asked. Not only because he was a man who had to do as women demanded but because he cared for her more than anything. He only wanted her to be happy and the best way to do that was to do as she said. She belonged in Pathins, he didn't.

Before his oars hit the water the boat rocked and Baya had to grab the side to keep from falling back into the water. A green light flickered over them.

She looked at Vicaroy with wide eyes.

"What was …" Vicaroy trailed off.

"We've left Shema's protection. We're on the outside. I can … feel it."

They looked back to where the island of Pathins should have been but there was nothing. Nothing but vast ocean all around them.

"The priestesses' protection makes Pathins invisible from the outside?" Vicaroy asked.

Baya's mouth hung open as she nodded. "Apparently."

The boat rocked again, this time harder and with a loud thud. Baya was thrown against Vicaroy, who deftly caught her. They quickly moved to where the sound had come from. Looking over the side they found the blue furry back of a large fish sticking out of the water. The fact that it was furry was not what was unusual, as most all fish had thick, water-resistant hair that covered their bodies. What was terrifying was the size of the fish. It was many times the length of their vessel.

"That thing could swallow this boat whole," Baya said.

"And not even know it," Vicaroy added.

"Set the sails! We have to get away from it before it decides to see if this boat is edible."

CHAPTER 36

At first light, Aga's eyes shot open. She quickly rose and looked out her window at the black diamond-shaped palace in the distance. Today was going to be a big day, she could feel it. She washed briefly in the washbasin and dressed in one of her best gowns.

Bek was still sleeping. Rus was making breakfast when she hurried past him.

"Good day, my darling," Aga said.

"You're in a good mood this morning and you're up early," Rus replied.

"Something big is going to happen today. If my intuition is correct this may be Baya's big day." She sang the last words.

"You think that there has been a calling from Ameris?"

"I hope so and there is no one better qualified than Baya. She is ready to take Shema's place." Aga frowned. "Well there is Fay, who is of age. She is skilled but not nearly as strong and powerful as Baya." Aga's smile returned. "Baya may become the youngest woman to ever become ruler. It's why she took her tests early, I can feel it in my bones."

Aga hurried toward the front door.

"Wait," Rus said. "Won't you at least stay to eat? It's the most important meal and if you have to begin fasting, you could use some food this morning."

"No. I have to get to the palace." She returned long enough to give Rus a peck on the cheek, then she was gone.

"Wish Baya luck for me," he called after her.

Once Aga entered the Great Hall her heart leapt. She was right! A calling and not just any calling but a call for a new Unawi.

The water in the fountain in the middle of the large room swirled high into the air. It formed two strands of clear water that curved around each other in a dancing spiral. Sunlight reflected off the water sending sparkling diamonds and shimmering rainbows around the room.

Aga had not seen this lovely sight since Baya was a small child.

Shema had been staring at the water intently, as if she were daring herself to believe that it was real. When she saw Aga, she smiled and opened her arms for an embrace.

Aga kissed her cheek. "Your day has finally come."

"Yes. I will be rid of the pressures of ruling at last. I have been Unawi for too long. Longer than most and I'm more than ready to retire to a life of peace and relaxation." Shema raised an eyebrow at Aga. "And this is good news for you as well, as there are no mistresses better suited than your wonderful daughter."

"At last, both our dreams will come to be." The light in Aga's eyes danced.

"You must inform the mistresses that they can go home for the next three days while we are fasting in prayer in order to determine who will take my place."

Aga wanted to run to the classroom where the mistresses would be waiting for their lessons. But she forced herself to walk slowly. It was early and the girls would barely be getting settled into their seats.

* * *

FAY SAT on a table facing her friends. "Well, if that silly lovestruck girl wanted to run off to certain death with some insignificant garden boy, then there was nothing I could do about that," Fay boasted.

One of the girls listening paled when she looked behind Fay. Fay slowly turned to find Aga glaring down at her.

"Surely you are not speaking of my daughter," Aga said.

"Oh, Madam Priestess … no. I mean … well…"

Aga was somehow able to scowl even harder. "Where is my eldest daughter? Why is she not here, reporting to her duties?"

"Baya left," Fay blurted.

"Where did she go? I will send for her at once."

"That may be difficult, High Priestess."

"Are you daring to question me?"

"No, it's just that —"

"I will find my daughter no matter where she is. Even if I have to search this entire island."

"You'll need a boat to find them." Fay had to spit it out, as Aga was not listening and she would have cut her off again.

"A boat! There are no boats on this island. The only one has been destroyed. And who is she with?" The realization caused Aga's eyes to widen with fear. "That boy — he built another boat and he … stole my daughter," Aga said out loud but to herself. She shook her head. This couldn't be. She had to find Baya.

Yet, what if it was true? It didn't matter if one mistress was missing. Ameris's calling must be answered. Aga's heart felt as if it had fallen into her stomach, crushing her previous excitement, her dreams slipping through her fingertips. Her heartbeat sped as she realized that she may have to perform her holy duty and let Baya slip even farther out of reach.

No. She would have a boat made and leave at once. As soon as Aga thought it she knew it would not work. It would take weeks or even months to make a boat. She had no idea how long it would take but she guessed it was not a day. Not to mention, how would she find Baya out at sea?

A knot formed in her throat and threatened to choke her. Baya was gone. Aga could feel it — her bones ached. Her oldest child was outside the protection of the priestesses.

"Madam Priestess?" Fay broke Aga from her inner turmoil.

Aga straightened. "The Great Ameris has given the high council a calling. The next Unawi is to be chosen. You are all dismissed. The new ruler will be announced by the end of the third day." Aga swiftly left the room.

Fay smirked, as she knew there was nothing anyone could do. Baya was out of even her mother's wide reach — gone forever — probably already dead. That left Fay as the most capable girl of age to become the next Unawi.

In three short days she would rule the world. Then she could exert her authority over everyone, even the great Aga. Her thoughts drifted to the harem of theos she would choose. Sure the gorgeous garden boy was gone, whatever his name was, but there were others, many others.

Fay's self-satisfied smile broadened at the thought.

CHAPTER 37

Aga searched for Baya despite what her brain told her. She knew that her daughter was gone. Perhaps it was maternal instincts that drove her to look anyway, even though her logic told her that she wouldn't find Baya.

Perhaps this was a cruel joke of Fay's and Baya had simply overslept — but no, she wasn't in her room, or in the garden, and she hadn't been at home either.

Despite logic, Aga couldn't give up, so she headed for the beach. She didn't know how to get to the cove where they'd found the canoe but she searched along the well-worn path to the beach below the palace.

The beach was empty … except for a crumpled-up piece of clothing. Aga's heart jolted as she raced to it. Holding it up it confirmed her worst nightmare, she remembered buying this tunic for Baya.

"No!" Aga scanned the ocean horizon for any signs of life — nothing. "How could you do this to me?" Sinking to her knees in the deep sand, she held Baya's tunic to her chest. Aga didn't remember the last time she'd cried, but the tears fell freely.

Finally, Aga was forced to accept what she had already known. No matter how much she searched, she wouldn't find Baya. Aga had to pull herself together. She couldn't keep the council waiting any longer.

She would have to force herself to go on even though Baya was missing. There was a job to do and the other priestesses would be wondering where Aga was. By the time she made her way back to the Great Hall her head was down and her shoulders were slumped but there was no sign of tears.

Shema had never seen Aga like this. "What in the name of Ameris is wrong?"

"Let's get on with the ceremonies," Aga's voice was flat.

"Aga?"

Aga walked by Shema as if she was not there. She moved mindlessly toward the prayer room. "Baya has left the island. She is out of our protection and completely out of my control."

"What? No! ... Then who ..." Shema trailed off.

The two women joined the other priestesses in the sacred room. The large doors were closed and two theos barred the door with a large board. The priestesses were not to be disturbed for three days.

Aga, Shema and the others received the clear message during the first day. A brilliant soft-spoken female voice that was all but audible, to the priestesses anyway, made it perfectly clear that Baya was to become the ruler of Pathins.

There was no close second, or third as was usually the case. On previous selections of the Unawi, the time was spent reviewing the strengths and weaknesses of each candidate to determine who was best suited to rule. However, only Baya was ready for the task. Yet something was wrong — very wrong.

Aga reiterated that Baya couldn't become Unawi because she had fled the island.

"You must choose another," the priestesses chanted.

By day three it was concluded that if Baya would not take the responsibility to lead then there was no other who was worthy.

Fay's mother insisted that Fay was ready and more than capable.

But the response was, "Fay's heart is not pure. She is not ready for the priesthood, let alone the position of Unawi."

"If Baya returns then she is the rightful ruler of Pathins. Until then Shema must remain in my service." The voice of the Goddess was lucid and the decision was absolute.

The priestesses were in a daze when they left the sacred room and it was not entirely from abstaining from food.

"That must have been the strangest calling in the history of Pathins," one of the priestesses murmured.

"Never has a mistress left the island before. In fact, I've never heard of anyone leaving," another offered as the two walked past Aga and Shema.

"She threw it all away. I gave her everything and Baya ..." Aga's head still hung low.

Shema could hardly stand to see the strong and rational Aga like this. Yet she was equally dejected. "I will have to rule for ... who knows how much longer?"

"I'm sorry, dear Unawi," Aga said.

"Don't be sorry. It's not your fault." Shema tried to smile but failed. "You should be proud. Your daughter is one of the finest to ever come through this school. Her heart is true and good. I have no doubt she is worthy of my position."

Aga shrugged.

Shema frowned. "The only thing we can do is to pray for Baya's timely and safe return." Somehow. The Unawi knew that once outside the protection of Pathins it was all but impossible to find the island again. Nothing could get through the shield that surrounded them.

A theo presented Aga and Shema with a large golden platter full of fruits of every color. Shema absently took a piece and plopped it into her mouth.

Aga thought she would throw up if she ate. "I kept thinking that Baya would learn to see the truth — that she would eventually see the world as I do."

"And how is that? That she would see the truth *or* that she would see the world as you do?" Shema prompted.

"They are one and the same."

Shema raised her eyebrows at Aga.

"Whose side are you on, anyway?" Aga asked.

"There are no sides. I don't even know if there is only one truth."

"Of course there is only one truth — the word of Ameris."

"And what is that, exactly?"

Aga didn't even try to answer. Her mind felt like it might melt from all that had happened the past month and for it all to end this way...

Shema was deep in thought as she gazed out the window. "I see Ameris's reasoning now. She didn't call Baya early to the trials so she could take my place but rather it was to prepare her for the world out there."

"Is that meant to put my mind at ease?" Because it didn't.

"She passed the trials; that means she is brave and powerful. She will be able to think her way out of the dangers that she will face. Now, thanks to the trials, Baya knows this about herself. She will believe she can survive as she has been through so much already. That is what will keep her alive and return her to us."

"I pray that you're right."

Both women stared out the large window, watching their dreams vanish far over the distant sea.

Shema rubbed her flat belly. The child she so desperately wanted would have to wait. "Yes, let's both pray that I am right."

CHAPTER 38

The blue hairy arch of a fish's back broke the surface of the water. A slight nudge from the large fish sent the boat jostling over the already rocky waters. Vicaroy struggled with the ropes. The stubborn knot finally came undone and Vicaroy yanked hard. The pulley-system sent a large white sail up the mast. The boat lunged forward as the wind filled the sail.

Baya lost her footing and ended up on her butt.

Vicaroy secured the rope to the sail and moved to help Baya.

"Don't touch me," she snapped as she scrambled to her feet.

They were speeding over the large waves now. The bow slammed down with each new wave, sending sprays of water that would fan out around the front of the boat. Baya held on tight to the side of the boat with her legs spread wide. She scanned the water around the boat for the fish. "There's no sign of it."

"Look!" Vicaroy pointed in the distance. "Out there."

They saw two blue curved backs cresting the water's surface and then disappear as the fish made their way toward the boat.

"Not more of them!" Baya all but screamed.

"Brace yourself." Vicaroy tried to place an arm around her waist to help steady her for the blow that was to come when the fish caught up to them. She pulled away and sat down bracing herself with her back to one of the benches and her feet secured against the other. She figured she would end up on her butt again anyway — or worse, she would be thrown overboard — so she might as well have a seat.

Vicaroy sat next to her as the boat rocked violently with another loud bang.

"Can the boat withstand such blows?" Baya asked.

"I reinforced her as well as I could but ... there's no way to know how much she can take."

"I guess we'll find out."

Another thud and this time Baya's head hit the side of the boat behind her.

"Eventually the boat will come apart," Vicaroy said. "I don't see any water coming in yet but it can't take hits like that for much longer."

"Okay, think. There has to be a way to get away from them." Baya closed her eyes tight in concentration. Perhaps she could communicate with them. But how? She couldn't see their eyes to make the connection. What would Ameris do? "I got it!" Baya said. "When I give the word, drop the sail."

In his panicked state, Vicaroy forgot his decorum. "What! That's crazy. We have to get away from the fish."

Baya glared at him and he moved to the other side of the boat.

Another hit from the fish sent the boat spinning and Vicaroy found himself in a heap, against the side of the boat.

Baya stayed focused on the space around her. She chanted the morning prayer that protected the island. Deep in her bones she could feel that it was working. It was like blowing an invisible bubble of protection around the boat. "Now!" she yelled.

Vicaroy untied the rope that held the sail up. It dropped from the mast and landed in a pile on top of the bow. The forward momentum of the boat instantly slowed.

Vicaroy braced for another hit, but there was nothing. The boat simply bobbed over the waves.

Baya stood and searched for the fish. "It worked."

"What worked?" Vicaroy scrambled to his feet.

Baya pointed to the backs of the two fish in the distance. "They can't see us anymore."

They were up ahead racing after where the boat would be if they hadn't lowered the sail. The fish were soon out of sight.

"But how?"

"I put a protection spell around us. If the priestesses can protect all of Pathins then surely I can protect this small ship. The fish can no longer see us. Nothing that lurks about should be able to harm us."

Vicaroy let out a sigh of relief. "You're amazing."

Baya glared at him. "You actually thought that you could survive out here without me."

Vicaroy sighed. "Baya —"

"Just raise the sail. I'll check for leaks and damage."

Vicaroy pursed his lips. She'd never been mad at him before. Of course, he'd never tried to leave her before either. What a fool he'd been. Of course, he needed her — in every way.

There was no way a man could survive on his own in the wild. Vicaroy would probably have already been a meal for a fish. Yet, here Baya was, right next to him. He smiled at the thought. At least they were together, no matter how short their lives might be. They wouldn't die alone. If only he could find the right words she would forgive him. Even if he did know what to say, she would not listen. When he tried to speak she cut him off.

The boat appeared in good order. "Thankfully it's sturdy." Baya studied the stars. "That way is west."

Vicaroy followed her gaze to where Pathins had once been.

She said what they both already knew, "Pathins is lost to us. Even if I wanted to go back I couldn't. Nothing gets in from the outside."

"So we follow the immotile star by night." Vicaroy pointed to the eastern sky.

"And the largest sun by day." Baya headed for the cabin. She needed food if she was going to have to use her powers this much.

Vicaroy manned the tiller and steered the boat eastward.

Rummaging through the supplies in the cabin, Baya heard a

rustling that startled her. She took a kitchen knife in her hand and carefully approached the noise.

A tiny voice hissed in her head. *Is it safe to come out?*

Baya squealed with delight and dropped the knife at once. Her squeal caused Vicaroy to appear in the doorway.

"Doba!" She threw some clothes off the bed, revealing the long dark insect. She scooped him up in her arms cradling him like an infant. "You made it! I'm so glad."

"What's that?" Vicaroy took a step back at the sight of the ugly creature.

Doba curved his thick segmented body around Baya, exactly as he used to do with Shema.

Vicaroy's eyes widened. "You stole Shema's pet?"

Doba clicked and hissed at Vicaroy, causing him to take another step back.

Baya ignored Vicaroy. She now had another companion — one she preferred. "I was sure that mean old boy left you behind, as he tried to do to me. How did you get to the boat in time?"

I left the night before, Doba was eager to explain. *I've been hiding in here ever since. I didn't want to miss my chance at freedom. I doubt Shema has even noticed I'm gone. Lucky for me, she's been very busy.*

Vicaroy looked between the two with growing dread. "Is it … *talking* to you?"

"He's a male and *his* name is Doba. I taught him how to get out of the cage where he was kept at night. I planned for him to join us all along. He's really smart." Baya rubbed under Doba's chin. "Aren't you so smart?"

Guttural sounds of pleasure came from Doba. Vicaroy furrowed his brow. He didn't like how Baya fussed over the creature. It seemed out of character for her, or maybe it was that he wished she was gushing over him like that.

He headed for the stern, to make sure they were still on course and that there was no danger lurking. "That thing is creepy." Vicaroy muttered.

A loud hiss followed by clicking sounds came from the cabin.

"He understands you — you know? Trust me, you don't want me to translate those angry sounds of his."

Vicaroy rolled his eyes and plopped down on the bench next to the rudder.

Wonderful, he thought. The only other living things on this boat hated him.

He focused on adjusting the rudder. It took some experimenting, moving it back and forth but it was fairly simple to keep the boat pointed toward the eastern star.

"Just ignore that bad man, Doba. That's what I plan to do." Baya's voice came from the cabin.

Vicaroy sighed. It was going to be a long journey.

CHAPTER 39

Vicaroy and Baya settled into a routine. They took shifts to make sure they were always following the immotile star by night and the largest sun by day. During the day they would take a brief break by lowering the sails for a time. This time was spent bathing in the ocean and fishing. Baya often studied the ancient scrolls she had found in the library — the ones that had been new to her.

Vicaroy would prepare the fresh fish in a small brazier and salt any extra fillets, hanging them out to dry. This helped supplement the dried goods they had on board.

However, drinking water quickly became an issue. In no time their supply was low and the only fresh water they had was dew that would condense overnight. Vicaroy devised a system for catching the night's dew in a spare sail.

After an entire cycle of the moons there was still no land in sight. Baya performed a protection spell every evening and every morning. They saw many furry sea creatures, some large and some small, none of which paid any attention to the boat, thanks to Baya.

At times the sea was calm; it would gently rock Baya to sleep. Sometimes it was impossible to sleep as they would be tossed about like a child's rag doll. The nights and days were clear with only occasional wisps of clouds. There was nothing to prevent them from knowing which direction they were heading, day or night.

Vicaroy's skin turned from a light black to a purplish-black and Baya's skin was no longer an olive tone. She turned into a golden-brown sun goddess. At least that's how Vicaroy saw her. He tried not to be too obvious — only stealing occasional glances at her — her long legs, her bare midriff …

Baya was true to her word. She spoke to Doba more than she did to Vicaroy. She was all business with Vicaroy. They spoke only when it was absolutely necessary.

It was his turn at the helm. He was so used to it that he hardly had to think about his job. At regular intervals he would glance up at the stars and then make any adjustments at the helm without thinking about it.

He was going through the same old motions, nothing more. His thoughts automatically strayed to the usual things; how to get Baya to forgive him and how it felt to kiss her … how it would feel to caress her soft skin …

A shiver passed through him. He focused on the water. All fantasies disappeared. He was suddenly yanked into the present. The sea had gone completely calm. Not a wave in sight. Not a puff of wind to propel them through the water. For the first time in a month the boat did not rock. They sat perfectly still in the water and the sail hung limp. He had no idea why but he didn't like the calmness. This was … eerie. "Baya, something is … not right."

But she was already crawling out of the cabin. "It's so still and I had a dream I was back in my bed at home. I thought I smelled Rus's cooking," she muttered, still half asleep. Her eyes widened when she studied the glassy water around them. "It's the calm before the storm. I've read about this."

She scanned the horizon but there was nothing but the dark sky and stars touching the black water.

"We can't see it yet but it's coming. We have to prepare the boat," Baya said.

Vicaroy didn't question her. He moved to secure the sail.

"No. We have to take it down entirely. Everything, if we wish to keep it, must be put inside."

He nodded and went to work.

Baya bit her lower lip, as she watched for any signs of the impending storm. She hoped that she was wrong, or that the scrolls had been misleading, or that she had somehow misread them.

Out of the corner of her eye she saw a flash of light along the horizon, then another.

"Vicaroy." She pointed to the south. It was coming fast and it was enormous.

Darkness was swallowing the stars and the waters. In no time, a wall of black clouds spanned across the entire southern horizon. Lightning flashed through the clouds giving away their true colors — variations of pink and pure orange. Distant thunder rolled and rumbled through the air with such force that Baya could feel it vibrate in her chest.

"It will be on us before we know it. Go! Get everything inside. We have to close ourselves in," Baya said.

She gave one last glance at the furious storm before heading into the cabin. A part of her wished that there was some way she could watch the beautiful power of the storm. But there wasn't, not if they had any hopes of surviving.

Vicaroy closed the hatch once Baya was inside. With no windows and no more moonlight it was pitch black inside. She lit a ball of fire so he could see to secure the latch to the hatch.

"That will keep the rain out." He looked at Baya with concern. "Will your protection … make the storm go around us?"

"No. The storm doesn't care if it can see us or not. My powers only work on humans and animals. It will pass right over us like it does everything else."

"Can you do something —"

"Like what?" Baya was losing her patience.

"Like force it away?"

"I can't control the weather if that's what you were hoping," Baya snapped.

"That makes sense, there was little need for that on Pathins where the weather was most always pleasant," Vicaroy mused.

"We aren't in Pathins anymore." Baya curled up on the bed with Doba. She held him close. "It's going to be okay," she whispered as she rubbed his chin.

The only place left for Vicaroy to sit was on top of the sail, which was on the floor at the foot of the small bed.

"I should conserve my energy." Baya put her fire out — plunging them into complete darkness.

It started slowly. The boat rocked gently at first. Baya tried to force herself to sleep. It could be a large storm and therefore a very long night. She could use the rest. But there was no way her mind would allow sleep to come.

The rocking grew more intense. The wall of torrential rain could be heard as it pounded into the sea, moving closer. Then rain drummed on the roof of the boat in a heavy rhythm. It could have been a relaxing sound except for the giant waves they were now floating over. It seemed like they were heading straight up. Then the bow of the boat slammed down with a loud smack as they headed down the other side of the wave.

It felt like they were free-falling for a mile before the boat would head up the next wave. Every sudden turn of the boat caused Baya's stomach to drop. She braced herself against either wall as did Vicaroy. This kept them from sliding from one end of the cabin to the other as they rode the monster waves.

The hours endlessly passed, each one just as dark as the last.

"Surely we must be about out of the storm," Baya's voice broke the black silence.

"It's like the storm is sitting on top of us. It's not letting up," Vicaroy said.

They had spoken too soon. The wind howled even louder through the thin cracks around the hatch. Up and up they went. As Baya's stomach turned again she found herself on her face. A thud beside her told her that Vicaroy had done the same. "We're ... upside down!" she yelled. The boat had capsized. It hadn't made it over the last wave. They were under water.

Darkness. Water.

Thoughts of being trapped in a well flooded Baya's mind. She couldn't breathe. They were going to die. As suddenly as she had found herself face-down she was now on her back on the bed. "Doba!" she remembered. She hadn't felt him in a while. There was no response.

Oh, Great Goddess, I've crushed him, she thought.

"Baya! I feel water," Vicaroy said.

That was it. She could no longer stand the darkness. She lit her fire and found Vicaroy standing on the sail. At least it had offered him some cushion when the boat righted itself.

Baya barely had time to put her hands out to keep her face from hitting the ceiling as the boat tried to top another wave and didn't make it. The shock broke Baya's concentration and the fire ball was extinguished.

She relit her light. This time Vicaroy was upside down. He had braced himself against the ceiling and floor with his legs and arms outstretched. Baya was in a pile on the ceiling of the cabin along with other loose belongings. She wanted to look for Doba but there was no time. Behind Vicaroy was the most terrifying sight.

CHAPTER 40

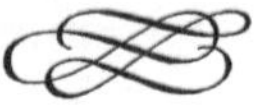

Water poured in around the frame of the hatch. Yet again, Baya found herself on the bed. Something hit her head but she didn't let it break her focus. She managed to keep her fire lit.

Vicaroy stood in a couple inches of water. They looked at each other with wide eyes.

"Get ready for another wave," he said as they headed upwards.

Baya was learning — she threw her arm up to brace herself against the ceiling that would soon be the floor. She couldn't fully support herself with one arm when the boat capsized again. More gracefully this time she caught herself with her legs and she was able to keep the light on. Which she regretted as it gave her a clear view of the water rushing in.

Her breaths grew quick and shallow. What should she do? She was no match against the raging sea and storm outside.

Two more turnovers passed. Vicaroy now stood in a foot of water.

"Think, Baya!" she yelled. But she couldn't stop the storm. She couldn't keep the boat upright.

Stop worrying about what you can't do and think about what you *can* do, she yelled to herself.

"I can —"

But she was upside down again. Water splashed in her face and belongings jostled around and slammed into her. What can I do…? she thought. I'm no match against a storm but I can … change matter.

"That's it!" she yelled. She crawled through the water to the leaking door. She held out her arms as the water rushed in through the cracks. She found herself sitting at Vicaroy's feet as the boat righted itself once again. Jumping up she worked quickly to seal the door.

Baya transformed the wood, making it one solid piece. There was now a wall where the hatch had been. Bracing for another upside-down ride she placed her hands against the ceiling. Water washed over her as it fell to the roof, which was once again temporarily a floor. She got to her feet and studied her work — no more water rushed in.

"You did it!" Vicaroy moved to wrap his arms around her in celebration but they both had to brace for the next go around.

Again and again — around and around but no more water leaked into the cabin.

Baya was growing weak and she had to extinguish the light to save her energy.

"Do you feel faint?" Vicaroy asked.

"I thought it was just me — losing my strength."

"No. I think we're running out of air."

Baya heard Vicaroy stumble. "Are you okay?"

"The cabin is sealed too tight. We need air," he sputtered.

"I can't make air."

"You're going to have to open the hatch when the boat rights itself."

"I don't have enough strength to reseal the hatch every time we go under."

They braced for another upturn. Nothing. They waited through another wave. Still nothing. The boat remained upright.

"Do you think …" Baya was afraid to hope that the storm might be calming.

A long silence as they waited in the dark. The pounding rain outside slowed to a drizzle. "Vicaroy?" Baya panted. She was terrified that he may have passed out in the water. He might be drowning. She lit her light.

"Open the hatch," he gasped.

She scrambled to her feet. It was a risk but she had to take it, knowing they were going to suffocate otherwise. Breathing in what little air she could, she focused all her remaining energy on the wooden wall where the door had been. The wooden slats and the metal latches reformed.

Vicaroy fumbled to open the hatch. He threw the hatch back and they fell out of the cabin, taking deep breaths. A gentle rain still fell but they didn't care. They were already soaked. What did matter was the sweet air that filled their lungs. And the fact that the worst of the storm was swiftly rolling away from them in the distance. They watched the lightning and clouds slowly move to the north.

Baya noticed that the boat sat lower in the ocean with all the water the cabin had taken in.

"You did it. You saved us … again." Vicaroy gave her a warm smile.

Baya put her head down. "Not all of us. I don't know how Doba could have made it through that. Surely he was crushed or drowned. I haven't heard his thoughts since the storm started."

"Let's look for him. He has to be in there somewhere."

The first sun of the day barely peeked over the water and they dared to head back inside. The cabin was a disaster and there was no sign of Doba.

"I'll start cleaning. He'll turn up." Vicaroy rather dreaded finding the large insect, dead or alive.

There was so much work to do ... and all Baya wanted was to somehow dry herself, eat twice her rations and fall asleep. But there was no way to do any of that. All their clothes and bedding were soaked. The food was in disarray. Goods that had not been sealed in jars were ruined.

"Well I'm not just going to stand around and watch you," she said.

Vicaroy smiled. "You never have. You always help, even though you don't have to." That's why I love you. He refrained from saying that last bit out loud.

"Don't be ridiculous. Of course I'll help. This is no time to make distinctions between men's work and women's work." Baya was at her wit's end. "You really need to give up on that old crap. We're not in Pathins anymore. We both have to work if we are going to survive out here."

Just get to work and don't argue, Vicaroy told himself. Yet his mouth opened anyway. "You already did so much — you kept us alive through the storm. You had to use a lot of your powers and I know it drains you. I wouldn't blame you if you needed to rest." Plus he worried that if she grew too weak to use her powers then all would be lost. He chose not to voice this last concern.

Vicaroy hated to see her like this; tired, uncomfortable and still having to work. She was royalty. She deserved better and it was his job to do the physical work. If he couldn't properly take care of her and keep her comfortable then he was a failure and that was why he hadn't wanted her to come. He knew he couldn't properly take care of her out here.

Baya glared at him and headed into the cabin.

They untied the bedding from the frame and placed it out to dry on top of the cabin. The ropes that were usually used for hoisting the sail were used to air their wet clothes. Baya was handing buckets of water from the cabin floor out for Vicaroy to toss overboard. After only the second bucket her arms shook with exhaustion. She needed food and rest ... and dry feet.

A jar floated out from the storage area which was under the bench seats in the back of the boat. Baya didn't notice it until it bumped her leg. When she looked down she let out a scream.

Vicaroy poked his head into the cabin to see what was wrong. It didn't take long for him to realize that it was a scream of joy. Inside the jar was Doba, who uncoiled himself and crawled out. The opening was barely big enough for him to fit through. He scurried up Baya's leg and wrapped himself around her as usual.

This place is a mess, he thought as he surveyed the cabin.

Baya laughed and broke into tears at the same time. "You're alright!"

"The damn thing just floated around in his own private boat in the cargo hold all night." Vicaroy had secretly hoped that the insect hadn't made it through the storm.

"You slept through the whole thing!" Baya yelled. "I could kiss you and strangle you." She plopped down in the water and let the tears fall — really fall.

Doba rubbed his head against her neck to comfort her.

Vicaroy lifted Baya to her feet. "Come on. We all need a break. Come out under the suns and let yourself dry while I find us something to eat." Vicaroy helped Baya stretch out on the bench in the back of the boat.

Thankfully the suns shone brightly in the clear purple-blue sky. The warm rays calmed her. She wrapped her arms around Doba and closed her eyes.

Vicaroy rummaged through the jars. Nothing was in its place so he had to pull the cork on every jar until he found the nuts. Baya needed food, and quickly, if she was going to keep going like this. He didn't have time to cook grains.

When he came out Baya was fast asleep with Doba tucked under her arm. He wanted to throw the insect overboard. She should have her arm wrapped around him, not that insect. Vicaroy was the one who should be comforting her.

He shook his head. I can't believe I'm jealous of a bug, he thought as he tossed a handful of nuts in his mouth.

Doba wormed his way out from under Baya's arm, as Vicaroy sat on the bench across from her. Vicaroy tried not to stare at her long bare legs drying in the sun. There were some dark bruises in a couple places. It had been a brutal night, but they were alive.

"Whoa!" Vicaroy started when he noticed that Doba was only inches away, staring at him intently with all four black eyes. Vicaroy pushed him away but Doba moved in even closer. "Don't touch me. Shoo, Shoo."

Doba hissed but was not deterred.

"What do you want?"

Doba made a clicking noise and appeared to be staring at the nuts in Vicaroy's hand.

"Here ..." Vicaroy tossed some nuts to the far side of the bench in order to get the creepy thing away from him.

Doba silently slithered away, his segmented body curving and weaving as his many legs moved him toward the food.

How can she stand that thing? Vicaroy wondered.

Doba turned his many beady eyes on Vicaroy and gave an open-mouthed hiss before he began chomping away on a nut.

It appeared to be able to read his mind as well as understand what he said. Vicaroy shivered.

CHAPTER 41

Baya woke with a start. The sea had gone completely calm ... again. It was the type of calm that filled her with dread. Her heartbeat increased as she searched the sky for another storm. The last sun would be setting soon. No storm in sight ... yet.

"I've slept all day?" She jumped to her feet. She was sore and bruised in various spots but she felt much better. At least her strength was back.

"It's okay. You needed the rest. And I took care of the boat," Vicaroy smiled with pride. He was feeling less a failure after taking care of things while she slept.

Baya looked over the side. The boat was sitting higher in the water. "You got all the water out of the cabin ... by yourself." Baya sighed. "I'm so sorry."

"Don't be. I'm glad you rested. You're going to need your strength for the next storm."

"Another storm?" She searched the sky. "Do you think we've entered a monsoon season?"

"I'm afraid so. Our time of peaceful sailing is over."

Baya slumped onto the bench.

Vicaroy handed her a plate of food. Her stomach growled when she saw it. "We can't keep heading east if we're stuck inside that cabin all the time," she said with her mouth full of food. She was starving and didn't care about manners. "There's no telling where the monsoons will take us. We may have been pushed westward last night, for all I know."

Vicaroy studied his surroundings. "I don't think so." He pointed to the south. "I think the storm last night pushed us north."

Baya looked to the south and her mouth fell open. The last sun was setting behind a rolling wall of clouds. The sky was an array of every color Baya could possibly name. The purple sky faded to a blue, then to a pink which faded into red and then a yellow. The clouds themselves were a bright orange trimmed with a golden light.

"I don't recall sunsets that beautiful on Pathins," Vicaroy said.

Lovely, Doba added in Baya's head.

She had barely noticed that he had wrapped himself around her. "Unfortunately what makes this sunset so spectacular is the massive clouds headed our way." Baya continued to shovel food in. She would need the fuel to make it through the night.

In no time her plate of the fresh flatbread Vicaroy had made that day and the dried fish were gone, all except some breadcrumbs, which she fed to Doba.

"Yes, let's get the rest of the supplies below deck. As I was saying, if the storms continue coming from the south then we will be pushed farther north each night."

Baya helped unfasten the bedding from the bow. It took them both, one shoving and one pulling to get the dried mattress back in the cabin. The last thing to be brought in was the sail and mast.

"What are the buckets for?"

Vicaroy had tied several of them to the bottom of the boat. "I hope to catch rain in them. We weren't able to collect any dew last night and our supply of fresh water is low. We lost a lot of dried cakes. Your parchments were turned to complete mush. I threw them overboard. Luckily most of the grains, nuts and dried fish survived. The corked jars saved them."

"We had secured the belongings against the back and forth motion but not for being upside down."

Vicaroy chuckled. "Hopefully, I took care of that. I pray we can stay dry through this storm and not lose any more supplies."

"And not sustain any more bruises." Baya examined a fist-sized black mark on her arm. She didn't remember hitting her arm — or something banging into her — that violently last night. She'd been too focused on staying upright, keeping her fire lit and trying to figure out a way to stop the cabin from flooding.

All three companions watched as the storm approached. No one was eager to spend another sleepless night cramped in the cabin.

When night had fallen and the rain reached them, Baya forced herself to go inside. Vicaroy had cleaned the cabin well. The jars of food were tightly packed in the cargo holds under the benches. He had nailed wooden slats across the storage areas under the benches to keep the jars from flying around the cabin.

He closed the hatch and their tiny world went black.

CHAPTER 42

Baya lit a candle with her mind. She studied the hatch. "We need the air to enter the cabin but not the water." She cocked her head to the side in deep thought. "You said the food that was sealed in jars didn't get wet?"

"Yes." Vicaroy didn't know where she was going with this.

"Do we have any extra corks?"

"We have plenty from empty water and food jars."

"I need the biggest one."

Vicaroy went right to them. Rummaging through a bag he handed a cork to Baya.

"Perfect." It was the size of the palm of her hand. She raised her arms to perform the transformation spell.

"Wait!" There was panic in Vicaroy's voice. "Not yet. The waves are barely rolling. We will suffocate if you seal us in too soon."

"I know." She raised her hands to the door again and chanted under her breath. The door became a solid waterproof and air-proof wall.

"Baya?" Vicaroy had never been confined before the previous night and he knew he didn't enjoy it. It felt like he was already short of breath as his chest tightened.

"Trust me." Baya gave him a sly smile.

It was his favorite expression of hers and it helped to calm him.

Placing her hand on the now-transformed door, Baya closed her eyes and chanted again, drawing a circle with her index finger. A hole appeared in the wall. "That should be about the right size." She forced the cork into the hole. It fit tight. It took all her strength to wiggle the cork out again. She tossed the cork to Vicaroy and crawled onto the bed. "Now all we have to do is plug the hole if we capsize. Otherwise, we should have plenty of air."

Vicaroy had not been aware that he was holding his breath, already trying to conserve the air in the cabin. He exhaled with relief, followed by a deep breath. "That's ... brilliant."

Baya smiled with pride. It was the first time she had done so on this journey. It was funny how life or death situations could lessen one's anger. She was no longer as mad at Vicaroy as she had been. The terrors of the previous night changed things — made her appreciate him. She looked at him, really studied him. She had largely been ignoring him which was difficult on such a small vessel.

Baya cocked her head to the side again. Vicaroy looked tired. There were dark circles under his eyes, ones she had never seen before. He was slimmer than he had been in Pathins as well. This voyage was taking its toll on both of them and it wasn't over yet. She patted the bed next to her. "Come. Get some rest before the storm will make it impossible to sleep."

Vicaroy didn't hesitate. Crawling into the bed, barely made for two, was what he wanted more than anything. The grueling night — the long day of work — it all hit him at once. They were safe ... enough ... for now. Sleep was his only thought as he lay next to her.

Doba hissed and clicked in protest of Vicaroy's closeness. He moved to Baya's other shoulder in order to put some distance between himself and the man.

It took no time for Vicaroy's breathing to grow heavy with sleep.

"Poor thing. He's been working so hard," Baya whispered.

Good. He's asleep. Now we can throw him off the boat.

"Doba!" Baya chastised.

That's what he wants to do to me.

"Don't be silly. Vicaroy would never do that."

Then how come he thinks it all the time.

"He doesn't ..." Baya's face fell. "Does he?"

Doba nodded vigorously.

Baya smiled at Vicaroy. "He needs to get used to you, that's all. Like I did."

Well, I won't ever like him, Doba huffed.

"Wait a minute. How can you read his thoughts? I thought you had only learned to understand our speech when we talk out loud. Not to mention men can't communicate with animals."

Men can't, but I can. It's easy once a connection is made, like the one I have with you. Usually, all I have to do is look them in the eyes. Then ... I'm in. I had to learn how to convey the images I get from others.

Doba bobbed side to side on her shoulder. *Usually all I get are emotions, which I can sense. Fear is the most obvious one to recognize. All animals, no matter how primitive, can read that emotion with ease. But I have learned to interpret many other emotions and thoughts over the years.*

"This's great. This means no one can lie to you."

I guess not.

Baya frowned. But she had to know. "What does he think about me?"

Oh, no I don't want to ... get in the middle of that mess.

"Please!" Baya rubbed his chin.

Doba melted in her arms and the soft guttural purr escaped from him even though he didn't want it to. *Okay, okay.* He conceded. *I don't like the way he thinks about you.*

A knot formed in Baya's throat. What did she expect? Vicaroy had tried to leave her behind. He didn't even want her here. So, of course, he didn't want her at all.

No. It's not that. Doba replied, as he had read her mind. *It's quite the opposite actually. He thinks ... nasty things about you.*

Baya furrowed her brow. "What do you mean, nasty?"

Like how it felt when he put his lips to yours and how he would like to touch you ... everywhere. He stares at you all the time with these thoughts running through his mind. I've noticed this over the years, human men tend to have only one thing on their minds. Doba's large eyes blinked at Baya. *Like I said, nasty. Human men are disgusting.*

Her heart leaped. He did want her! Baya, with her skinny body. She frowned at her toothpick legs. Like Vicaroy, she too had lost weight this past month and Baya hadn't had much to lose to begin with. No. She sighed. No man would want her. Especially, one as handsome and strong as Vicaroy. She watched him sleep. His face looked younger while he was at rest — relaxed and carefree.

I don't know what makes a human attractive. You are all very ugly to me but I do know that he fancies you. Doba mused.

"Then why did he try so hard to leave me behind?"

That ... I don't know. It's like his brain shuts down when he thinks about why he left early. He doesn't have the words. He is really quite dense.

"He's not dense!" Baya snapped.

Vicaroy stirred beside her.

"Shhh," she said. The boat was only gently rocking. Vicaroy could still get some much-needed sleep.

I'm not making any noise. You are, so shush yourself.

Baya stifled a chuckle. She continued to watch Vicaroy. He was lovely. Could it be that he wanted her? He had taken the initiative to kiss her first. It took guts for a man to make the first move. So maybe, just maybe, he did desire her.

Her gaze settled on his full lips. Memories of what it had done to her body when he kissed her overwhelmed her. She resisted the urge to run her finger along his lips.

Okay, now you're as bad as the boy. I've had enough of you sick humans for one day. I'm going to find a safe place to sleep. Doba scurried off the bed and buried himself in the cargo hold.

She hoped Doba was right. If Vicaroy did indeed love her, then she must find out. And she needed to understand why he had tried to leave her.

The waves grew larger as the night wore on. Baya knew this because it took longer and longer for the boat to top each wave.

CHAPTER 43

When the rain stopped Baya reformed the hatch of the cabin. The night's storm had been gentle compared to the previous one. Thankfully, the boat had stayed upright. They emerged on deck dry and unharmed to greet the early morning darkness. Vicaroy had managed to sleep most of the night. He set the sail at once and steered the boat eastward.

Baya had dozed some as well. She was ready to take on the world. Or at least the sea and even Vicaroy. It was time she figured out what was going on with him. Even if he broke her heart again. She had to know.

Baya cleared her throat. "Vicaroy. Why did you leave without me?"

His shoulders visibly sank. He looked out at the sea. "I don't know …"

"You mean you won't tell, because of course you know why you do the things you do, and I'm finally ready to listen."

He swallowed hard.

"Damn you, Vicaroy. I deserve to know. Would you at least look at me?"

He looked toward Baya but was distracted by four solid black eyes. Doba was perched on her shoulder, staring intently at him, as if he was just as interested in what Vicaroy had to say as Baya was. Vicaroy shrank away and adjusted the rope on the sail, even though it didn't need to be done.

"Vicaroy." Baya demanded.

"Yes. You have every right to know why I left. I regret it every day. If I could do it over again I never would have left without you. You being mad at me is the worst thing in the world and I thank the Great Goddess every day that you're here ... with me." Once he started talking it all came out fast.

Baya narrowed her eyes at him. "Of course you're glad I'm here. I've saved your life, how many times now? You'd be dead if it wasn't for me."

"It's not that —"

"You honestly think that you'd be alive without me?" Baya's voice was louder than she'd meant it to be.

"Of course not and I thought you were ready to listen?" He finally met her intense stare and didn't shy away.

She crossed her arms in front of her chest and waited, challenging him to go on.

"I don't want you here because of your powers. ... Well, they are incredibly helpful. But I want you here because I ..." love you. He was too afraid to say the words.

He says he loves you or he thought it, Doba whispered in Baya's mind.

Baya's expression softened and her arms fell to her sides. "Say it ... finish your sentence." She desperately wanted him to speak those few, yet precious words and she wanted them to be true.

Vicaroy shook his head. "I can't because you don't feel the same way about me."

"I do love you and you broke my heart when you left without me. You still have not answered my question. Why did you leave?"

She loved him! Vicaroy felt a shift inside himself — a glimmer of hope. "I left because ... well ... you had everything in Pathins. I couldn't take that from you just because I had nothing."

"I didn't *have* everything. Not without you. Don't you get it? I chose this." She gestured to the boat around them. "I didn't want my life in Pathins. I want you. That's why I'm here." Baya said.

"And I've put you in mortal danger. I didn't want to risk your life. My life is worthless but yours — you had a good future, a life as a wealthy ruler. I wanted that for you — not this." It was his turn to gesture to the boat.

"Well, it's my life and you should have let me make that decision." Baya's heart was heavy — it was something he had said. He felt like his life was meaningless. "Your life is worth everything ... to me."

He wanted to take her in his arms, press his lips to hers. The love was back in her eyes — he had missed that even more than he had realized. He would do anything to keep that light in her color-filled eyes.

"If we survive this journey then I promise to never make decisions for you again." He took her hands in his. "Every day I'm grateful that you are with me and not only for your powers but for your company. Even with you angry at me, it's been better than being without you."

He was drawn to her lips but the beady stare of the insect on her shoulder stopped his advance. Baya hadn't looked this full of life since they started the journey.

"I'm starving. I'll find us something to eat," she said.

"That's my job. And I'll get your morning tea for you as well. We don't want you to have a baby when we don't know what the future holds."

Baya sighed and took the tiller, making a minor adjustment to steer the vessel eastward. One thing at a time. They would work on the gender-segregated chores another time.

Vicaroy lit the small brazier with his stones. He liked it that he didn't have to bother Baya with something as simple as lighting a fire for him. At least it was one thing he could do for himself.

He set a steaming hot cup of the women's brew next to Baya on the bench.

When Baya reached for the plate of food that Vicaroy held out for her, he didn't let go of it until he had her full attention. He waited until their eyes met. "I do love you."

Baya smiled playfully. "I know. Doba told me." She ran a finger along the insect's chin. Doba appeared to be more interested in the food than anything else.

"He can tell you my thoughts?"

Baya chuckled. "Yep. So be careful. You can't lie to me."

"That's … creepy and I have no intention of lying to you."

"Good." Baya shoveled some food into her mouth.

Vicaroy smiled warmly. It was a relief to see her happy. Leaving her had been the stupidest thing he had ever done. It wouldn't happen again.

Baya snickered as Doba relayed Vicaroy's latest thoughts to her. She fed him from her plate as a reward.

That creature, however, was going to be annoying. Vicaroy didn't like it that Baya knew what he was thinking at all times.

CHAPTER 44

The rains came early that day. Just after mid-day Vicaroy and Baya had to quickly pack everything inside before it got too wet. The storm came quickly and it grew fierce. This time Baya's hole in the wall was put to the test. The cork did its job to keep the water out even when they were turned upside down. By nightfall the storm had passed.

Baya used her light to assess the boat for any damage. "Thankfully she's sturdy. You built her well."

Vicaroy hoisted the sail but when he moved the tiller something was wrong. It was too easy, there was no resistance. He unfastened the tiller and let out a curse.

"What's wrong?" Baya asked.

"The rudder must have broken off in the storm." He looked around frantically. "I don't have any spare wood to fix it."

Baya laid the tiller and what was left of the rudder out on the bench in front of her. "I got this." She gave him a playful wink and held her arms out. Faint golden wisps, like clouds, came from her hands. In no time, the missing part of the rudder had been replaced with a hard, amber-like substance that sparkled under the moons' light.

Vicaroy rapped his knuckles against the strange substance. "What is it?"

"Just a nifty little trick."

"I'd say so. Where does it come from?"

"I don't know, Mother said it's like a spiders web, or something. It comes from inside us."

He shook his head in amazement. "How come you never showed me before?"

"There was never a need and it takes ... a lot of practice to acquire the ability." Baya lowered her head. "It's very similar to transformation spells, which were the hardest skills for me to master. I still mess that up sometimes."

"Well, this looks perfect."

"Not to mention it requires a ton of energy. Speaking of that..." Baya headed into the cabin for some food. Making the new rudder had made her so hungry that she felt queasy.

They headed east at once under a clear night's sky. Three moons shone bright and the fourth was on the rise.

"All four moons are full tonight. They will be celebrating in Pathins." Baya's heart sank at the thought of her family having to celebrate without her.

"Azod will be all alone tonight." Vicaroy's thoughts had drifted home as well. "At least one good thing has come out of the monsoon season."

Baya frowned at him. "And what is that?"

"We have plenty of fresh water. However, our food supplies are down."

"How much do we have?"

"I guess no more than two weeks if we keep eating as much as we are now."

"We need to fish." Baya rose to get the poles. "We should cut back on our portions. Who knows when we'll find land? With these storms blowing us north it could take even longer."

"I'll cut my portions in half but you can't." His stomach growled with hunger at the mention of less food. He had already been giving

Baya more to eat. "You have lost weight and you need the fuel for your powers."

She turned to glare at Vicaroy. "You've already been eating less than me?"

Vicaroy was really starting to hate that insect. Before he had just disliked it but now it was all he could do not to wrap his hand around its neck and strangle it. "Stop telling her my thoughts! She doesn't need to know everything." Vicaroy yelled at Doba.

Doba hissed and clicked at him in return.

Baya took Vicaroy's hands. "We are partners in this — equals." On the one hand, she felt overwhelming love for him. It was incredibly kind that he had let her eat more. But then there was also overwhelming guilt. "If you can't eat as much neither can I."

THERE WERE many more nights and many more storms to weather. They made their way east as best they could when the storms were not forcing them north. Baya was careful to watch how much Vicaroy ate and she refused to eat more.

The energy it took to perform the protection spell and to protect them from the storms caused her to lose weight rapidly. Her cheekbones became more prominent. Vicaroy begged her to eat his rations but she stubbornly refused.

After two weeks Baya hardly left the bed. On top of this the weather grew cold as they made their way northeast. Vicaroy had never been more grateful that he could light the coals in the brazier by himself. At least he was able to keep the cabin warm for her.

Fish had been harder to catch in the turbulent waters. Vicaroy studied the last of their food supply; only one jar of grain and one jar of nuts remained. He lifted his shirt to examine his thin frame. His ribs stuck out in an almost unnatural way. He didn't recall ever being this skinny before.

His gaze turned to Baya — fast asleep on the bed. Under the pile of covers it was hard to make out her dwindling body. He pulled back the blankets and lifted her tunic. Her ribs stuck out even farther than his. She was burning through calories faster than he was. Yet her breathing was steady and for that he was grateful. Yet, he worried that her ribs might come out of her skin with each breath.

What kind of a man couldn't even feed one woman? This made him want to take back his promise. He had done the right thing by trying to leave her behind. She shouldn't be slowly starving to death because of him. Baya belonged in Pathins, safe and healthy, probably the Unawi by now. Of course, he would be dead but at least she would be safe. That was all that mattered.

Doba nodded as if in agreement with Vicaroy's thoughts. Doba rubbed his head against Baya's cheek and issued a guttural purr.

Vicaroy covered them both.

Baya had no idea either of them were there. She was lost in a deep sleep, to conserve energy.

"I hope you're dreaming of Rus's cooking." Vicaroy whispered in her ear. He headed out into the brisk night air. He was not accustomed to the cold. Una Sitka was never this frigid. He wrapped a blanket tightly around his shoulders and studied the dark sky. He set his sights upon Ameris's constellation. She was standing upright in the eastern sky.

"Ameris is with us." Then he prayed ... "Please get her off this boat. She deserves a better life than the one I can provide for her. I beg you Ameris, save her."

Vicaroy didn't know how long he had been in deep prayer when he suddenly became aware of his surroundings. Perfect calm.

"Oh come on! Not another storm." He yelled at the sky. He prepared for yet another icy rain. The waves grew more intense but Baya didn't wake. She was used to the motion and she was too tired to get up. Vicaroy didn't bother her. He hoped the storm would not be too bad. Plus he didn't think Baya had the strength to seal the hatch anymore.

He took Baya and Doba in his arms and wrapped blankets tightly around them to help keep her warm. He had learned to accept that

Doba was part of the deal. What did bother him was how little she weighed. He barely knew she was there.

Hours into the storm came a terrible bang and the forward motion of the boat stopped in an instant. This sent them flying forward.

Vicaroy barely had time to register that the keel must've hit something when the boat swung violently to the port side. The sound of wood splitting tore through the droning of the rain. Something had broken through the cabin. Vicaroy reached out to touch the dark intruder, as if he needed tangible proof that his eyes were not failing him. His hand fell on a large black boulder that had punctured the wall of the cabin.

CHAPTER 45

"Land! Baya!" Vicaroy barely got the words out before freezing water flooded in on them. Baya let out a moan and curled herself tighter against his chest.

He carried her — and Doba — to the stern of the boat. She moaned another protest when cold drops of rain hit her face. He covered her head and held her tighter to him. Surveying their surroundings, he quickly discerned that they had indeed hit land.

The storm clouds blocked out any moonlight so he couldn't see far or make out much beyond a dark rocky shoreline. The boat creaked and groaned against the rock that held it in place. With each new wave the boat slowly splintered apart.

"Baya! We don't have much time before the boat sinks."

"Then why wake me? Let me die … in peace." Baya mumbled.

"No, Baya!" He gave her a slight shake. "The boat is sinking because we've hit land."

She opened her eyes. The cold night air and his words forced her to wake. She wiggled trying to get out of his arms.

Vicaroy gently set her down. "Can you walk?"

Baya had not stood in a couple days and her legs buckled. She leaned on his shoulder for support. Doba made his way to his perch on her shoulder.

"Land …" Her voice was little more than a whisper.

"Let me carry you across the rocks to the shore. Then I can come back for some supplies — though there isn't much left."

"No. I can walk. You carry what you can. We have to get out of this freezing rain."

Baya wrapped as many of the blankets around her as she could and stepped out onto the rock that had punctured the boat. The fact that the rock didn't move confused her sea legs. She stumbled before catching her footing. It was a strange sensation to be back on solid ground — ground that didn't constantly sway beneath her.

The rock was slick and she stumbled and fell onto the beach. But she didn't care. They were on land! Real land. She hoped it was not a dream, and feared that she would wake only to feel the endless motion of the sea, surrounded by wooden walls that were too close. Was it true? Could they really be off that wretched cramped boat?

Vicaroy joined her with his arms full. He had gathered what he thought was most important. "Can you make it to the tree line?" he asked. Thankfully it was not a driving rainstorm but they would still be soaked and frozen by morning if they didn't get out of it.

"I'm fine." Baya said. There was finally a reason to be awake. There was actually someplace to go. "I feel like I could fly."

Vicaroy headed for the shelter of the branches. One of the larger trees provided some relief from the rain but water still dripped through in places. Vicaroy broke limbs from a neighboring shrub and wove them into the lower limbs of the big tree. This made a temporary roof. He went straight to work gathering the driest twigs and branches he could find from under the trees.

Baya and Doba sat against the trunk wrapped up tight. Baya held out her hands to light the branches.

"No. Save your strength. I got this." Vicaroy used his magic stones and soon had a fire roaring.

She warmed her hands.

"I'll make us more food than we can eat tonight." Vicaroy poured Baya a handful of nuts from the jar. "Start with this, while I make us some flatbread. Tomorrow I can hunt for small game and gather fresh plants. I will have you back to your old self in no time."

Baya laid a hand on his arm. "Is this real? Are we on land?"

He smiled. "We made it."

* * *

AFTER EATING until she could not swallow another bite, Baya curled up on Vicaroy's lap with Doba in a ball on her lap. This way they could all share the blankets and keep each other warm. Baya struggled to keep her eyes open. She was afraid that when she woke the land would be gone.

Being off the boat and the feeling of having a full belly — it was more than she had dared to hope for in some time. How many times had she dreamt of such luxuries these past weeks? She couldn't count. Eventually sleep got the better of her and she dozed off into a deep dreamless rest.

Vicaroy couldn't sleep. He sat with his back resting against the tree. He easily held Baya's too-light frame. He watched the fire and kept it stoked as needed. Late into the night, he thought he might have dozed a moment but was woken by a sound, a rustling in the distance. He couldn't see anything beyond the firelight. Maybe his mind was playing tricks on him?

Yet, it happened several more times during the night. He would jerk awake at a sound, or what he thought was a sound, only to find nothing but silent darkness and nothing in sight.

He had to remind himself that while it was great to be on land, the untamed world in which they now found themselves was a deadly place. Hopefully the fire would deter any man-eating animals lurking in the dark.

* * *

BAYA WOKE to the rays of the first sun. She wasn't rocking back and forth. There was only stillness. She sat up and Vicaroy's arm fell to the ground between them. He had been holding her close as they slept under a pile of blankets. She was not imprisoned by thick wooden walls.

Wide-open space was all around her and something cold and soft was under her hand. She ran her fingers through the damp yellow grass. She hadn't known if she would ever feel grass again. They really had made it! This was not another dream of finally reaching land.

Excitement raced through Baya. The earth seemed to give her strength. She slowly stood and carefully tucked the covers around Vicaroy. He must not have slept much last night. His breathing was heavy as he remained fast asleep.

Baya surveyed her surroundings. There was nothing familiar about this place. The air smelled different than home, it was cool, damp and fresh. None of the smells that accompany humans could be sensed. The trees were nothing like she was accustomed to.

Unlike the tall skinny tropical trees which had a tuft of green leaves at the top, these trees had leaves from top to bottom. She moved to examine the closest tree to her. They looked like dark green leaves from a distance, yet up close she could tell that they were not. The branches were covered in pointed cone shapes. "How strange," she murmured.

The beach was sprinkled with large dark-red stones. To the south, rolling grassy hills led right into the water. The last of the season's flowers proudly flaunted their vibrant colors of orange, red and blue. Sunlight sparkled off snow-covered mountain tops in the distance. Baya's mouth hung open as she slowly spun around taking in the foreign landscape. To the north the beach gave way to rocks. This was where they had landed. What was left of the boat continued to drift into the rocks with each wave. Baya was not sad to see that it was mostly destroyed.

Doba was already helping himself to some of last night's bread.

"Good morning, Doba!" Baya sang.

It is a great morning. We're alive and on land.

Baya stirred the coals in the fire and added more wood for warmth. "This land appears to be lush. We should be able to gather plenty of food." Baya's stomach growled at the mention of a fresh meal. "And now you can find a mate."

Doba scampered off through the tall grass.

"Wait! Where are you going?" Baya was worried that he was leaving to find his own kind this very moment.

It is wonderful to be free. I want to have a look around.

"Are you coming back?"

Doba paused on a rock and looked back at her with his many blinking eyes. *Of course. You guys have food and a warm fire.*

Baya laughed with relief. "And what about good company?"

That part is debatable. Haven't we spent enough time together lately?

She chuckled. "Be careful. We don't know what's out there." She didn't want him to leave her for good, not yet, maybe not ever. Baya tossed some nuts into her mouth. But someday he would leave them, when he found others of his kind.

He didn't know how to survive in the wild. She frowned. Maybe they couldn't survive in the wild either? All three of them were accustomed to a very different lifestyle.

Baya tried to be patient while she waited for Vicaroy to wake or for Doba to return. There was so much to be done. They needed to make a better shelter and hunt and … make a plan.

CHAPTER 46

Baya and Vicaroy ate their fill, almost wiping out the last of their food supply.

"I had come across some interesting information in the scrolls that I brought with us," Baya said. "They didn't survive the voyage but I had been reciting them in order to commit them to memory."

"What are you talking about?" Vicaroy asked.

"Before we left I found some long-forgotten scrolls in the library. One of them told a different tale."

"Different? How?"

"We're told the story of how Ameris led all people to Pathins to keep them safe."

"Yeah?" Vicaroy had no idea where she was going with this. Even though he was not educated like Baya, he had heard many stories of his people. All children were taught the basics of Ameris's life and the origin of Pathins, even if it was simply their mothers' theos telling them bedtime stories.

"Well ... I found an ancient scroll that contradicted what we were taught. This scroll stated that not everyone willingly followed Ameris to Pathins — the Land of Plenty. It stated that there was political strife and nobody wanted to go to war over their differences. It would have been a hardship that the people couldn't afford in already dire times. So Ameris chose to leave the city with only Her followers."

Vicaroy's eyes grew wide. "That means … "

"There may be people outside of Pathins." Baya and Vicaroy spoke in unison.

Baya laughed. "Doba is right, we've obviously spent far too much time together lately. If the people who rebelled against Ameris were able to survive the drought and the wild beasts that plagued them back then, then yes, there may very well be others out here somewhere."

Vicaroy frowned. "But where? The maps you showed me were of vast lands, many times larger than Pathins, and none of them gave the location of a city."

"Yes, that's true. But another scroll that I found gave clues as to how to find the Abandoned City. Which, I think, is a reference to Merth."

"Merth? Is that the city where Ameris first lived, the city She left in search of Pathins?"

"Yes. And I think we can find it."

"Why didn't you tell me this before?"

"I was mad at you, remember?"

"Right, you weren't speaking to me. Well, this does change things. Do you trust this information?"

"There's only one way to find out."

Vicaroy sat back against the tree. If they had managed to find land, he had imagined them making a life for themselves — alone. They would build a home, a strong one to keep out the beasts. He would have a magnificent garden and he would raise Baya's children. This life sounded peaceful. Perfect.

If there were descendants of the survivors still in Merth, what would they be like? Vicaroy was sure it would be more strict rules to live by. He furrowed his brow.

"Don't you want to find other people?" Baya asked. She didn't need Doba to be able to guess what Vicaroy was thinking.

"I'm … not sure. We left to get away from people. I don't know if we should spend our time trying to find more people." He shook his head. "Strangers, with strange customs ..."

"Maybe they're better than the ones in Pathins and if not we'll leave again."

He had imagined life in the new land as being just the two of them. Much like now, sitting by a fire. It would get lonely. "Perhaps having company wouldn't be so bad."

"It will be the Dark Season soon. We're much farther north than we had hoped, thanks to the monsoons blowing us northward. Let's head south along the coast. We should be able to reach warmer weather. Neither of us is used to the cold. I don't know how to survive in it."

"We need fresh plants and game and soon this place could be a frozen wasteland with little of either."

Baya nodded.

"Then we head south and see what we find." While Vicaroy was not sure how he felt about searching for people, he knew that trying to survive a cold dark season without supplies was not a good idea. They were already too thin.

He studied Baya's sunken cheeks and the dark circles under her eyes. "We need to take some time to gather supplies and regain our strength before we try to make our way south. Surely we can spare a few weeks to hunt and gather food for our travels."

"That sounds ... smart," Baya had to concede.

CHAPTER 47

There was too much ground to cover. After much debate it was decided that they needed to split up. Vicaroy would head east and Baya would explore to the south. This way they could cover more ground in search of food and shelter. Neither was thrilled about the idea. It was most likely dangerous but this was a vast land and they needed to find resources — and fast — if they were to survive.

There was no telling what terrible things could be out there. They hadn't seen any signs of the dangerous animals that the scrolls warned about. Yet, Baya knew that they most likely existed. They were out there … somewhere.

She watched with apprehension as Vicaroy headed off on his own. He might very well be the only other person in this new world. The thought of being alone for the rest of her life made her shiver. "Be careful," she called after him.

Armed with his bow, quiver of arrows and a spear which doubled as a walking stick, Vicaroy disappeared into the thick forest.

Baya fought the urge to follow after him. She didn't have time to stand around and worry about him. She forced herself to head south.

But he didn't have powers. He would be fine, he was strong and capable with his weapons, she tried to convince herself.

Baya studied her own bow with apprehension as she secured it over her shoulder. She doubted that she was strong enough to pull the string back. Hopefully she had the strength to explore the southern coast and use her powers if the need arose. She paused and took a deep breath.

"I can do this," she whispered.

The tickle of many legs could be felt as Doba scurried around her own leg and his feet made their way up her body.

"Doba! Thank the Goddess you're back!"

He secured himself in his usual place, resting on her shoulder with his head next to Baya's.

"What did you see out there?"

Mostly trees, lots of trees ... and grass.

"No terrible woman-eating beasts?"

Nope.

"No others like you?"

Nope. So did you finally ditch the boy?

"No! Doba, you two are going to have to learn to get along. We're supposed to meet back at the campfire at dusk, if not before."

Doba hissed his disappointment.

They made their way south along the coast.

Baya was glad she had someone to talk to. "Everything is strange in this place, the trees, the plants, even the air smells different.

I hate it. It's cold, Doba said.

Hours passed and Baya's pace slowed. She was weak and malnourished from the long boat voyage. They saw nothing but shore and grass and trees. There was nothing that could be used as a shelter. She didn't recognize any plants as edible. On the positive side there were also no giant animals trying to eat them.

She sat by a small stream and they both drank their fill.

"I hope Vicaroy is having better luck than we are." All Baya wanted to do was rest in the warm midday sun, but she had to keep going…

Baya woke with a start. The suns were getting low in the sky. She wasn't sure how long she'd been dozing but she would be lucky to make it back to Vicaroy before dark. She struggled to her feet and headed north, back up the coastline. As she walked, she nibbled on some bread, which she shared with Doba.

The night was almost fully upon them when she saw a faint light ahead. Baya ran to close the distance. She was eager to get to safety and the delicious smell that came from the fire ahead.

Vicaroy paced by the large fire. When Baya stepped into the light his shoulders slumped with relief. "I was about to head out after you."

Baya's legs ached and her lungs stung from her short jog. "We're fine." She sucked in some air. "Sorry to worry you. I …" she lowered her chin to her chest.

"What is it? Are you okay?"

"Yes. I fell asleep, that's all. I'm sorry." She felt like a complete failure. "I hope you had better luck than we did."

Vicaroy gave her a broad smile. "This land is fruitful. I was able to kill two birds and I found many plants. Here …" He gestured for Baya to sit by the warmth of the fire. "Try this."

Baya took the steaming bowl from him and the delicious fragrance was almost more than her senses could handle. It took all the restraint she could muster not to devour the scalding-hot stew. She stirred the contents of the bowl and blew on it.

Her mouth salivated in anticipation of a much-needed fresh meal. When she was confident that it was cool enough to eat she took a mouthful. The juicy taste of fresh meat and veggies caused her mouth to water even more. A moan escaped her lips.

"I found several different roots." Vicaroy's eyes shone with pride. "Not to mention some herbs to help flavor the meal. The plants are not quite like the ones I'm used to, yet they're similar enough that with some digging and searching I found what I was looking for."

Baya could feel the strength flow into her body as the stew went to work restoring her health. "This is the best food I've ever tasted." Baya spoke with a mouth full. In no time her bowl was empty.

Vicaroy puffed his chest out. Nothing made him feel more like a man than being able to provide for Baya. He filled her bowl again and she didn't object. It was a luxury to have seconds. They'd had to go long enough without eating their fill.

"I didn't find any shelter, though. And you said you didn't have any luck?"

He posed this as a question and Baya felt as useless as a rock. "Well … no. We didn't find anything." She sighed and couldn't bring herself to tell him that it was not just a short nap she had taken but rather most of the afternoon she'd wasted away in a slumber.

Yet Vicaroy had accomplished so much. He'd hunted and found food, then prepared it and managed to salvage more stuff, including the cookware, from the wreckage of that dreaded boat — all while Baya slept.

"It's okay," Vicaroy said. "We can look for shelter tomorrow. The sky is clear tonight so hopefully it won't rain."

"I suppose we don't have a choice anyway, rain or not we're stuck outside," Baya said. "We'll have to rely on the fire to keep us safe."

"We need the heat anyway."

"Let's pray our luck holds out and there are no wild animals lurking about in search of an easy meal."

She hated feeling weak and useless. Her strength would come back if Vicaroy was able to find plenty of food, and then she could be of more help. She didn't think she had the strength to set a protection spell yet.

Baya's face lit up. Lots of rest and a belly full of warm stew had her feeling more energized than she had in a long time. She collected four long branches and pulled strips of tree bark from some nearby trees. She wrapped one end of a branch with the tree bark.

"Torches?" Vicaroy asked.

"They can be placed around our camp while we sleep."

"Good idea."

"Hopefully they will help keep us alive through the night. Now, you get some rest. You've had a full day. I'll stay up on first watch." At least she wasn't utterly worthless. Baya smiled to herself.

A full stomach had the opposite effect on Vicaroy — while Baya was more energized, he was content to crawl under the covers. His breathing soon grew heavy.

CHAPTER 48

After a large breakfast of leftovers Baya and Vicaroy decided to split up again but this time they would stay within earshot of each other.

"We want to head south to warmer lands so —"

"And to find the path to Merth," Baya interrupted.

"There's a path?"

"I doubt it's a wide cobblestone street like we had in Una Sitka but I think one of the parchments left clues to get back to Merth." Baya looked to the sky in deep thought. "It was titled, 'A way back' …

To return to the abandoned civilization
The key is to follow the unmoving star
Let these clues be your guide
The secret lies with the snake
Nestled in its belly
You will find what you seek
Yet the problem remains
How to find the elusive creature

One mighty obstacle will change your course
The birds of stone will show you the way
But first you must seek the sentinels who carry the morning sun
Then you know you are on the right path

THERE WAS a brightness in Baya's sunburst eyes that Vicaroy hadn't seen in a long time. "What in the name of Ameris does that mean?"

"It could be a map, of sorts, that will guide us to other people."

Vicaroy frowned. "Or it could be just an old poem. We have no idea who wrote that. There is no telling what they meant by all that nonsense."

"I think it means that the secret is Merth and to find it we have to find a snake and stone birds ... and two sentinels. Only in reverse."

Vicaroy made no attempt to hide his confusion. He only stared at Baya with raised eyebrows.

"Okay look, the scroll also had symbols." She drew in the dirt with a stick, two finger shapes with a sun rising between them. Underneath she drew a circle.

"That doesn't look familiar."

"Of course it doesn't, we've never been here before. It's a landmark that we have to find, the sun rising between two sentinels. See..." she pointed to the two finger-like figures.

"And the circle underneath? What's that?"

"I don't know. But if we had sailed directly east then it may have been easier to find. The scroll said that the most direct route to land was east, yet we were blown off course. So we need to head south in order to find the first clue that will lead us to Merth."

"And that vague drawing and a cryptic poem are our only clues?" Vicaroy shook his head, not fully following what she was saying. "It doesn't matter why we make our way south, as long as we head toward warmer weather as soon as we can."

"Fine." Baya said. She didn't like the skepticism in his voice. "At least we're in agreement about that." Baya grabbed her bow and quiver throwing them over her shoulder.

She had already explored some of the southern beach so they both moved inland before making their way southward through the forest. They stayed within earshot of each other, yet out of sight.

This way they could cover more land and increase their odds of finding a cave or a rock overhang that could be used as shelter from the weather and wild animals.

Baya had a sinking feeling that it was only a matter of time before they came upon the dangers of these lands, the ones promised to them by the old texts.

She scoured the foreign plants in search of ones that would lead to edible roots. Vicaroy had shown her what leaves to look for. They seemed to be the only vegetables in season this close to the cold months of equal darkness and light.

"Baya!" Vicaroy's voice boomed.

Her heart leapt. Sure that he was in terrible trouble she took off at a full run in the direction of his voice. Her legs protested but she forced them to move faster. She really needed to get back in shape.

"What's wrong?" she tried to yell but couldn't find the breath to get the words out.

She came up over a hill to find Vicaroy standing in front of a pile of huge rocks. He held his arm out. "Do you think this will work?"

Baya bent over, lungs heaving and sucking in air, before she even tried to figure out what he was talking about. He's okay, he's okay... her, on the other hand ... she was not so great. She gulped in another deep breath and stood to examine what he had found.

Several rocks were piled on top of each other. One large slab had fallen across other stones to form a triangle. The space beneath it was open. It wasn't a cave, per se, but it would provide shelter enough for two to sleep comfortably.

"It's perfect!" Baya threw her arms around Vicaroy. "It will make a great home while we gather food for our journey south."

So the work began. Vicaroy left to hunt and Baya headed back for their supplies. She found a large plank that had washed up on shore by the camp. It had been part of their boat and it was about the size of a door. Tying all the supplies she thought they may need to the plank she dragged it through the forest. Her arms shook from the effort and her legs screamed at her.

She was tempted to use her powers to float the supplies but that would drain her even quicker. Plus, Baya needed to make her body strong again. It was terrible to not be as strong as she had once been.

Baya glared at Doba who sat on top of the belongings like a sentry. "You could help, you know? Or at least carry yourself."

Doba only replied with a short click and hiss.

Covered in sweat she eventually collapsed in front of the fallen stones — their new shelter.

* * *

THEY SPENT their days hunting and searching for useful plants. Vicaroy grew skilled at hunting birds and they both learned more about the local plants. They used the panel from the former boat as a door to their triangular room.

Each day that passed seemed colder than the last. In the evenings, Vicaroy sewed them jackets and pants out of two of the thickest blankets. Using cured hides from their supplies, he made them leather boots. The extra pieces of blanket material were used to line the makeshift footwear, which they wore over their stockings and shoes.

Vicaroy smoked thin strips of poultry. The resulting jerky would make good travel food.

He was glad to see the dark circles disappear from under Baya's eyes and her cheeks slowly filled out. At least he could once again keep the woman he loved well fed.

As Baya regained her strength she was able to start using her powers again. She set a protection spell around them every night.

"You know I could get used to this," Vicaroy said over the campfire one night.

Baya smiled in answer. It was peaceful.

The following morning they woke to find a solid white landscape.

The snow was up to Baya's knees and still coming down. None of them had been in snow before. They had only heard about it. It didn't take Baya or Doba long to decide they didn't like it.

Supplies were rolled up in blankets that fastened to their backs. Their time had run out and the journey south began.

CHAPTER 49

For days on end staying warm was their greatest challenge. Vicaroy was sure his hands were going to freeze solid and fall completely off, so he sewed mittens for Baya and himself. With their new heavy clothing they were warm enough as long as they kept moving. At night Baya would use her powers to help keep them warm.

Any plant life had frozen, making the edible roots impossible to find. Small game was also scarce. They ate largely from their supply of roots and dried meat. It was not nearly as satisfying as Vicaroy's hot stews but it kept them healthy. Baya dreamed of a day when she would never have to eat smoked meat again, or feel the bite of the bitter cold on her face.

They made their way south down the coast. It took a week before they were out of the snow and several more weeks passed before the weather grew noticeably warmer. Supplies were getting dangerously low. So they decided to stop at a rock overhang along the beach. They had to take some time to dry more meat and gather what little plant-based food they could find.

Baya plopped down under the overhang, taking the opportunity to rub her sore feet. "Hopefully we have finally escaped the rainy season." Baya frowned at the foot she was massaging. "The blisters have turned into calluses," she mindlessly observed. "What is it?" she asked when she noticed the concerned look on Vicaroy's face.

"The nights are growing shorter. We are heading into the warm season."

"The Time of Daylight. Yes, that's a good thing." Baya longed for the hot sun on her skin.

"But, I've been thinking ... There seem to be more small animals in the south ..."

"And?" Baya still didn't see the problem. "That means more food for us."

"Yet, what if predators follow the prey as well, and we're headed right for them. That could be why we didn't see any large animals in the north."

"It's definitely possible. We don't have a choice do we? We can't survive in the cold and the snow. Let's hope that my protection spell is enough to keep us hidden from predators at night."

"We've been lucky so far ... too lucky. I'm worried that ..." He left the thought hanging.

"That ... our luck will run out and that there are likely to be more threats the farther south we go," Baya finished his sentence.

"Yeah. That's it." He admired how she could always find the words to sum things up nicely. Expressing his thoughts and feelings was not one of Vicaroy's strengths.

"It's wise to be worried," Baya admitted.

* * *

THUS THEIR JOURNEY WENT. They crossed the strange and lovely land that grew greener as they traveled. They stopped to re-supply as needed. Like life on the boat, before the monsoons, they fell into a monotonous routine. But instead of taking turns sailing, their life consisted mostly of walking ... endlessly walking.

One warm morning Baya woke to an amazing sight. She had to rub her eyes to make sure she was actually seeing what was in front of her.

Vicaroy woke to her scream. He'd been dreaming of a large beast. It moved gracefully around him on three powerful legs. Her scream came as the beast leapt for him. The next thing he knew, he was awake and on his feet, his spear in his hand. The spear was always by his side, never out of arms reach.

"Look!" Baya pointed.

Doba scampered around Baya's feet hissing and clicking. He'd been rudely startled by the sudden awakening as well.

There was a lake in the distance. The morning rays glistened off the crystal blue water in waves of white light. But that was not what had provoked her outcry. On the other side of the lake stood two tall stone structures. Between the thin rocks rose the first sun of the day.

"Yes!" Baya screamed again. "That's it! The first sign. We set up camp in the dark last night and couldn't see it." She drew the symbol of the two fingers with the sun between them and the circle underneath. "The circle represents the lake. See?"

Vicaroy stared opened-mouthed at the sight of the round lake and the peculiar pillar-like mountains on either side. He glanced back and forth between the view and Baya's drawing from the scrolls. It was an exact match. "I'll be damned."

Baya leapt up to throw her arms around Vicaroy's neck. "If we head east we can find Merth ... or at least the next indicator that we're on the right path."

Vicaroy put his arms around Baya in return. "Do you think there might be others out there?"

"I do."

Vicaroy sighed. Part of him enjoyed having Baya all to himself, well mostly. He could do without Doba's company. Yet, Baya deserved more. She needed a home, a real one. Vicaroy desperately missed having a garden as well. It would be nice not to have to work so hard just to survive. Perhaps they could have a better life in a city, with companions.

"What do you want?" he asked.

"I think we need to find other humans if we're to survive for much longer."

Vicaroy nodded. "Then we head east."

Baya squealed before pressing her lips to his.

He tightened his arms around her waist, pressing her body against his. His hands slid down her back. Her body exploded with a need she hadn't let come to the surface in some time.

Since the monsoons their life had been consumed with survival. Find food, prepare food, eat food, stay warm, sleep, walk — that was it. But their kiss ignited the dormant desire. It was like being reunited with an old friend — pleasure, urgency, comfort all in one.

Baya ran a hand through Vicaroy's curly black hair and kissed him harder. She leaned her body into his. Her lips parted and his tongue brushed lightly against hers. The escape had been so complete that she hadn't noticed the familiar tickle of hundreds of legs crawling up her body. A loud hiss followed by irritated clicking broke the spell.

What are you two doing? Doba's voice rang in Baya's head.

Baya pulled herself out of Vicaroy's arms with a nervous laugh. She had momentarily forgotten about her little friend.

Vicaroy glared at Doba, who held his stare with his four unblinking eyes.

"That thing's got to go," Vicaroy's voice was husky.

"Oh, don't be that way." Baya moved to pack up camp. "That leaves two more clues. Next we have to find the stone birds and then the serpent which holds the ancient city."

"The only problem is that none of that makes any sense."

"Well, neither did the first clue — two sentinels that hold the morning sun. But we found it. Let's hope that the other signs will be as obvious once we find them."

By the time they made it to the lake, both suns were high in the sky. The nights were brisk but the days grew warm. This day was the warmest since the rains had first pushed them off course.

The clear blue water allowed them to see the lake's rocky bottom.

"This is too lovely to pass by. We could use a good washing." Baya was eager to soak her entire body. The occasional splashing off in a cold stream didn't get her as clean as she liked. She threw off her pack and began to undress.

Vicaroy tried not to watch — too closely. He busied himself with unpacking the soap root and lav. They rubbed the two together under water to form suds that smelled of a spring garden. The scent made Vicaroy long for the palace gardens.

Baya couldn't wait to rub the soap all over her body. It felt like ages since she'd had a proper bath. The water was cool on her toes but not freezing. Wearing only her stained and threadbare undergarment, she waded into the crystal water and dove in headfirst. She wanted to get the shock of the change in temperature over with as quickly as possible. She came up gasping at the refreshing coolness.

Vicaroy had not meant to stare after her but his world had stopped as he watched her enter the lake. This time it was more out of relief than male desire. Baya was filling out again after almost starving to death. Her long legs were lean and strong once again. The slight, yet perfect curves of her breasts and hips were back.

Okay, so there was some desire, he admitted. More than anything, though he truly was relieved that she had gained her health back.

"Come on. It's wonderful once you're in," Baya yelled.

Vicaroy began to undress. He wanted to jump in the water and scoop her up in his arms. It would start with a kiss, then he'd carry her to the shore, dripping wet and …

Baya's attention turned to Doba who was sunning himself on a rock beside the lake. her cheeks flushed purple and she laughed.

It was a joyous sound to Vicaroy's ears, yet he frowned. "What did that thing just tell you?"

"Not much. Just what you'd like to do with me … dripping wet …" She gave him a playful wink, her cheeks still a shade of purple. Baya couldn't have been more pleased that he found her long lanky form attractive. He was probably the only man who would.

"I'm glad you kissed me. It means you're feeling better. I told myself that I wouldn't be the first to kiss you, not again. It was your turn and you would when you were good and ready."

Baya smiled. He was always putting her first.

A flash caught her eye. As she turned toward it, Vicaroy was thrown to the ground by a streak of colors. She hadn't had time to yell out in warning.

The sudden impact sent Vicaroy flying. It felt as if he'd run full speed into a stone wall. The next thing he knew he was on the ground. Something had slammed into his shoulder sending him through the air. He hit the ground with a thud and turned over to find a large snarling mouth full of sharp teeth. A wild animal was on top of him.

Baya let out a piercing scream, much different than the excited scream that had awakened him that morning. This was a scream of terror that turned Vicaroy's blood to ice.

Yet the scream worked to wake all his senses at once. He rolled out of the way as a large mouth lunged for him. He made a quick movement heading for his spear but the beast blocked his path. The animal growled and Vicaroy took a cautious step away.

Baya quickly positioned herself between the man and the beast.

Vicaroy couldn't believe his eyes. "Baya, no! Run!" Was she out of her mind?

The beast showed its teeth and a low guttural sound started deep in its belly and came out as a deafening roar.

Baya held out her arms with her palms facing the beast, as if this would slow it or stop it somehow. "Shhh. It's okay. … Shhh." Her voice was low and soft as she tried to calm the animal. "We won't hurt you, if you don't hurt us." She tried to make a connection with the beast by looking into its four wild eyes.

The creature resembled Mook but was smaller and its eyes were crazed. They blinked and darted about as they examined its prey. This was the look of a starving animal in the middle of a hunt. Now it was Baya's blood that went cold as she realized that there would be no reasoning with this wild creature.

It lunged for Baya.

CHAPTER 50

Baya sent up a cloud of thick smoke from her hands and grabbed Vicaroy to pull him out of the path of the beast. He wasted no time in lunging for his spear while Baya disappeared entirely.

The beast snorted and wheezed in protest as it inhaled Baya's smoke.

"Run!" Baya's voice came out of thin air. She was nowhere to be seen.

The beast turned its four eyes to Vicaroy who now held his spear. Something told him that he couldn't outrun this thing. So he braced himself and readied his spear.

The beast crouched in preparation to lung forward with its powerful back leg. Vicaroy heard Baya scream, even though he still couldn't see her. This scream was different than her previous screams that day. This time it was a determined battle cry. The beast began to flail around as if it was going mad. It bucked and snarled. It threw its head back and jerked around in circles, snapping its teeth only to find nothing but air.

It wasn't biting at the air. It was acting like something was on its back, something that it desperately wanted to get off. Fear pulsed through Vicaroy. Baya must have thrown herself onto the animal. He just couldn't see her.

"Baya!" he yelled.

"Run!" she screamed.

"I'm not leaving you."

There was no reply as the beast continued to growl and leap and bite at seemingly nothing.

Baya didn't want the beast to die but no other options came to mind. Time was running out. It was either the beast or them.

"Kill it," Baya yelled.

Vicaroy stepped closer, raising his spear higher. "But I can't see you. I don't want to hurt you."

Baya's hands struggled to hold onto the beast's feathery neck. Her muscles strained from the effort it took to cling to the beast. She couldn't hold on much longer anyway. She let go of the glistening rainbow-colored feathers. She materialized as she hit the ground and rolled away.

Vicaroy didn't hesitate. As soon as he was able to locate Baya, he lunged with all his might. The spear slid into the scaly-flesh of the animal's chest. A loud growl was cut short as he drove the spear deeper into the beast.

Panting, Baya got to her feet and brushed herself off. "Are you hurt?"

The animal lay at Vicaroy's feet. Its front paws twitched and dark blue blood pooled around the beast's head and chest. Vicaroy was covered in splatters of blood. Baya didn't care, she buried her head in his bare torso.

"I don't think I'm hurt. You?" He held her tight and scanned his surroundings in search of any other threats. He couldn't see any. "It came out of nowhere." His fear and the instinct to fight gave way to shame. "I'd been …" he lowered his head and shook it.

Baya narrowed her eyes. "Don't do that." Her words were short and pungent.

"Do what?"

"Lower your head, like you did something wrong — like you're beneath me because I'm a woman. Look at what you did." She gestured to the slain creature. "You saved me."

"But I shouldn't have let myself get distracted. I should've seen it coming. My guard was down and it put you in danger."

She lifted his chin so she could see into his dazzling golden-brown eyes. "The only thing that you did wrong is not look at me. Please don't shy away. Don't hide from me. In this land I'm not the daughter of a high priestess and you're no longer a garden boy. We're partners — equals. It will take both of us working together to survive out here. Do you understand?"

"But I can't do all the things that you can. You made yourself invisible. That was amazing."

"And yet it was *you* who managed to stop the beast. In fact, you made it look easy. We make a good team. My powers and your strength, together we can make it in these wild lands." She gave him a wry smile. "Let's get cleaned up and get out of here in case there are any other hungry monsters out there."

They wasted no time in cleaning up. So much for enjoying themselves in the lake. The beast was a clear reminder of the dangers of this land. No more teasing and relaxing. They would have to stay alert at all times.

Once they were clean and packed, Baya headed in the direction from which the animal had attacked. She studied the ground and headed north.

"Where are you going? I thought we were heading east?" Vicaroy asked.

"We are or will. I need to … find something first."

Vicaroy raised his eyebrows.

"The beast was desperate. I tried to communicate with it — to convince it not to harm us. But she was too hungry and —"

"That was a she? And you could communicate with it?"

"Yes. She was desperate to feed her starving baby."

"In case you've forgotten, we were supposed to be the 'food' you're talking about."

"Yes. We would have provided lots of meat for her baby, much more than the small game she'd been forced to try and survive on. I think we can help though."

"Help who?"

"I've seen her kind before. Only much bigger." Baya was glad to find that she was able to talk about her trials now. Once outside of Pathins the spell that kept her silent before must have been broken.

"You mean to tell me that that thing was small?"

Baya nodded. "The ones I've seen were kept in captivity and better fed. They must've been able to grow larger. This one was struggling to hunt for herself and her baby. That must be why I wasn't able to convince her not to eat us. The one I met before was not starving and only wanted to play."

Vicaroy looked baffled, so Baya told him about her second trial and about Mook.

"That still doesn't explain what we're doing now — heading in the wrong direction."

"Without her, her baby will die."

"That's a good thing — one less wild beast in this land."

"I don't want the baby to die. It's the least we can do for an animal that was only trying to provide for herself and her offspring."

"Then it will grow up and try to eat us."

"Not if I can befriend it, like I did Mook and we keep it well fed."

"We don't need another mouth to feed, especially a potentially dangerous one."

Baya gave him a crooked smile with her head cocked to the side. It was a look that said the debate was over.

Vicaroy lowered his head. He should've known better than to argue with her.

She grabbed his chin more gruffly this time and lifted his gaze. "Head up." She demanded. "That's a terrible and all too ingrained habit of yours but we'll keep working on it. You have every right to question me."

Baya's expression lightened. "Let's keep our eye out for fresh game to feed the little guy when we find him."

CHAPTER 51

Vicaroy shot two birds and Baya managed to shoot her first animal. It was a scaly creature that didn't make it back into its burrow before Baya's arrow found it.

She held her prize up by its thick back leg. It was heavy. She'd never seen anything like it in Pathins. "It's fat and juicy, perfect for feeding a baby meat-eater."

Vicaroy shook his head as they made their way back to the faint trail of the beast who had attacked them.

They traveled until the suns were getting low in the sky.

"We need to make camp soon so that I can cook these birds for dinner," Vicaroy said.

Baya nodded. "Just a little farther. The den must be close." There was a desperation in her voice.

Vicaroy frowned. Why was the offspring of a beast that tried to kill them so important to her?

Dusk was upon them when it began to rain.

"No! The paw prints are hard enough to follow. Now the rain will wash them out."

Vicaroy picked up some branches and began tying them together to make a lean-to.

"You got this, right?" Baya asked.

"If you mean, can I make a shelter and a fire? Then, yes."

"Good." Baya headed off in the rain.

"Wait. Don't go looking for that thing in the dark ... alone. What if there are more of them?"

Baya smiled and then vanished. "I'll be fine," she said, when she materialized again.

"Be careful." Vicaroy bit his lip.

But she was already headed off into the night.

She was soaking wet when she returned — empty-handed. Baya plopped down under the lean-to by the fire. Vicaroy stirred a lovely smelling stew that made her stomach growl.

"Damn rain! I lost the trail. I looked all around but ... nothing. Now we'll never find the little guy. Poor thing, out there all alone. Waiting for a mother that won't come home."

Vicaroy tried to feel sorry for the animal whose mother he had killed but he couldn't understand Baya's desire to save the creature. He decided it was best to remain silent as she was visibly upset.

They both jumped to their feet at a light rustling sound that came from a nearby bush — Baya with a bow drawn and Vicaroy with a spear ready to issue a deadly blow. Doba deftly buried himself in their belongings.

"What was that?" Vicaroy asked.

She moved away from the fire so she could better see her surroundings before cautiously heading toward the sound. Vicaroy moved around the other side of the fire.

There was a hiss and the sound of crunching leaves. Baya moved toward the noise. A flash of sparkling feathers and scales caught her eye as the light from her fire ball reached the small creature. It disappeared into a den under a rock.

"There it is!" Baya yelled. "In there." She pointed to a mostly concealed hole.

Vicaroy studied it. "It looks like someone covered it with branches to try to hide the entrance. Like we used to do to cover the trail to our cove."

"Its mother must've done that to hide her baby while she hunted."

"Animals can't possibly be that smart, can they?" Vicaroy's brow furrowed with concern. The wild beasts of this land were not only as fierce as the ancient legends claimed but they were also intelligent, making them even more of a threat.

"Look at Doba, he's smart. Mook seemed pretty smart as well. I'll try to lure it out with some meat."

Vicaroy went back to tend to his stew. He prided himself on never ruining a meal.

Baya waited with her kill. Thankfully the rain had stopped. She laid the gutted varmint by the den. It seemed like ages before a long scaly nose came into view.

"That's it, little one. Come and eat." Baya whispered.

Four dark eyes blinked at her followed by a hiss. The creature retreated once again.

Maybe it didn't like fire? She quickly extinguished her fire ball and waited.

The little nose sniffed the air before venturing farther out of its den. It eyed the meat and then Baya.

When she was able to get a good look into its eyes, she used the opportunity to try to make a connection. "This is for you. Come and eat. I know you're hungry."

The creature's four eyes blinked at different times while it debated whether or not to take a chance with Baya. In the end its hunger won over its fear as it slowly moved toward her and the fresh kill laid out in front of her.

"That's it. Come on." Baya took a step back.

The creature tore at the flesh of the varmint. It took ravenous mouthfuls of meat with each bite.

Baya laughed. "You poor starving baby."

The creature jerked its head toward her, apparently understanding something she had said.

"You don't need to eat so fast. Your food isn't going anywhere." Yet Baya remembered what it was like to want to swallow all the food in front of her at once.

She sat crossed legged and waited patiently for the creature to eat its fill. When most of the meat was gone it backed away toward its den.

"Wait. Do you have a name?"

Four eyes blinked in confusion and it scurried away.

Baya sighed and headed for camp. "Well, I'm learning a lot. Apparently, it doesn't like fire. Our campfires most likely do help to keep predators away at night."

CHAPTER 52

The next morning Baya woke to a sharp hiss followed by familiar irritated clicking noises. The shiny rainbow-colored baby had knocked over the stew pot from the previous night and was licking the insides clean.

Doba scurried to hide behind Baya.

"Good morning, little one," Baya said.

The baby moved away from the pot but didn't run to its den.

"Good girl. You don't need to run."

Yes, it does. Shoo. Shoo. Doba's voice sounded in Baya's head. He finished with a loud hiss.

The beast took another step back. When Vicaroy got to his feet the animal ran for shelter.

"You scared her. I think she was coming around," Baya said.

"That thing is a female? As skittish as it is, I would have thought it was a boy."

"It's a girl for sure."

"We don't have time for this." Vicaroy was already packing up their camp. "What are you planning to do, take it with us?"

"Of course. She will die all alone out here."

Vic can't see what the problem is with letting it die and for once I agree with him, Doba protested.

Baya laughed.

"What?" Vicaroy said with reluctance.

"Doba must not be able to say your full name. He calls you Vic. Hmm ...Vic." Baya rolled the name around on her tongue. "I like it."

Vicaroy frowned. "I guess I'll start calling you Bay."

It was Baya's turn to scowl. "That sounds like a boy's name."

"Well we wouldn't want that."

"Okay, I won't call you Vic ... too often."

He chuckled. "We have to travel quite a while just to get back to our eastern path. We should get going."

"We can't leave without the poor little creature."

"It's terrified of us. How will you convince it to come with us?"

"I have to try." Baya dug around for a piece of dried meat and headed for the den entrance alone. "Come on little one."

Nothing.

"Please, come out. We'll take care of you."

No response.

Baya placed her finger to her lips. It must not have been as hungry as it was last night.

More time passed. She could feel Vicaroy's mounting impatience.

"Come on, baby. Please!"

Baya heard its thoughts before she saw the tiny black nose peek out. *Baaa...beee.*

Baya's heart jumped. "Yes. Yes, you're a baby."

Ba...by. Four black eyes peered out at Baya.

"Yes. Come out. I won't hurt you."

Baby, mama calls me.

Relief flooded through Baya. It could communicate, at least a little. "Baby is what your mother called you?"

It took a couple cautious steps out into the early morning sunlight. Baya inhaled sharply at the lovely beast. Iridescent hues of blue, green and orange danced off its feathers and scales.

"We must give you a proper name." Baby would not do as that would be like calling Doba, Insect. The name popped into Baya's head and she knew it was perfect. "I will call you Tara."

Tara. The animal tried out the name.

"Do you want this, Tara." Baya held the meat out.

She sniffed the air but didn't come any closer.

"Come on Tara. I'm your friend."

Fend?

"A friend, it's someone you can trust. Someone who won't hurt you."

Mama says, no such thing. The world outside is bad. All bad.

"Not all bad. Would I bother to feed you if I wanted to hurt you?"

The animal blinked in confusion or deep thought — Baya wasn't sure which. It was difficult to understand the creature's thoughts. They were muffled and garbled at times. Tara's language was simple and Baya knew that the young creature didn't understand half of what she said.

Baya tried anyway. "Take the food from my hand. Trust works both ways. You have sharp teeth and claws, so you could hurt me and I have powers, so I could hurt you. But we won't hurt each other. This is how you build trust."

Tara eyed the meat and then Baya for a long while. *Mama brings meat.*

"Yes. And so do I."

Tara inched forward. Step by step. Slowly, until her sharp teeth gently snatched the meat from Baya's out-stretched arm. Tara all but inhaled the food.

"You kept your mama hunting all the time with that appetite." Baya slowly reached out to rub the shiny feathery neck.

Tara let out a guttural purr when Baya's hand found the right spot behind her tiny ear. Instinctively Tara's head leaned into Baya's hand for more.

"Tara." Baya spoke softly. Four wide eyes peered back at her expectantly.

"We're heading east. We have to keep moving. You won't make it on your own. Please come with us. We'll care for you."

Mama come back.

Baya's heart sank. "No Tara. Your mother ... will not come back. She's ... gone."

Mama never leave.

"She didn't want to leave you but she ... had to. Your mother is gone for good, Tara. I'm sorry."

Tara looked back to the den. *Gone long time.*

"Yes. Tara your mother has been gone longer than usual and she is not able to come back. Although she wanted to."

Where go?

"She had to leave."

Why?

"Tara, she's dead."

The creature took a step back and sat down hard on its back leg. *No.* A whimper escaped from her as she fell to the ground, her two front paws spread out in front of her.

Baya wanted to weep for the poor creature. "I'm here to take care of you now." Her voice broke.

There was a long silence.

"We have to get moving," Baya finally ventured.

Tara didn't move.

It was as if she had given up. Tara no longer cared if she lived or died.

"Come on Tara. I know you miss your mother but she wouldn't want you to die."

Only a whimper came from the little creature.

"Will you let me carry you?"

No response.

Baya ran her hand over the soft feathers and along the hard-scaled body. She rubbed behind Tara's ears. Another whimper but the animal leaned into the touch. Slowly Baya worked her hands under the creature and lifted it into her arms. Tara was heavy. Not much bigger than a toddler but much heavier. "You're solid muscle aren't you?"

Tara lay her head on Baya's shoulder and let herself be carried away. She watched her den disappear in the distance. *Mama,* she murmured in Baya's head.

"I know. We're your family now."

CHAPTER 53

A shiver ran up Vicaroy's spine and he suppressed a yelp. "What…" Vicaroy snapped his head to the side only to find Doba's four black eyes staring at him. Doba sat perched on his shoulder. The shiver had been caused by Doba's many legs as they crawled up his body. He barely resisted the urge to swat the insect away. How does Baya put up with this creature?

Doba gave him an irritated click but the insect's attention quickly turned to Baya and the beast that was in her arms.

Vicaroy sighed at the sight. "And now it seems she's collecting animals. And I guess I inherited you out of the deal."

Doba gave a quick hiss to indicate that he wasn't happy about the situation either.

"Well, let's get going." Vicaroy waved them on with his hand.

They made their way back toward the lake and the peaks that held the morning sun. They didn't want to get off their eastern path, which started at the lake. Baya's arms quickly grew tired from carrying the heavy creature which lay limp in her arms. She paused to rest, setting Tara down.

Tara plopped down beside Baya. Baya worried that the creature had lost its will to live. It didn't care about its safety or anything else. "Hey there, it's going to be okay." Baya rubbed behind its ears.

There was an involuntary guttural purr that came from Tara.

Baya waved a piece of dried meat in front of Tara's nose.

After a couple sniffs Tara's head was moving in time with the meat that Baya moved in front of her.

"That's it. Now you can have meat whenever you want. But I want you to walk on your own, okay?" Baya stood and slowly moved away.

Tara bounded after her.

"That's it, come on." Once she was sure that Tara would follow she let Tara take the meat from her hand.

Baya was relieved not to have to carry her. They could make better time with Tara walking on her own.

When the two fingers of the sentinels came into view they headed east. As the day wore on they topped a grassy hill only to find an incredible sight.

Baya's mouth fell open as she took in the vast field of wildflowers that lay in front of them. Bright pinks, blues, purples and oranges lay before them. The flowers stretched as far as they could see. Tara leapt forward without hesitation. She fully disappeared into the flowers. Her brightly colored feathers and scales blended in perfectly. The only thing that gave her away was an occasional movement of the flowers. Her head could be seen briefly when she leapt through the foliage.

"Tara seems right at home here," Baya observed.

"Tara?" Vicaroy questioned.

"That's her name."

"I guess you're not the only one who can disappear into their surroundings."

"Tara was made to be in a field like this and it definitely lightened her mood."

Tara darted toward them and Vicaroy tensed.

She ran around Baya's legs and back into the field. *Come on.* Baya heard Tara's voice. *Mama used to bring. Good hunt and play.*

"Your mother used to bring you here to play and practice hunting?" Baya bellowed after Tara as she waded into the knee-high foliage.

Yep, Tara yelped as her head peeked out of the flowers and then quickly disappeared.

Is it dense, like Vic? Doba asked.

"No. Neither of them is stupid," Baya answered. "Tara is young and has never seen humans before. She will have to learn how to communicate better. Like you did. How old are you, Doba?"

At least ten.

"You see? You're much older and you've been around humans your entire life. You're used to the way we talk and how we act. Tara is not even a year old. She has a lot to learn. Like I'm sure you did when you were young."

"I have to admit, she is a lovely creature," Vicaroy said.

Doba only clicked his disapproval in Vicaroy's ear.

They hunted for small game in the flowery meadows and by nightfall they were still surrounded by flowers. The colorful fields seemed to go on forever.

Exhausted from a day of walking, Tara fell fast asleep after dinner. On one side of Baya lay Doba and pressed against her other was Tara.

Vicaroy couldn't help but smile as he stayed up a bit longer to make sure the fire was stoked good for the night and to make sure they were safe. He didn't sleep deeply anyway, not while they were out in the open. After being attacked by Tara's mother he was even more on edge. It didn't ease his mind that Tara preferred these lush hills. That meant there would be others like her in these parts. Vicaroy hardly let himself doze.

CHAPTER 54

The following morning Vicaroy poked at the campfire coals without seeing them.

"What's on your mind?" Baya asked.

"I've been thinking —"

"I can tell."

A ghost of a smile crossed his lips. "Yeah, well, now that we've been attacked … do you think it's time to set protections spells around us? I mean, if you're strong enough and all."

"That's a good idea." She rubbed his shoulder. "You know you can always tell me what's on your mind."

He nodded.

Baya set a protection shield around them before they headed out.

The day brought about more of the same vibrant fields.

"This land is so vast and completely uninhabited … by people. It's a shame that Pathins is over-crowded when there's all this lush land in the world," Baya said.

She stumbled forward.

"Are you okay?" Vicaroy asked.

Baya felt dizzy and her legs were wobbly. She placed her hand over her stomach when it growled. "I don't think I can walk all day and keep a protection spell around us. It's only been an hour and I'm hungry again." She lifted the spell and the dizziness faded.

Vicaroy looked like he was ready to catch her if needed. "I guess it was easier to maintain the protection when we were sitting around on a boat."

Baya nodded. "I guess so. It would help if there were other women around. Together we can magnify our powers." Baya bit her lip and shook her head.

"It's okay. We'll be fine." He handed her some flatbread.

A distant rumbling, like thunder, could be heard. Yet there were no clouds in the sky. Tara scrambled to hide behind Baya.

"It sounds like it's coming from the east." Baya shoved the bread into her mouth.

"I'll see if I can get a better view." Vicaroy headed for the tallest tree not too far off.

Baya notched an arrow. Little bumps formed on the back of her neck and there was a sinking feeling in her stomach. She scanned the horizon for signs of any threats.

Once he was high up in the tree, Vicaroy let out a low whistle. "Baya, you've got to see this."

She placed her bow over her shoulder and reached for the lowest branch of the tree. A growl came from behind, causing Baya to instinctively make herself disappear.

"Climb, Tara!" Baya yelled. She helped it get its front paws around the tree.

Four black eyes and a large toothy mouth lunged for Tara and unknowingly for Baya as well. Tara was able to claw her way up the tree, as sharp teeth chomped at her hind leg but only found air.

Baya spun around the tree slamming her back into it. The attacking animal breezed by. Although it was multicolor and iridescent it didn't look like Tara. It had a hump on its back and its nose was longer and thinner. It also had large floppy ears and a short curved tail covered in feathers.

It spun around and both Baya and the beast looked up to find that

Tara was using her powerful back leg to leap up the tree, holding on with her front claws as she climbed.

There were more snarls and the beast lunged for Tara.

Tara flicked her tail sending the sharp spike at the end into the predator's nose. There was a yelp and the circling beast backed away. This gave Baya her chance to grab the nearest branch and crawl her way into the tree. Another beast snapped its powerful jaws but missed Baya as it couldn't see exactly where she was. It was only able to smell her.

Baya's heart sank. The bottom of the tree was now surrounded by these creatures. She scrambled onto another branch as one jumped for her, driven by her scent.

"Baya!" Vicaroy yelled.

Another yelp rang through the air. Baya paused her ascent and turned to find an arrow sticking out of one of the animals.

Vicaroy shot another arrow as an animal lunged for the tree trying to claw its way up after Tara. Baya let herself materialize and called up to Vicaroy. "We're all in the tree and it doesn't look like these animals can climb. Don't waste any more arrows."

Vicaroy exhaled with relief. She and Tara made their way higher up into the tree.

"Look." He pointed to the northeast.

Baya took in the sight with a sharp inhale, her jaw slack.

Tara tried to make her way to the branch Baya was on but the bark under one of her paws gave way and Tara roared in fear as she hung on by only one paw. Baya lunged for her loose front leg. Tara panted heavily as Baya strained to pull her into her arms.

"It's okay, you're safe," Baya whispered.

She could not keep her gaze from the horizon as she patted Tara's feathers. There were too many animals to count. Herds and herds. She could make out several different types. The largest beasts were bigger than a common house, with three thick legs the size of tree trunks.

The creatures moved slowly and in unison as they used the long arms coming off their faces to pick grass and flowers and shove them into their large mouths. Each one had three such arms where their noses should have been. This way they could continuously shovel food in as they walked.

"Look at how much they eat. No wonder they are so huge." Vicaroy's voice was full of awe.

"They're so large they shake the earth when they walk. They must be causing the thundering noise," Baya added.

All the animals were covered in scales and had three legs. This was where their similarities stopped. Some of the species had different colors and markings. Yet they all blended into the rainbow-colored vegetation. Some had glistening stripes of blue, green and purple, while others sported hues of red and orange. Some were thick and slow and yet others were lean and fast. They ran around one another and leapt into the air with ease, as they played in the meadow. The different types of animals were clumped in herds largely of their own kind.

Baya reluctantly pulled her eyes from the view to study their situation. The pack of predators circled the base of the tree that they were now trapped in. "What do we do about them?"

"We don't have enough arrows to shoot them all," Vicaroy said.

"I guess we wait them out."

"Look." Vicaroy pointed to two distant figures. They were difficult to make out. The grass bending around them was the only thing that betrayed their presence. Upon closer inspection, Baya could make out that the two creatures were like Mook and Tara. The two animals split up. One startled an animal on the outskirts of the herd.

The animal broke into a full sprint. The predator was not in a hurry. It made a weak effort to chase its prey. The second predator hunched down in the tall grass. It was almost too easy. When the prey ran by, the crouching animal lunged with its powerful back leg. It took its prey to the ground twisting its neck in the same motion. The second predator joined its hunting companion for the feast. The grass and their faces were soon covered in shiny dark blue blood.

The pack of predators at the base of the tree sniffed the air. With a couple barks and snaps they headed in the direction of the fresh kill.

"They're off in search of an easier meal." Vicaroy observed.

The pack of predators circled the two hunters. They may have been smaller but they greatly outnumbered the hunters.

"Now is our chance. We have to get off these plains." Vicaroy made his way out of the tree.

"How?" Baya was immensely curious to see who would win the battle over the carcass. She wanted to stay and watch. Plus, the tree was safe, as the ground was crawling with large beasts and vicious predators. Yet she knew they couldn't spend the night in the tree. They needed to get somewhere safe by nightfall — somehow.

"There's far too much prey on these plains and with them come predators and lots of them," Vicaroy said. "Our chances may be better if we can get far away from here."

That all made sense. "I guess that's why people don't live here." They hadn't seen land quite this lush and they hadn't seen near this many animals. In fact, until a couple days ago they hadn't seen any large animals. But the problem remained. "Where should we go?"

"We head to the southeast. To those mountains." Vicaroy pointed and then jumped to the ground.

Baya followed. She held out her arms to Tara. "Come on little one."

Tara wiggled her back end as she readied herself for the leap into Baya's waiting arms.

"That's the nearest change in scenery and it keeps us heading eastward, as much as possible."

"Brilliant. Now let's move." Baya headed toward the mountains at a slow run. This place was overrun with large plant-eaters and the predators that fed on them. They had to get across the plains as quickly as possible. She had the sinking feeling that their chances of making it to those mountains unscathed were slim.

CHAPTER 55

A flutter of hope filled Baya as the southeastern-most mountains grew close.

They had to slow their pace after Tara began to fall behind.

"We're almost out of the plains," Vicaroy said. "We need to make it to the base of those mountains. I know we'll be safer the farther away we can get from the herds."

"But Tara is tired. Can you carry her, so we can move faster?"

Vicaroy sighed.

"Give me Doba." Baya held out her arm and Doba moved from Vicaroy's shoulder snaking his way across to Baya's arm and wrapping himself over her shoulders.

But I'm still mad at you for bringing that hideous creature along. Doba's voice announced.

"Come on. She's just a baby. Someday she will be big and strong and then you'll be glad she's around," Baya replied.

Vicaroy quickly secured his spear to his back with his bow and easily lifted Tara in his arms. They picked up the pace, not quite running but a brisk walk. Tara's head rested on his shoulder and her four eyes quickly grew heavy.

"Poor little thing. She's so very tired." Baya rubbed behind the animal's ear.

"Little? She's really heavy for a baby." Vicaroy complained as he adjusted the animal in his arms, trying to get a better hold.

The suns were getting low in the sky. He couldn't carry this animal all night and they needed time to gather wood for a large fire to help keep wild beasts away.

A low growl to Vicaroy's left caused his heart to jump into his throat and the now-familiar surge of energy coursed through his entire body. Another growl came from behind them.

Baya had turned toward the threatening sounds but Vicaroy had a feeling that they were distractions. As a hunter himself he knew that you never gave up your position to your prey until it was too late. So the only reason to growl before an attack would be if the attack was not coming from that direction.

Damn, these animals were smart, Vicaroy thought as he sat Tara down, trying not to make any sudden movements. As he turned away from the growling sounds he swiftly readied his spear from where it had been secured to his back.

Baya heard a scuffle coming from Vicaroy's direction but she didn't have time to look as four dark eyes emerged from the tall grass. Her bowstring groaned as she pulled it tight. When the beast bounded for her she let the arrow fly. The scaly beast slid to a stop at her feet with her arrow sticking out of its chest. It looked like the same type of animals as the ones that had treed them earlier. Another of the pack had halted its attack; it was now more cautious as its prey had easily taken out its companion.

Baya tried to talk to the animal but she could only make out that it was hungry. All it wanted was to sink its sharp teeth into Baya. So she disappeared as the beast leapt for her. It found nothing where it landed. She merely stepped aside and drew her knife.

Her movement came naturally, she didn't have to think. Some deep instinct took over. Her only unfeeling thought was that the threat must be eliminated. How to alleviate the problem came naturally. She wrapped her arm around the beast's shoulders. With a quick forceful jerk of her arm the knife entered the animal's neck slicing it open.

Baya wasn't sure if the pain-filled cry had come from the beast or from somewhere else. She scanned the area for any other threats as she turned toward Vicaroy.

Horror pulsed through her veins as she ran toward him. One of the beasts lay dead with Vicaroy's spear wedged deep in its chest. Yet another beast had its teeth deep in his left arm. He struggled to reach his knife with his right hand. He gave up on the knife and sent his fist crashing into the animal's face. The animal tightened his jaws and shook his head.

Vicaroy's scream filled Baya's ears causing her blood to turn to ice. Every second seemed like a minute. She could not move her feet fast enough to get to him. She was still invisible as she drove her knife into the spine at the base of the animal's skull.

The jaws instantly loosened and Vicaroy's arm fell free of the animal's mouth. Baya scanned her surroundings only to find Tara's long tail disappearing in the grass as the last of the beast chased after her. It must've decided to go after something smaller.

She ran for her bow. Her quiver was still on her back. She quickly moved into the tall grass after them.

Vicaroy tried to stop the bleeding from his arm with his good hand. He scooted across the dirt toward his knife in case any more animals were still out there. He heard a faint whimper and then Baya calling for Tara to come back.

She must've shot the last one, Vicaroy thought as he winced in pain. He strained to reach his knife. He would feel better if he had it on him.

Baya rushed back into the clearing. No Tara. She knelt down beside him. Tears filled her eyes at the sight of the dark blue liquid on the ground —Vicaroy's blood. Panic rose in her chest. What could she do?

A woman's education only included some basic medicinal techniques. If a woman showed aptitude she might receive a calling which would include further education in the healing arts.

Shema's lecture rang in Baya's mind ... We can't make wounds disappear and we can't make the sick healthy. For that they had to rely on medicine, which was far from foolproof.

"When Mook injured my shoulder one of the priestesses used an ointment and bandaged the wound."

"We don't have any such ointment with us, but I believe it was made from the cockelle root."

"So for now I'll bandage your arm to stop the bleeding. We can look for the root as we go."

Vicaroy nodded. "We have to get out of here and I can't be dripping blood as we go."

Baya gave him a sideways look, not understanding. She moved for her pack.

"This place is covered in blood and will soon be crawling with predators. We have to get out of here and I can't leave a trail of blood for them to follow us."

"Right." Baya said. "You seem to have the ability to understand how predators think."

"I've become a predator myself since we found this Goddess-forsaken land. We've had to hunt for our food every day. I've found my wounded prey before by following the trail of blood it left behind," he explained.

That's right, Baya remembered. She rummaged around in her pack for an old tunic that could be used as a bandage. But first she found Doba coiled up in tight circles. "It's okay. It's safe now."

Doba scurried up to her shoulders again.

"It's a good thing you're so good at hiding."

Vicaroy gritted his teeth as Baya lifted his arm. He didn't want to scream in front of her. Yet, he'd never felt such pain.

"Sorry. I'm trying to be gentle," she whispered.

When she tightened the cloth around his arm a fierce yell escaped his lips.

"I'm so sorry." She kept her voice down trying to remain calm. She couldn't fall apart now. She tried not to look at the injury too closely but the large gashes were hard to ignore. Blood-stained muscle was practically falling out of the gashes on his arm. She caught a glimpse of something white as well. *Bone*. She tried not to think about it. "You just rest."

Vicaroy didn't protest. He wasn't entirely sure he could get up anyway. Intense pain pulsed through his arm while a duller pain throbbed in his leg. It was all he could think about as he struggled to remain conscious. They had to get out of there. It wasn't safe in these open plains.

The tunic was soon soaked with Vicaroy's blood. Baya quickly gathered their belongings. When she was done she inspected the bandage. "It looks like the bleeding has stopped or at least slowed. It's not dripping, anyway."

She helped Vicaroy up by his good arm and supported him until she was sure he could stand. "I pray that you can walk."

He nodded and winced in pain as he took a step. "I don't have a choice. We have to get out of here. More beasts will arrive any minute."

Baya headed in the direction that Tara had run off. "Tara!" Baya yelled.

"That creature is going to be the death of us," Vicaroy muttered.

"This isn't her fault."

"She slowed us down and we can't waste time looking for her now. We have to get as far away from here as possible."

"I know. She's hiding somewhere nearby and she'll find us … or we'll find her."

He winced with every step. His left leg sent a painful throb through his body every time he put weight on it.

Baya was right. They hadn't gone far when Tara came bounding out of the grass and leapt into Baya's arms.

Vicaroy was in too much pain to be startled by the animal's sudden appearance. The last of the suns was setting for the day. They made their way toward the mountains as fast as they could, which was not fast enough.

CHAPTER 56

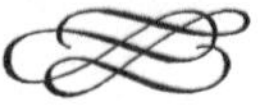

Two moons lit the way as Baya and Vicaroy walked well into the night. The distant orange glow of the third moon could be seen barely peeking over the horizon. Vicaroy's wound had soaked the cloth and blood trickled down his arm.

Baya helped him to sit down on a stump. She wrapped a fresh cloth around his arm. "You need to rest. Let's stop here for the night. I'll set a protection spell to help conceal us." Surely she had the strength for that, while they were at rest.

Falling into a deep sleep and possibly never waking sounded like the best thing in the world to Vicaroy. "No. We need to get to the tree line, at the base of the mountain. That will offer more protection and we're almost there."

Tara lay panting next to Baya.

If he wouldn't stop for himself then maybe he would stop for Tara. "Tara is too tired to go any farther. We have to stop."

But Vicaroy awkwardly and with a couple loud grunts got to his feet. "We can make it — we have to, or none of us will make it through the night. We're not safe out here on these plains. What if they can smell us, even with your protection spell?"

Baya buried the blood-drenched tunic in a shallow hole in an attempt to cover up some of the scent. She took Tara in her arms and hurried to catch up with Vicaroy, who actually hadn't made it very far.

The sight of the dark trees up ahead was the only thing that kept them pushing forward. Baya's back ached from carrying all their supplies and Tara. Yet, with one look at Vicaroy, she knew she had nothing to complain about. The trees were not getting close enough fast enough. It felt like every time she took a step, the trees would move two steps away. "We should be to the forest by now," she said.

* * *

LEAVING the plains behind and entering the tree-filled land was like arriving home after a long day of work. A sense of safety flooded through Baya. She had never been more relieved than when Vicaroy gingerly sat down against a large rock. She lay Tara down next to him and let the packs fall to the ground. She lit a ball of fire so she could better examine his injured arm.

"It looks like the bleeding has pretty much stopped."

But Vicaroy was already dozing. She laid his bedroll out and he barely moaned as she helped him onto it.

Her feet ached but she still had to gather wood. She thought about using her own fire ball instead of finding enough wood. She couldn't afford to deplete her powers by keeping a fire lit all night. Plus, if she fell asleep the fire would go out. Not to mention she had to conserve enough energy to set a protection spell around them for the night.

Once she had a raging fire burning, she watched Vicaroy with concern. Her eyes scarcely left his chest, watching every rise and fall of his breath.

He had to be okay. She couldn't lose him. He had been right when he called this land Goddess-forsaken. Ameris abandoned this land for good reasons. The old tales about the wild untamed beasts were true.

Only they were smarter than she had expected — cunning at catching their prey. That pack had surrounded them and then used decoys to distract them while others attacked from the opposite direction. Baya shivered at the thought. What other horrors awaited them out there?

Vicaroy didn't look well. His skin was much too pale. He'd lost a lot of blood — too much blood.

She distracted herself by setting a protective layer around them. After another silent hour of watching Vicaroy breathe, the adrenaline had left Baya's body. She forced herself to keep her eyes open. She listened intently for the slightest sound but thankfully the forest was silent.

The morning light caused Baya to wake with a jerk. She'd dozed off sitting with her back to the large rock. Her neck was stiff and her feet still ached when she stood. In fact, most of her body ached, especially her back.

Vicaroy remained fast asleep, yet still breathing. She had to find that root — what had he called it? Cockelle? What had it looked like? If his injury became infected it would be the end of him.

Baya stoked the fire, forced some dried meat and nuts down and headed into the forest to see what she could find. A nearby stream provided water for their bladders. She carefully dug up any plants that looked like they could be cockelle.

Baya woke Vicaroy when she returned. He struggled to sit up against the rock.

"You have to drink," she coaxed.

CHAPTER 57

Vicaroy and Baya camped there for several days, with the large rock protecting their backs. Vicaroy's upper thigh swelled to twice its normal size. He slept most of the time as a way to escape the pain from his injuries. When he was awake he taught Baya how to make the ointment from the cockelle plants to treat his arm.

"It's a good thing you know so much about plants," Baya mused.

"Azod taught me to make all the medicines and poultices for the Unawi's healer." Vicaroy flinched as she poured water over his wounded arm. He ground his teeth together and moaned as she gently dried it and applied the medicine.

"Sorry," she breathed.

Baya did the hunting and the cooking, which tasted horrible. Vicaroy tried to guide her in how to season the meat but Baya had never cooked before. "Maybe this is why women don't cook. We're terrible at it."

"It takes practice. I couldn't cook at first either," Vicaroy said.

On the fifth day Vicaroy was determined to move on. Baya was worried as his skin had not regained its proper color and there was still some swelling in his leg. Nevertheless, they moved on. It amazed

Baya how stubborn Vicaroy could be when he put his mind to something.

The following days were tedious as they slowly made their way up the mountain. They stopped in the afternoons, long before dark, so Baya could set up camp and Vicaroy could rest. The higher they climbed the colder the nights grew. She reminded herself to be grateful that they weren't seeing any large predators in the mountains. It was similar to the western coast, before they'd entered the plains. They only saw birds and small game, which supplied them with fresh meat.

The apex of the mountain revealed a breathtaking and lonely view. The vibrant lands stretched as far as they could see in every direction. To the north and south stood many more mountain tops. The rainbow colors of the plains stretched out across the lands to the west. The view to the east didn't reveal much about what they were to face.

Baya's heart sank at the sheer vastness of it. The land bore no sign of people. Only wild nature lay before them. To the east, trees and grass could be seen but the landscape changed dramatically, as if someone had drawn a line on a parchment and colored one side with lovely hues of greens, blues and yellows, while the other side was left a dull tan color.

Vicaroy's eyebrows were raised. "What do you think it's like to the east?"

Baya tried to sound normal. She didn't want her voice to give away her fears, "I don't know. It can't be any worse than where we came from."

Going down the mountain was easier. The swelling had gone down in Vicaroy's leg and it was no longer as painful to walk. He could move his arm now but it had a ways to go before it would be fully functional. Thankfully, the wound appeared to be closing up nicely and they'd avoided infection.

The plains at the base of the mountain were warm and lush. While the nicer weather was a plus, the land resembled the plains on the other side. They constantly looked over their shoulders — on high alert for anything that might try to eat them. On the third day of travel through the plains their path eastward came to an abrupt stop.

Baya and Vicaroy stood at the edge of a cliff. Tara stayed back, leery of the edge. It wasn't just any cliff, it was a great ravine spanning many lengths down and just as many across. Far below a blue river snaked its way through the mighty valley.

"There doesn't appear to be any way down. Well ... no safe way down," Vicaroy said.

Baya was in deep thought. She studied the sides of the canyon to the north and to the south. Indeed there was no path or way to climb down — only a sheer drop. "The obstacle."

"What?" Vicaroy asked.

"The ancient text, it spoke of a mighty obstacle."

"Oh, right. The parchment with the vague text from who-knows-where." Vicaroy had almost forgotten about it.

Baya ignored his skepticism. "I can't think of any greater obstacle than this." Baya swung her arm out toward the intimidating view before them. "And the stone birds will show us the way."

Vicaroy looked around. "I don't see any stone birds."

"It's difficult to know how to find them. Hold on..." Baya's eyes lit up. "They should lie directly to the east of the first clue which was the two sentinels. Remember?"

Vicaroy nodded, trying to hide his impatience.

"But we veered slightly to the south to get off the plains as quickly as possible. So that means we must be due south of the stone birds." Baya headed north at once. On her way by she caught the concerned glance that Vicaroy gave Doba.

Doba had taken a liking to riding on Vicaroy's shoulders ever since Tara joined their little herd. The insect was still mad at Baya for bringing the creature along. Doba preferred being the only non-human around. It was all he knew — his entire life had consisted of him and his human companions. Tara was nothing but a stupid and scary beast.

"What's wrong?" Baya threw her arms up in exasperation. "Are you two conspiring against me?"

"Annoying, isn't it?" Vicaroy's golden-brown, almond-shaped eyes danced with the amusement of playful revenge.

Baya smiled and rolled her eyes. She was thankful that he was feeling better.

Vicaroy looked to the north and then to the south again – weighing the options. "Maybe we should head south, the weather will be warmer. Perhaps we can walk around the canyon. It can't go on forever, can it?"

"There's no way of knowing how far it stretches. From what we can see it is hundreds of lengths out of our way. Heading north to find the birds is our best option."

"Wasting time looking for a statue does not sound like a good idea. If we were to head south what is the worst that could happen?"

"That the valley extends much farther than we can see making it thousands of lengths out of our way."

Vicaroy bit on his lower lip as his mind mulled over the best course of action.

"We found the first sign, didn't we?" Baya continued. "And we'll find the next one. It should be obvious – like the first one and it shouldn't be too far to the north. I don't think we ventured too far off the eastern path. So let's give it a couple of days. If we don't find it we'll reassess the situation."

She was entirely too intelligent and logical. Vicaroy could think of no further objections. "Alright." He held his arm out toward the north indicating for her to lead the way.

CHAPTER 58

On the second morning of hiking north they came to a rock face. Baya let out a screech when she saw it. "I was right!"

They found themselves staring up at a large carving of two stone birds. The structure blocked their path along the canyon. There was no way they could have missed it. The birds' smooth wings were outstretched to the sky, as each perched on its one leg.

Baya wrapped her arm around Vicaroy's waist, careful not to touch his bandaged arm.

He smiled down at her. "I shouldn't have doubted you. Really, it was the scroll that I doubted — not you. I guess whoever wrote it knew what she was talking about."

Yet Baya's initial excitement had already vanished. "The next problem is to figure out what the birds are telling us. I thought they would be clearly pointing to a bridge or some obvious way around the canyon but their wings only point to the sky."

"Maybe we'll be able to see the way across if we climb to the top."

Baya raised her eyebrows at Vicaroy — impressed.

Up they went. Nothing but a dizzying view lay before them. There was no clear path in sight.

Baya sat down hard in dismay. "I'm such a fool for feeling so hopeful. There's no short cut. Maybe it was an ancient bridge that has long since rotted away. The canyon could add months of endless walking. I'm so very tired of walking."

"Don't give up. Not after all we've been through. Let's take a careful look at the birds. There must be a clue. We've found two of the three clues. They can't be wrong. After all, how many other giant birds have we seen carved from stone in this land?"

Baya huffed. "None."

"Then we must be on the right path. We just have to figure this out ... somehow."

They studied the stone birds carefully. Their beaks were worn from centuries of weather. Yet they were still clearly intact. Both birds faced to the right, staring out over the canyon. Vicaroy cautiously ventured to peer over the edge in the direction of the birds' gaze.

"See anything?"

"Nothing but certain death if you fell."

Baya investigated every carved line with a furrowed brow. One bird's talons were worn almost completely off. The foot of the other bird was bent awkwardly to the left.

As a last resort she placed her hands on the stone and concentrated. It was a long shot but maybe there was a secret door she could open. Maybe it would contain a map.

Nothing. No secret passageway revealed itself. No light of power shone to lead the way.

She plopped down in dismay.

"Why did they carve the bird's foot like that?" Vicaroy asked.

"It's hard to carve front-facing. So they draw them to the side so it's clear what they are." She turned to Vicaroy with wide eyes. "Unless —"

"The foot is pointing the way," they said at the same time.

Baya jumped to her feet. She ran her hand along the cliff face, inspecting every inch in the direction of the pointing foot. Above her head was a small rock ledge. She couldn't see over it but she assumed it was a shallow stone shelf. As she neared the end something appeared on the top of the ledge. Her heart leapt at the sudden movement. It was the four beady eyes of Doba that stared down at her.

She placed her hand over her heart. "You scared me!"

Are you coming or not? Doba said with unmistakable impatience. Then he disappeared.

"How in the name of Ameris?"

"What's wrong?" Vicaroy stopped his investigation of the birds and moved to her side.

"Doba just … disappeared into the rocks."

Vicaroy's brow wrinkled. "Are you going mad out here in the wild?"

Baya gripped the stone lip and tried to pull herself up. Her feet slid against the smooth stone so Vicaroy helped her up with his one good arm.

She peered over the ledge. "Whoa," and almost fell back in surprise. Baya managed to steady herself before she landed on Vicaroy. "Lift me up all the way?" Her voice was full of excitement.

Vicaroy shoved and she easily swung herself up. His mouth fell open as one of her legs disappeared entirely.

"What …? How…?"

"Its … well … I've never seen anything like it. I'm actually straddling a stone wall, of sorts. It's not a shelf at all. There's a thin, and I mean thin, gap between the lower part of the cliff and the upper part." She used her right hand to pat the cliff face that was smashed against her left shoulder.

Vicaroy still looked baffled.

"I wonder where it goes." Baya laid her torso on the wall and peered into the long skinny space between the rocks. Darkness. She lit a fire ball in her hand. This only revealed a dirt floor. In the distance she caught the reflection of four tiny eyes. "Doba, what do you see?"

It's a cave. I can't see the end. It appears to head down into the mountain.

"Wow."

Baya started at the sudden closeness of Vicaroy's whisper. She turned to find his face right by hers as he examined the long gap in the rock. He'd busied himself by piling up rocks to stand on.

"This must be the way across the mighty obstacle," Baya said.

"How can a cave be the way?"

"It must lead down to the bottom. I'll check it out." Baya swung her leg over the wall so that she was facing Vicaroy. She carefully lowered herself down as far as she could then let go. It wasn't far to the bottom. The gap was so thin that she had to turn her head to the side so her nose wasn't ripped off by the stone.

As Doba had said, there was a dark passage at the far end of the small cave, leading down as far as her firelight would reach.

Her heart pounded in her chest. Thoughts of being trapped in the dark — stuck in wells with no way out, caused sweat to break out on her forehead. She had no doubt that this was the way or at least it had been the path a thousand years ago. She also knew that she had to put her fear aside — somehow. She forced herself to enter the black hole.

"Come on. Let's see where this leads." Her voice broke and she wondered if Vicaroy noticed the panic in her words.

Vicaroy threw their packs over the wall into the gap in the rocks. Next came Tara. She had to squeeze through as well. Vicaroy had the toughest time. He was almost too big to fit. Having only one good arm made it all the harder.

Baya thought his broad chest might not let him through. She debated about trying to help him by pulling on his legs. That would have only made matters worse.

With a painful moan he landed on his feet. "I sure hope there's another way out because I don't think I can make it through that thin gap again."

"This must be the way past the Great Obstacle."

"Well, the bird's foot seemed to be pointing to this hidden entrance."

They gathered themselves and their belongings. With a long knowing glance, Vicaroy and Baya shared a thousand unspoken words before they headed into the darkness of the waiting cave.

Tara was the only one who was happy about this. She bounded into the black abyss. *It's like my old den.* Her footsteps echoed off the stone walls.

CHAPTER 59

Baya and Vicaroy made their way downward — deep into the earth. Baya's breathing grew heavier with each step. Being surrounded by darkness led to memories of inescapable black wells — drowning.

We're fine. We're not drowning. It's only a cave ... leading to ... who-knows-where? Baya thought.

Her breathing turned to gasps and she bent over — greedily sucking in as much air as possible, as if the supply might suddenly run out. She couldn't get enough and what air did enter her lungs was dank and putrid — like trying to draw a breath out of the mouth of a mummified corpse.

"Are you okay?" Vicaroy placed a hand on her shoulder.

She straightened and forced herself to hold her breath in an attempt to get it under control. "I'm ..." she was going to lie by saying that she was fine. But why? So she didn't cause Vicaroy any extra worry? There was a time when she would have lied in this situation but not anymore. There was no point. It was obvious that something was wrong.

"No. I feel like I can't get enough air. I can't stop thinking about being trapped in a freezing well. I hate confined dark places, especially when I don't know where they lead."

"It's okay. No one likes to feel trapped and no one likes not knowing what lies ahead. It's terrifying ... well, for everyone except Tara."

Baya waved her fire ball around to see if she could spot Tara. No sign of her. She was most likely far ahead of them.

Vicaroy's eyes were full of affection and understanding as he took her in his arms. "Tara will be our eyes. She'll warn us of any danger. We have each other and there is plenty of air in here. We'll be fine."

Baya let him hold her tight. She rested her head against his hard chest. Her breathing slowly returned to normal. "Thank you," she whispered.

"For what?" Vicaroy blinked at her — puzzled.

"For helping me calm down."

"That's what companions are for." He took her hand as they moved deeper underground.

Baya still had to focus on taking deep and regular breaths. This was *not* the trials. They were safe, she reminded herself. She had never been more grateful for anything than she was now for Vicaroy's hand in hers.

Deeper they descended. To keep from panicking, she forced herself to think only of the air flowing in and out of her lungs. She fell into a trance-like state as she matched her breathing with the regular beat of her footsteps. This helped to block out her many worries for a time.

As time passed Baya's thoughts strayed again. What if the bottom was filled with water and there was no way out? What if the passage had caved in and they reach a dead-end? Or maybe there was a giant beast waiting for them up ahead. Her increasing panic caused her to yell for Tara.

Tara bounded back to them.

Vicaroy squeezed her hand. "See, everything's fine."

Baya took a deep breath to calm her pounding heart. She tightened her grip on Vicaroy's hand. Another long stretch of time passed and her fears threatened to take over once again. What if the cave fell in on them, trapping them ... or crushing them? She wasn't sure which was worse.

Stop! Baya scolded herself. At least she managed not to burden Vicaroy with her endless fears. Inhale, exhale. That was all that mattered.

After a long time they stopped for a brief meal. Tara ran circles around them while Vicaroy fumbled through the packs for some dried meat, nuts and fruit. Doba watched Tara with an irritated glare.

Baya didn't sit down to rest, she was desperate to keep moving. The rock walls glistened with moisture in Baya's firelight. For a moment they appeared to be closing in on them and she shivered. "Let's walk while we eat."

Time began to blur. Vicaroy commented that the path wasn't as steep anymore, but it barely pierced her panic. It could have been another hour or two, maybe three when the air grew lighter — fresher. This lifted their spirits and kept Baya from turning back, which she had seriously been debating. Within the next hour a light appeared up ahead.

Baya rubbed her eyes and squinted to make sure the light was still visible. When it remained, she ran for it. She was frightened that the darkness would swallow it. A gulp of sweet fresh air filled her lungs and she sprinted toward the light — the way out!

Blinking and covering their eyes from the intense sunlight, they stepped out of the cave to find that it was late afternoon. Once Baya's eyes adjusted she let the sun warm her face and she fully enjoyed each breath of fresh air.

Vicaroy stared up at the sheer rock face behind them, then took in the large river in the distance and the mountain on the other side. "This place is incredible."

Baya lowered her head and shook it. All that worrying over nothing, as the cave had led safely to the bottom of the canyon.

"The birds did point the way to get around the obstacle," Vicaroy said.

"Well, half of it anyway. We still have to get across the river and climb out of here."

"The other side doesn't look to be nearly as steep. We should be able to make our way up the far side easy enough."

"We made it to the bottom of the canyon in only five or six hours." Baya was incredulous. To her it felt like the tunnel had warped time. Her mind had blocked out parts of it as if she had been in a trance. It felt like they had been standing at the top of the great ravine only an hour or two prior. Yet the suns' locations indicated that it was getting late.

"Maybe it took us eight hours. The suns are staying longer in the sky as we move into the daylight months."

They came to an embankment and peered over the edge. The river raged far below.

"How are we going to cross that?"

"It must have been a wet dark season. The river is full and swift."

Baya's mouth fell open. "Does that mean we have to wait until the days start getting shorter again before we can cross?"

Vicaroy didn't answer.

"It was only a thin line of blue water when we viewed it from the top." Baya pointed to the massive cliff face behind her. She doubted that she would be able to throw a pebble all the way across it.

Vicaroy furrowed his brow at the water furiously rushing by. "Let's rest here for the night. Maybe if we sleep on it we can think of something. We'll look for a way to cross in the morning."

The excitement of reaching the end of the cave faded and Baya was suddenly weary. Another problem to solve. Food and rest would make the situation appear less dire. "Let's set up camp." Baya had barely taken one step away from the river's embankment when a terrible grinding sound echoed off the cliff wall.

She turned toward the sound. But Vicaroy wasn't there. The embankment where he had been had vanished as well. She took a step forward but more of the earth along the shore fell away. Instinctively she jumped back.

"Vicaroy!" she bellowed.

All she could do was watch in horror as more of the bank vanished. Her heart pounded in her chest as she ran to the nearest rock ledge overlooking the river. Without consciously thinking she'd known she had to find stable land in order to be able to assess the situation.

Her gaze followed the path of the earth that had been swept away by the water below. Panic rose as she faced the fact that Vicaroy had slid into the river. She screamed for him again as she searched the water for any sign of him.

"Vic —!" Her yell stuck in her throat, as she had spotted a tiny black dot being carried swiftly downstream. Baya shrugged off her pack and without further thought, moved to follow Vicaroy over the embankment and into the rushing water below.

CHAPTER 60

Baya's shirt snagged on something, stopping her from stepping off the rock outcropping and falling into the raging river. She grabbed her tunic to jerk it free and found that it was Tara who held the cloth tight between her sharp teeth. The young animal pulled with all her might to keep Baya from going over the steep embankment into the river.

"Tara! Let go!" Baya tore her tunic free, leaving a piece of fabric hanging out of Tara's mouth. "I have to save him."

Tara sat down with the piece of Baya's tunic hanging out of her mouth. A heart-wrenching whimper escaped from the animal and Baya heard her tiny voice, *Please don't leave me too.*

Baya glanced desperately back at the river. "You mean like your mother did? You don't want me to die too."

Tara whimpered again.

Baya cautiously moved to peer over the edge. Water rushed swiftly over large rocks. It would lead to painful injury and certain death. She fell to her knees and a sob stuck in her throat. That meant the fall would have killed Vicaroy as well.

He was dead.

That had been his lifeless body floating away. Another sob escaped as the reality of the situation hit her. For a moment she still wanted to step over the edge. But this time it was not to save Vicaroy but to follow him in death.

Baya shook her head. "I can't give up. I have to try." Baya ran along the bank heading downriver. She didn't make it far before she came to the end of the ledge. There was a muddy bank below at the river's edge. The sheer rock wall guided the river south from there. She could go no farther.

Now on all fours, her mid-day meal came up, splattering over the rock supporting her. "Doba was with him and now they're both gone." Another painful cry jammed in her throat.

She moved away from the edge.

With a whimper Tara nudged her shoulder.

Baya wrapped her arms around the animal and they lay in a ball.

Darkness came and Baya didn't move. She made no attempt to make camp or even a fire. She stared at the moonlit cliff without seeing it. She couldn't bear to look at the river that had taken Vicaroy. She could hear nothing but the endless noise of the rushing water — mocking her. Normally it would have been a pleasant sound but on this night it pierced her ears — the noise drove her mad. She slowly turned a hard stare to the raging waters that had taken her love. "Shut up!" She screamed.

The river continued to roar back, utterly oblivious.

Baya finally fell asleep to escape the pain. She woke with a start from a nightmare. It had ended with a voice pleading, yelling, demanding that she continue her journey eastward. As the dream faded and the voice faded she wondered if it was her mother's, or Shema's. Perhaps it was Ameris calling her — guiding her.

The dream quickly faded and the real nightmare returned. It soon had Baya wanting to heave up the contents of her stomach. The problem was that there was nothing left to come up. She lay on the bare earth looking up at the thin slice of purple sky. It looked like a snake as it curved and weaved, following the outline of the mountains on either side of them. "He's gone ... dead ... just like that. Here one minute and taken the next. I had no time to react — to help him."

Tara stirred from her slumber at the sound of Baya's voice.

Baya jumped to her feet, startling Tara, and studied her surroundings. Her mind was sharp and determined. She had to find him, even if it was only his … body.

The far riverbank was a gradual slope and she could more easily follow the river south from that side, which was the direction that Vicaroy had been swept away.

"That's it. We have to cross here." She made the brief walk back to retrieve her belongings.

She tossed her pack down to the river's edge. "We have to slide down."

Tara peered over the edge and whimpered.

Baya took Tara in her arms and tried to run down the embankment. It was too steep and Baya ended up on her butt sliding down most of it.

"Ouch." They landed in the mud. Baya stood and rubbed her backside. Her pants, like her tunic, were torn and her skin was scraped. She didn't care. Glaring at the river, it was clear that there was nowhere to go but across it. The river ran directly alongside the steep cliff face. "I could shoot an arrow into a tree on the far side with a rope tied to it. Then tie the other end to …" Baya looked around. "This big rock. I can hold onto the rope so that the river won't carry us away." Baya frowned. "Of course, all our food would get wet and how will I carry you and hold the rope?"

Tara's four black eyes blinked up at Baya. She clearly couldn't make out all that was being said.

Baya cocked her head to the side in concentration. "I'm going to have to use my powers ... somehow. Perhaps I could float our stuff over my head to keep it dry. Overhead, that's it." She gave a wicked smile to the raging river. "Better yet, I will bend this river to my will." Focusing all her hatred and grief onto the river. She threw her arms straight out in front of her, palms toward the river.

The river yielded. A tunnel formed before them — a rainbow of water for them to pass under.

"Come on, Tara." Baya led the way under the water.

They made their way over round river rocks and through the slippery mud of the riverbed while the crystal-blue water rolled harmlessly over their heads. Colorful furry fish swam above them. The fish took no notice of Baya and Tara.

"I wish Vicaroy could see this." Baya's heart fell at the mention of him and a spray of water cascaded down. Focus! she told herself. She couldn't afford to lose her concentration or they would be swept away.

As soon as they were on the far bank Baya let the water resume its natural course. Her stomach growled, louder than the river. The last thing she wanted was food, but her powers required fuel. She took some snacks out of her pack to feed herself and her companion and kept moving south as she ate. She had to find Vicaroy.

There was no sign of life in the canyon, only the two of them. They walked until Tara was too tired to go any farther and then until Baya grew too tired to carry her. The animal was growing by the day.

* * *

He is lost to you. You must head east ... east ... east.

Baya opened her eyes to the echo of the word 'east' still ringing in her ears. It was the same female voice as before, urging her to continue on her journey. Sitting up, she shook her head. "No," she grumbled. Then more adamantly, "No! He can't be gone. What if he's alive ... somehow? What if he needs my help?" Tears ran down her cheeks. "I have to find him. ... I need him."

The only thing that had made this entire insane voyage to the mainland worthwhile was that they were together. Now that he was gone, everything was pointless. This was all for nothing. "I will find him or I do not go on." Her voice caught. "I can't go on without him."

She lay back down, determined to never get up again. Yet, her mind would not let go. She had to try. One thing she had proved in her still-young life was that she was not a quitter. What if he was only badly injured? Maybe he needed her. She rose and began making her way south at once. "No! I will not leave him." She argued with the voice from her dreams.

On the second day of following the river south Baya and Tara came to a narrowing. The riverbank disappeared as it gave rise to a rock cliff-face. The water was forced between the two towering stone walls on either side. There was no way to continue south from the river basin.

Baya slammed her hands against the stone wall blocking her path. If only she could move it — transform it. It was too heavy and there was too much of it. She kicked the stone causing her toe to throb. Looking to the east the terrain was steep but they could climb out easy enough. Nothing sounded better than getting out of this wretched hole — away from the loud mocking river. She would find another way to get to Vicaroy.

Up they went.

* * *

FROM HIGH UP on the east side of the great obstacle, Baya could survey the lay of the land. To the south the two tall cliffs gave way to a large waterfall. There was no way Vicaroy would have survived if he had been carried over that cliff.

Baya sat down hard. She let the possibility that he might really be gone sink in. Either way, there was no way to find him, or his body at that point. If he had gone over the waterfall, then not much would be left of him. Her stomach heaved but she managed not to throw up. She lay her head on her pack and let the tears fall. She gave in fully to the sorrow and exhaustion. The dab of hope she had held onto faded away.

* * *

THE VOICE BIDDING her to head east woke her again. She didn't fight it this time. Her body and mind were entirely numb as she turned her gaze to the east. Once out of the canyon she could see far into the distance. A gradual slope of colorful trees and shrubs ended abruptly in the lower lands at the base of the mountain. From there the view was bleak — nothing but a dull brown could be seen. She remembered Ameris's tales of crossing the drylands — brutal. Baya would have to gather as much food and water as possible if they were to survive.

CHAPTER 61

Not only had Vicaroy made the journey into the unknown bearable he had made it enjoyable. With him at Baya's side, she felt she could do anything. It was fine that they didn't have a home, fine that they slept on the ground.

He had even made the adventure fun. She tried not to think about the playful flirting, that had almost gotten him eaten. How he often looked at her with an intense longing, yet always with love in his eyes. Now she could find no reason to go on.

Why bother? Baya thought upon awakening. She and Tara were following a small stream down the mountain. Being off course after the detour south, Baya adjusted their direction to head slightly northeast.

Bright orange clouds hung in the purple sky and the weather seemed to grow hotter with every step she took down the mountain toward the wastelands that lay beyond.

Tara licked her cheek by way of a morning greeting. Baya absent-mindedly rubbed her companion behind an ear. "At least I have you. ... Doba..." She moaned. "I'd brought him here to free him, so he could find his own kind. All I did was get him killed."

He was a funny little thing. Tara hadn't said much lately. She didn't know what to say to make Baya feel better.

"Yeah, he was."

Tara pawed at Baya's pack in hopes of finding some breakfast.

"We're running low on food. I'd better hunt. We'll have to stock up on supplies if we're going to make it across that desert. You may have to carry supplies as well."

Wait. What?

Baya gathered her bow and quiver and set out. She would not have bothered if it was not for Tara. The need to care for the young animal was the only thing keeping her going. Baya would have been content to go hungry.

BAYA STOCKED up with extra bladders of water, even tying a couple to Tara's back. The creature tried to shake them off, but Baya stopped her. "There is no telling how far it is across the desert. You have to help me carry supplies — otherwise we will not make it."

You mean die?

"Yes. We will die."

Tara let out a low growl of protest but didn't try to shake the water containers off.

"I know. I don't like it either. But this may be the most challenging terrain yet." Baya ventured a longing glance back up the mountain.

"Goodbye, my love." Tears filled her eyes. She had not been able to give Vicaroy a proper burial. His body would be devoured by … Baya stopped herself from finishing the terrible thought.

She and Tara stood at the edge of the tree line. She reluctantly turned her gaze from the lush mountainside. The trees and shrubs grew sparse to the east until they disappeared altogether, leaving only a dry parched earth.

* * *

THE NIGHTS GREW SHORTER as each day passed. The time of the sun would soon be upon them, in which night would not come at all. At least one of the suns would remain in the sky at all times. Baya had decided that bringing wood was not a good use of the limited supplies they could carry. Fire was no longer needed for warmth. She hoped that it was not needed for protection. Surely no animals could survive in the desert.

She unrolled her bedding after a long day of walking in the intense sunlight. Tara was more than ready to lie down. Tara shook her rainbow-colored mane when Baya untied the water from her back. She stretched her back and then curled up at the foot of Baya's blankets.

They were both fast asleep before the last sun had set.

Baya woke to a faint tickling sensation and a rustling sound. There were two moons in the night sky. One was full, providing ample light for her to see that her pack was moving. She jumped to her feet and lit a fire in the palm of her hand. At first she thought it was Doba, or many Doba's, all over her pack. Yet, their long segmented bodies were tan, not black like Doba. They were tearing into her food pouches.

"Stop." She tried to shoo them off with a wave of her hand. No luck. Picking the food bag up she shook it hard, sending some of them to the ground. They disappeared as they burrowed into the dry dusty soil. A couple still had secure grips on the pack. "Get your own food."

Several sets of large black eyes blinked at her. *That's what we're doing, getting food. It's rare to find so much in one place.*

This will last us a month, another one of the creatures said as it took a mouthful of nuts.

"This is our food and it has to last us. I'm sorry but I can't feed you all."

They ignored her and continued to munch away.

"I'll have to ..."

To what? one of the large insects challenged.

"I don't want to hurt you but if you don't leave our food alone ..." She pulled one off the pack and threw it to the ground. The other hissed at her before leaping off, both of them disappearing into the dirt.

Baya sighed and began repacking and repairing the damage as much as she could. Finally she had found creatures like Doba but not until it was too late. The irony settled in her gut like a boulder. Doba would have been excited to meet them.

Something flickered at the corner of her eye. She jerked her head toward the light and wiped the tears away to better make it out. It looked like a fire — back toward the West. It was a small campfire, one like humans would make. Could there possibly be others like Baya out here?

Baya slung the food pack over her shoulder worried that if she set it down it would soon be crawling with Dobas again. "Tara. Wake up." She gave the animal a nudge.

Tara grunted and rolled over, putting a paw over her long snout.

Tara was too tired. She needed to rest. Baya looked between the distant fire and her only companion. The thought of leaving Tara bothered her. Yet, that fire had to be the sign of another human. She had to find out. Baya would return before Tara woke. Surely she would be fine here ... alone...

Baya took off at a jog. Once she'd made up her mind there was no time to waste. Excitement coursed through her veins. There were other humans in the world after all. The long-forgotten scroll might be right. She wondered what they would be like?

It wasn't long before she drew close enough to see a lone figure sitting by the fire. Baya slowed her pace. What if she's hostile? Her heart pounded in her chest and it wasn't from the jog. She readied the bow and an arrow, keeping them casually in her right hand. Yet, she could have the arrow nocked and aimed in less than a second if it turned out to be necessary.

CHAPTER 62

As Baya drew closer, it became apparent that the figure was that of a man. This was surprising — how could a man survive alone in the wild? She was careful to keep her steps as silent as possible. Her fingers twitched around the bow and arrow as she drew closer.

That body. It was familiar. Too familiar. Within a couple hundred yards she realized that she knew every curve and line of that beautiful, perfect body. Hardly daring to hope, she dropped her bow and pack and sprinted the rest of the distance between them.

"Vicaroy!" Her voice rang out in the silence of the night. She threw her arms around the figure almost knocking him over.

The man didn't respond. He didn't wrap his arms around her. Not a word. Baya pulled back to study him. He met her eyes briefly, with no hint of recognition, then turned to stare blankly at the fire.

"Vicaroy? It's me."

He didn't look at her. The vacant look in his eyes chilled Baya's entire body.

The thrill at finding him alive vanished. She placed a hand on his shoulder. "Vicaroy. I thought you were dead. … How did you survive the river?"

Nothing but a blank stare at the fire.

Baya! Is that you?

She jumped at the sound of the familiar voice. Her focus had been entirely on Vicaroy.

She felt a tickle moving up her leg. She picked the insect up and held him close to her chest. "Doba! You're alive!"

Can't ... breathe.

"Oh. Sorry." Baya loosened her grip. "I'm so happy you're okay ..." She held Doba out so she could look at him. "What's wrong with him?"

Doba lowered his head and all four eyes closed. *I don't know. He's been acting odd ever since we fell into the river. He took a nasty hit to the head.*

"Where?" From what she'd been able to see, he appeared to be fine.

He must've hit his head on a rock while we were tossed around in the river.

Baya's heart jumped into her throat threatening to strangle her.

Doba scurried along her arm and secured himself to her shoulder and waist. The normalcy of the gesture gave her strength. It felt right, which made her think that everything might be okay, somehow. At least she was able to take a deep breath.

Baya gently moved Vicaroy's overgrown curls to the side. He didn't flinch away from her touch. The fact that he didn't acknowledge her at all caused her chest to tighten.

Above his right ear was a terrible crescent-shaped gash. Baya inhaled sharply through her teeth. The wound was a deep blue, yet clean, most likely from the river. It appeared to be healing well even though it would leave an awful scar. She inspected him carefully. Aside from some healing bruises, and the pink scarring on his arm from the animal attack, he appeared to have no other injuries.

"How did you get here?"

Vicaroy didn't so much as blink at her question.

So Doba answered, *Thankfully he wakes most mornings mumbling about heading east. So we made our way out of the canyon and down the mountain. I'd hoped the fire would guide you to us. I pushed the fire stones over to him and stacked the kindling. He eventually lit the fire.*

"At least he was able to do that? That must be a good sign." She scratched under Doba's chin. "You smart little critter, you."

Doba clicked with affection.

Baya studied Vicaroy. "Head east, huh?"

"Go east." Vicaroy recited in a monotone voice.

"That's right." Baya lit up. At least he had spoken! She knelt down in front of him and took his hands. "You're correct. We are heading east to find people. You and me and our animal companions, remember?"

Only a blank stare.

"You remember me. I'm Baya."

Nothing.

Tears ran down her cheeks. "What's wrong with you?" She rested her head on his chest and let the tears fall freely. "I thought I lost you. Only to find you … like this."

No response.

Baya was not sure how much time passed before Vicaroy lay down and fell fast asleep. No bedding, no clothes for a pillow. He sprawled out flat on the dirt.

He sleeps odd hours now, Doba said.

He had only a mostly empty pack. Baya gently put it under his head. His bow and quiver were gone. They must have been lost in the river. The short night would be over soon.

Where's that wild beast? Doba asked.

"I'd better go back for her. Tara's sleeping no more than a length away."

Oh, I'd hoped —

"Doba, how dare you? We all need each other. It would be terrible to be alone out here in this strange world that we know nothing about."

The insect shuddered at the thought.

"Speaking of alone. We found some other creatures that looked like you. Well … sort of."

Where? Doba's dark eyes suddenly glittered in the firelight.

"Right here in the desert. They burrow underground."

Doba scanned the ground intently.

When they made it back to Tara, it looked like the ground around her was moving. "That must be them — the others like you."

They live in the sand? Doba's voice was full of disgust.

"Maybe that's where your kind is supposed to be. They probably came up looking for food again."

As they approached Tara the ground went still. There was no sign of them.

The first sun of the day was on the rise. Baya was barely able to wake a very grumpy and very tired Tara. "I know. The nights are too short this time of year. But we have to get back to Vicaroy." She rubbed behind Tara's ear.

Tara's eyes widened at the sight of Doba. *You found him!* Tara put her front paws on Baya's chest and gave Doba a long lick across his upper body.

Doba hissed his greeting. *Disgusting! Don't let that thing near me.* He weaved his way up onto Baya's head to get as far away from Tara as possible.

What are you feeding that thing? It's huge.

Baya hadn't really noticed, other than the fact that she couldn't carry her anymore. "Apparently, her kind grow fast."

Tara bounded around them, propelled by her powerful back leg. *Where's the man?*

Baya's shoulders sagged. "Let's go get him." She rolled up her bedding.

CHAPTER 63

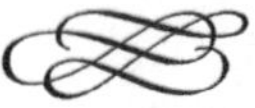

Baya and her companions found Vicaroy already awake and heading east, carrying nothing but the pack in one hand. She had to jump in front of him to stop him.

"Vicaroy. We need to go back to the mountain to get more supplies. You can carry more than this bag. We have to take as much water with us as we can."

"Head east."

"I know. We will head east but look what we have to cross." Baya gestured to the endless brown that lay before them.

With a blank stare. Vicaroy sidestepped her and continued eastward.

"Vicaroy, please. We need more water. You don't even have a bedroll."

Nothing.

She looked back to the mountains in the distance. Only a day's walk. She glanced back to Vicaroy. "I'm going to regret this but I won't lose him again."

Tara's four eyes blinked up at Baya. *What's wrong with him?*

"I don't know. I wish my calling had been that of a healer. Maybe then I could help him."

I'm scared.

"Me too." Baya whispered.

Maybe Tara's not as dumb as I thought, Doba added. *It's wise to be afraid when we are heading off into a desert with few supplies.*

They followed Vicaroy deeper into the wastelands.

* * *

BAYA WATCHED Vicaroy as he stared blankly at the night's sky. She practically had to feed him, putting dried meat in his hand and reminding him to eat.

"What matters is that we're all together again." Baya rubbed under Doba's chin while he made himself comfortable on her lap. He didn't move as smoothly as he once had. His legs used to flow in a graceful even pattern. "Doba! I'm so sorry. You were hurt too."

Only a couple of legs missing. I have plenty to spare. They don't hurt anymore. He wiggled a section of his legs, tickling Baya.

"I'm glad you're okay. You're both alive and I'm grateful for that. We have to find people as quickly as possible. They may be able to help Vicaroy." … she hoped…

There's no hope for him. Doba hissed. *The man you knew is gone.*

Baya frowned. "I refuse to believe that."

* * *

BAYA WOKE to the familiar clicking sound of an agitated Doba. The ground around them moved in snake-like waves. A couple of the brown Doba-like insects were making their way to Baya's pack.

"There they are, Doba. More of your kind. They must only come out at night." Baya rose to her feet and picked up her pack to keep it out of their reach.

The heads of a couple of beady-eyed insects popped out of the ground. Doba hurried down Baya's body to greet them. His shiny black body was in stark contrast to their dull brown ones that blended in perfectly with the desert. These insects were smaller than Doba as well, yet otherwise they looked and sounded very similar.

The insects blinked at each other for a moment before the clicking and hissing began.

Baya caught the gist of it. It was an all-around loathing.

Doba retreated quickly, making his way back up Baya's leg.

The creatures soon gave up on finding food and headed back underground.

"I take it that didn't go well?" Baya said.

They are pathetically primitive. They can't possibly be my kind, Doba replied.

"Hmm, so there is no hope of finding a mate with them?"

A shiver ran through Doba's long body. *They are terrible, wretched creatures.* Doba hung his head.

"Don't give up. Maybe ... there are others out here who are more like you. Perhaps you're not a desert dweller. I would venture to guess that you won't find any insects as smart as you. You have spent your life around people, remember. You're always going to be a bit different than other insects. Maybe you shouldn't be so picky."

Doba hissed at her.

* * *

As soon as the first sun's rays lit the sky, Vicaroy was up and heading east. Baya felt like she'd hardly slept. "The nights are too damn short in this season." She rubbed her puffy eyes and scrambled to pack up camp and catch up with Vicaroy. "Well at least he's headed in the right direction."

He's insanely driven, Doba thought.

"Or ... he's been driven insane."

Or both.

By the fourth day they were almost out of water. Baya gave only a sip to everyone in the morning. She tried to block out Tara's incessant complaining about being thirsty.

Shut up. We're all thirsty! Doba snapped.

"That's not helping, Doba."

Only Vicaroy appeared unaffected by the heat and the lack of water. Their skin blistered and their lips were so dry that they cracked and bled.

Baya did the best she could to keep the sun off them. She covered Tara's back with a cloth, and she kept a hood pulled over her head, shading Doba as well. Vicaroy's hood kept slipping down. Baya continually had to pull it back up.

The fifth day they walked with no water. There was not a drop left. Baya sucked on dried fruit to keep some moisture in her throat.

At least the complaining had stopped. "I'm afraid we won't make it another day without water."

As the day dragged on and they plodded along in silent misery, figures appeared far up ahead. "Are those people or some type of animal?" Baya asked no one in particular.

Doba narrowed his four eyes to get a better look. *They are too short and too crooked to be humans.*

Baya was beyond hot and tired and too thirsty to worry much about what lay ahead. She made no move toward her bow as she trudged onward behind Vicaroy. "They are not moving. They must not be people or animals."

Strange plants, different from anything Baya had seen before came into focus. They were gnarled and knobby with bright orange bark. Tufts of sharp pointy leaves, or at least Baya thought they were leaves of sorts, stuck out in every direction at the top. The extreme heat and lack of moisture must mangle the poor plants.

The number of plants increased and they found themselves moving up a gradual slope. But there was no sign of water, nor of an end to the desert.

"This area must get at least some rain if it can support any plant life, even these ugly things." Baya tried to glean some sliver of hope from the slight change in scenery.

Out of desperation, she focused on an empty water bladder. She gathered all the power left inside as she tried to transform the air inside into water. The bladder remained deflated. She felt her power trying to draw moisture from the air around her. But there was none. Even though she had never created water before, she knew that if there was any moisture in the air, she would have been able to get some of it into the bladder.

Baya let out a frustrated yell. “I’m useless here. I can’t make water … and I can’t fix Vicaroy’s mind.”

CHAPTER 64

The following morning Baya woke with a start. The voice of the female who had guided her east continued to ring in her head. Baya suspected that it was the same voice who pushed Vicaroy to move eastward as well.

"The plants are the key," Baya mumbled, repeating the message from her dream. She let out a curse. "What does that mean?"

Vicaroy was already up, relentlessly heading east, as always. She was too weary to move and every muscle ached. She felt as if they might collectively dry up and blow away in the hot breeze. She wanted to surrender herself fully to the dry earth. It was calling to her.

"I'll try to catch up later … or maybe not." She pulled a blanket over her head to block out the brutal sun.

"The plants are the key."

Baya bolted upright, turning to Vicaroy who had only gone a short distance. He was digging at the base of one of the orange plants. Those were the only words he had uttered besides, *Go East*. Now Baya was sure that the same voice was guiding them, helping them on their journey.

"Vicaroy?"

He ignored her as usual.

"The plants! They must have moisture in them — in the roots. Tara! Help us dig."

Baya joined Vicaroy. They dug at the hard earth until their fingertips bled. Thankfully Tara helped, she was a much better digger than her human companions. When the large root ball was exposed it felt cool and moist compared to the dirt around it.

Baya began cutting shavings off the root, giving them a good squeeze. A drop of water fell to the earth. She was tempted to lick the ground where it had fallen. Shaving more of the root she gave a handful to Vicaroy.

He expertly tilted his head back, raised his arm and squeezed the root shavings in the palm of his hand, letting the moisture run down his thumb and into his mouth.

"How did you ..." Baya vaguely remembered having seen the gesture in her dream. "Ameris is with us. She is showing us the way, while we sleep." Baya crushed some of the root shavings in her palm and let the water run down her thumb and into her mouth. It felt wonderful even though it burned her scorched throat on the way down. "I should have listened to the voice sooner."

When no more moisture came from the handful of shavings, she cut more off the root. "Your turn, Tara. Hold out your tongue."

Tara eagerly did as she was told, licking Baya's thumb clean when no more water came.

"You can have more. But it's Doba's turn."

They drank until there was not much left of the root. Baya gave them all food and they headed east once again, feeling better than they had in days.

* * *

OVER THE NEXT couple of days, the vegetation grew more dense and more diverse. They began to see some small animals and birds, which allowed them to have their first fresh meal since they had entered the desert.

It was partway through the following day when Tara burst into a run almost knocking Baya over. That was when she smelled it too — something they needed. Something they hadn't smelled in a long time — moisture. Another hundred yards or so and she could hear the faint trickling of water. She pulled at Vicaroy's sleeve. "Come on!"

They burst through the shrubs to find a south-bound stream. It was small but that didn't diminish their joy. Tara was completely wet as she bounced through the water.

Baya threw her arms around Vicaroy in celebration. The gesture was not returned but even that couldn't dampen her relief at finding fresh water. They let the crystal-clear water rush over them and they drank their fill until their stomachs distended.

THE VEGETATION CONTINUED to grow more lush with each passing day, accompanied by more streams and wildlife. Baya thought she would go mad with only the two animals for companionship as Vicaroy showed no sign of improvement. He said nothing and would only stare blankly to the east as they sat around the campfire at night. By day he led the way — ever driven eastward.

The more welcoming lands also meant that predators would be out in full force. Baya was careful to set burning torches around their camp at night. She only dozed briefly as the sounds of nearby animals were all too common. Even during the day, she found herself on high alert. She carried her bow in hand instead of having it slung over her back. "Do you feel that — like we're constantly being watched?" Baya spoke to anyone who would listen.

Yes. Doba and Tara said in unison.

Baya tightened her hand around her bow.

Other than small game and distant herds of strange animals, they didn't see any predators. Yet Baya knew they were there ... waiting for their chance. Waiting for them to fall asleep without a fire or a protective spell. "I won't give them that chance." Baya mumbled to herself.

Another week passed. Night no longer came, as they reached the height of the warm season. There was always at least one sun in the sky. They topped a hill — the view stopped Baya in her tracks.

What is that? Tara asked.

Baya couldn't answer. Her mouth hung wide open — incapable of forming words. There was an unrealistic fear that if she spoke, the vast city that lay before them might disappear ... somehow. She didn't even want to blink because the city might not be there when she opened her eyes again.

The wide river valley below glistened. Every inch of it appeared to sparkle as if it were filled with stars so bright that they could shine during the day. The countless buildings below appeared to be largely made of glass. Tall stone walls surrounded the city. In the center stood the tallest of the buildings. Ten sharp-pointed crystal towers rose high into the sky around the palace. Baya — still unwilling to blink — scanned the mighty river that ran through the middle of the city. It was nothing like the raging river that had created the mighty obstacle; this river was wider — slow and lazy as it made its way south.

The river slithered amongst the buildings. Giant metal grates in the wall allowed the water to flow into and out of the city. But what captured Baya's attention was the large head of the stone beast that sat atop the wall. Its mouth stood open in lethal warning. Its long fangs were fully visible and its glassy red eyes were aglow with sunlight.

"The slippery creature ... the ... the serpent," Baya breathed, her voice little more than a whisper. Could it be? "Merth ..." She finally allowed her eyes to blink. It was a test to see if the city would still be there when she reopened them. A screech escaped her lips when the city still lay sprawled out in front of her.

"Vicaroy! We found it! We found the ancient city nestled in the serpent's belly. It really exists. There are other people in the world. We haven't been chasing shadows this entire time." That's when she noticed that he had already headed down the hill. She sprinted after him and leapt onto his back. "We did it! We found Merth!"

CHAPTER 65

Vicaroy didn't seem to take any notice that Baya had jumped on his back.

"Wahoo!" She pumped a fist in the air.

Tara bounded around them, Baya's excitement was contagious.

"Maybe they have a healer who can fix you?" Her thoughts whirled. What would these people be like? What if they weren't friendly? Would she even remember how to act around others?

Baya felt like they had been alone for a lifetime. Oh, to have the protection of walls ... the comfort of a bed ... She hardly allowed herself to hope for such things as they made their way down the hill.

Silent and fearless, Vicaroy marched toward the walls of the city, which looked plenty tall enough to keep out any type of wild beast. There appeared to be only one metal door at the base of the wall underneath the massive serpent's head. It was ridiculously small compared to the wall and the statue above.

The sound of a horn boomed through the air as they approached.

Tara halted and gave her tail a nervous flick. She sniffed the air. *It smells ... funny.*

"You haven't smelled this many people before."

Figures ran along the top of the wall. There were more than Baya could count. Vicaroy was not deterred and continued his approach.

I don't know about this. ... What if they're hostile? Doba whispered into Baya's mind. He crawled into her pack hiding himself from view.

Baya slowly advanced as did an antsy Tara.

A male voice rang out. It sounded similar to the word, "Beast!" An arrow flew through the air and landed at Tara's feet. Then came another and Tara leapt out of the way just in time.

"Stop!" Baya yelled. She swiftly moved to stand in front of Tara and raised an invisible shield around them as two more arrows harmlessly bounced away. "The animal is with us. She is our ... companion."

Some of the figures looked at each other and murmured. Baya was too far away to make out what they said.

Vicaroy remained focused on the door to the city as he continued forward, relentlessly determined in the face of flying arrows.

Nocked arrows and strained bow strings lined the top of the wall as a female voice called out. It sounded to Baya like the word "Halt!" but it was heavily accented. The woman wore a metal breastplate and her upper legs were also covered in a protective metal. Baya studied the figures on the wall. There were more men than women and all wore armor and were well-armed.

Baya grabbed Vicaroy's arm to stop his advance.

The woman yelled again.

Baya was only able to make out a couple of words. She must've been asking where they were from. "We're from Pathins." Baya yelled up to them. She held on tight to Vicaroy to keep him from moving forward and being impaled by an arrow.

The people on the wall murmured in awe at the mention of Pathins.

The woman, clearly the leader of the guards, spoke again this time more slowly.

One word rang out — beast. Baya was able to discern that the woman was inquiring about Tara. Maybe she wanted to know why Tara didn't attack them.

With numerous arrows pointed in their direction, Baya moved slowly. She knelt down by Tara and rubbed her chin and ruffled the iridescent feathers on her neck. "Lick my cheek." Baya whispered.

Tara did.

"You see. She is our friend." Baya yelled up to the woman on the wall.

It sounded like the woman said something to the effect of, "Impossible."

"Please. We need help. My friend is ..." Baya gestured to Vicaroy. "He's sick. He needs a healer."

After much murmuring and some commands being thrown around, the metal doors in the city wall swung open.

The leader of the guards gestured for them to move forward, even though the arrows remained ready to fire.

Once inside the city they found themselves surrounded by men and women holding spears. They were mostly focused on Tara.

Tara bared her teeth and growled.

"Tara. Be nice. That's no way to convince them that you're harmless."

If they make any sudden move, then I won't be harmless.

"Tara!" Baya chastised. *Sit tight. Don't make any aggressive gestures.* Baya spoke directly to Tara through their mental bond.

Tara sat on her back leg and closed her mouth, concealing her sharp teeth, yet her tail flicked in warning.

The armed people parted to make way for a woman. She was dressed in the finest gown Baya had ever seen. It was of the purest white. Small pieces of clear gems hung down on threads anchored all over the gown. The precious stones moved and shimmered with every step. Long pieces of sheer white fabric flowed behind the woman as she approached. The crown atop her head contained more white jewels which, like her gown, glistened in the sunlight.

She must be the Unawi of Merth, Baya thought.

Unlike the others, this woman had dark skin. Almost the color of Vicaroy's. Many were pale, but most were a golden brown — like Baya. She was suddenly acutely aware of her attire for the first time in months. They looked like the poorest of the poor, even worse actually. Her hair was ratty and her clothes were torn, stained and threadbare in many places.

The armored leader of the guard stood close to the woman in the white dress. The guard held a spear and appeared ready to leap in front of the crowned woman, especially if Tara were to make a move.

"I'm Unawi Nacora, the ruler of Merth, and you are from Pathins?" She didn't seem surprised — simply curious.

"Yes." Baya was relieved that she could understand her. Baya hardly paused to question why this woman didn't have the same heavy accent as the leader of the guard.

The ruler briefly studied Tara and Baya. Her eyes stopped on Vicaroy. After a long moment they widened. "What is your name?" she demanded of Vicaroy.

Vicaroy stared blankly past the Unawi.

"Please." Baya ventured. "He is ... sick."

The Unawi narrowed her eyes at Baya. "What is wrong with him?" she snapped. "He looks fine."

Baya thought she sensed a hint of panic in the woman's voice. Baya slowly took a step toward Vicaroy, leery of all the spears pointed at them and gently moved Vicaroy's overgrown hair in order to reveal the long curved pink scar. "Ever since he hit his head, he ... hasn't been right. Do you think you can help him ... heal him?" Tears had filled Baya's eyes. She tried not to get her hopes up ... too much.

Unawi Nacora lifted her chin high. "His name?"

What does that matter? she thought. "Vicaroy."

The woman's eye's widened again. She spun on her heel causing her gown to flash with white light as the sun reflected off the gems. "Get the healer at once," she all but yelled to the people behind her.

The head of the guard inquired about the beast — that was what Baya guessed anyway.

"Lock it up with the others," the Unawi ordered.

Baya's relief was replaced with fear.

Tara snarled as a net was thrown over her. Tara's tail wildly slashed through it as she swiped and snarled at the approaching men.

Baya ran for Tara but a man took hold of her arms.

"No! Don't lock her up. You can't take her from me!"

Unawi Nacora turned to glare at Baya. "Are we going to have to lock you up as well? You're insane, girl, for bringing that animal in here. It will try to kill us the first chance it gets."

CHAPTER 66

Baya looked frantically between Vicaroy, who was being gently led away and Tara who had ropes around her neck and legs. Men struggled to drag her off in the opposite direction. "No. Please! Just don't hurt her."

Tara. Baya used her mental bond to communicate silently. *Calm down. It will be okay. I'll come for you as soon as I can.*

"Let go of me!" Baya tried to jerk her arms out of the man's grip but failed. She had never been treated like this before. "What are you? Heathens? Men should never handle a woman like this." If he hadn't been wearing metal armor, she would have gladly kneed him in the groin. Baya was about to use her smoke on the man when the Unawi rounded on her.

Fury flickered through the leader's dark almond-shaped eyes. "Shut your mouth, girl. You know nothing of life here. These men will knock your teeth out if I give the word." The Unawi gave a slight nod to the man who held Baya.

He released her at once.

With one last glance toward Tara, Baya headed after Vicaroy. The thought of letting him out of her sight in this place was only slightly more unbearable than having to leave Tara. "Please don't hurt her." It was a soft plea this time, not a demand. *I'll find you as soon as I can, Tara. I promise.*

They led Vicaroy and Baya down a wide cobblestone street. People lined the road to get a peek at the newcomers.

Baya wished she were clean and dressed in her finest gown. She had never been looked at with such sorrow and pity. They must've looked dreadful, like they had been dead for a long time and recently came back to life.

They were escorted straight toward the largest building in the center of town, directly toward the giant palace. It was even more impressive up close. Numerous pointed spires rose high into the sky. It consisted of much more glass than stone, making the palace shimmer in the sunlight like a giant crystal.

They were taken into a large white room with glass walls. Evenly spaced stone columns were the only things holding the building and the glass in place. Baya glanced around nervously as she wondered about the integrity of the structure.

An old woman sat by a large bed — the healer was already there waiting for her new patient.

Nacora gestured for Vicaroy to lay down.

Baya was surprised that he did just that, without hesitation.

The healer placed her hands on either side of Vicaroy's head. He instantly closed his eyes and went limp.

It seemed to take forever before the healer shook her head.

"It's not good." The Unawi translated for Baya.

"What's not good?" Baya said. Her heartbeat throbbed in her ears.

Baya grew more anxious with each second she had to wait for Unawi Nacora to translate what the healer was saying.

"His brain is too full."

"What does that mean?" Baya's voice came out higher than normal. "You can fix him, right?"

"It means that some of it has to be released. My healer will drill a hole in his head —"

"What?" Baya yelled. "You're going to open up his head and what … let his brains spill out!"

"The pressure in his head is keeping his brain from functioning properly," the Unawi spoke through gritted teeth.

Baya slowly reached for the knife at her side. She quickly drew it as she turned to stand in between Vicaroy and the others gathered in the room. "You are not going to put a hole in his head!"

Nacora glared at Baya. "I've had quite enough of you, girl. And I only met you moments ago."

The healer laid a gentle hand on Baya's arm, which held the knife. She started at the sudden and comforting contact. The old woman looked deep into her eyes.

It is the only chance he has. I've done this procedure before.

"Why is your voice in my head and how can I understand you?" Baya asked.

Mind to mind communication does not need translating.

Baya thought about how she knew what Doba and Tara were thinking without knowing their language per se. This appeared to be rational. "Will he be okay?"

It is a risky operation. Once it was successful. And yet another time ... not so. The old healer shook her head in sorrow.

Baya had lowered the knife. "So, he is equally likely to be fine or ... he will die?"

The healer smiled with warmth and sadness. She gave a slight nod.

"No!" Baya raised the knife to the Unawi. "I won't risk it. It's my job to protect him and I can't let you do this."

The Unawi nodded to the healer, who moved behind Baya with surprising speed and placed both of her hands on Baya's head.

Baya tried to move away from the old woman but instantly felt dizzy. Her head bobbed and she swayed when she tried to turn toward the old woman. The knife clattered to the floor and she stumbled forward. Baya felt the ground coming up to meet her.

Strong arms caught her. The room was nothing but a blur. The muffled voice of Nacora could be heard, "Good riddance. Take that crazy girl away."

Baya was taken to a bright room. She couldn't focus on the face of the person who carried her but he appeared to carry her with ease.

She was too tired to struggle or even move. "Vicaroy..." she mumbled. "They're going to kill him."

The man carrying her sat her on the bed and took off her pack. She tried to protest but couldn't. He gently laid her down and covered her in bright white linens. She vaguely registered the sound of the door closing behind him as he left.

Baya tried one last time to get up — to move but she could no longer hold her eyelids open, let alone raise her body. The familiar tickle of Doba crawling across her and nestling against her was the last thing she remembered. Her heavy arm fell over him and Baya knew no more.

CHAPTER 67

Baya had to be shaken awake. When she finally came to, she swung at the hands that held her shoulders. The pounding of her heart was all she could hear. The healer stood by the bed with two other women.

Baya started again at the sight of her hands. They were … clean. No more dirt and grime, even the black was gone from under her nails and someone had smoothed the chipped edges. She looked down to find that she was wearing a long white nightgown. A quick glance told her that Doba was nowhere in sight. He was good at disappearing.

Unawi Nacora stood in the doorway. "My healer has informed me that he is awake and he is asking for you."

Baya was on her feet and shooing away the woman who tried to help her. "Is he okay?"

Nacora frowned. "Yes. No thanks to you."

The Unawi's entourage walked far too slowly for Baya's preference. She wanted to run to Vicaroy but she didn't remember which room he was in. She had to slow her pace and wait to be led down a wide hallway.

"How long was I asleep." Baya asked, in order to break the

awkward silence and distract her from the anxious energy that was threatening to boil over.

"Eighteen hours."

"Really? I don't think I've ever slept that long before."

The Unawi shot her a brief glare.

Baya obviously hadn't made a good first impression. All that had happened after they arrived was still somewhat blurry.

When they entered the large sun-lit room, Baya's name rang out. The sound of it coming from his lips was the most beautiful thing she had ever heard. He knew who she was! He was back!

Vicaroy tried to lift himself out of bed but winced and placed a hand on his head. Baya sprinted for him. With no regard for anyone else in the room she leapt on top of him. Straddling him, she gently kissed his forehead then his cheek. She pressed her lips to his.

Her face was soon streaked with tears of happiness as his hands gripped her waist pressing her against him. His touch was loving, passionate and strong. "You know me." She breathed before she kissed him again.

Vicaroy pulled away enough to look at her. "What're you talking about? Of course I know you."

Baya studied his lovely honey-colored eyes. They were no longer vacant. She could only answer with a laugh. He *saw* her, really saw her. Even though Baya's lips were wet with tears, she kissed him again. It was easy to lose track of how much time had passed before someone cleared her throat — a reminder that they were not alone.

"Where are we?" he asked.

Baya let out a choked laugh. "We made it. We're in Merth." Tears continued to stream down her face. Vicaroy's eyes were full of light and love but even more importantly they were full of recognition.

Vicaroy didn't loosen his strong hold on Baya's waist. When he finally pulled his gaze away from her, his face fell. His eyes narrowed on the person standing behind Baya. It was not the empty stare that would haunt Baya forever. No — this was an angry stare. Baya turned to find that it was the Unawi who had brought about this change in him.

"Mother?" Vicaroy asked.

Nacora studied him with a gentle warmth. "Yes, my son. You have found me."

The End of Book One

Help others find this book by leaving a review on Amazon.

Sign up to Lynne's email list at www.lynnehill.com to get a free eBook. Plus, never miss a new release.

LOST POWERS

BOOK 2 IN THE WOMAN'S WORLD SERIES

Baya has been chosen to restore balance.

The friends she can't save.

The family she can't help.

The lover she can't live without.

And don't forget about the world.

It all rests on Baya's shoulders.

She must piece together the truth about their history.

Her path leads her to face her greatest regrets and her worst fears.

Warning: nothing is what it seems, so don't say we didn't warn you.

Get your next adventure today!

What Critics are Saying...

Baya and Vicaroy's journey continues in this sequel and the story keeps getting better and better. Our heroine and hero are caught up in even bigger intrigues and threats in Merth and, as they learn the ways of their new home, they have to contend with forces much greater and darker than they can comprehend. But, who loses their power?

This is the question so huge and terrifying, you will have to read on to find out. This book will leave you wanting more!

— Addicted to Books

Lost Powers does not disappoint! It brings new challenges and adventures with new friends, creatures, and characters. It is beautifully descriptive and had me on the edge of my seat! Learning more about the culture of Merth and Pathins as well as Vic's past was illuminating. The ending had me dumbfounded and longing for the third book to find out what ultimately happens to Vic and Baya and how the surprise ending fits into the world. As far as I'm concerned this series is another home run and I would recommend it to anyone wanting something different from the now cookie cutter literary world!

— Jennifer V.

ALSO BY LYNNE HILL

The Lords and Commoners Series

Of Lords and Commoners Book 1

Of Princes and Dragons Book 2

Of Gods and Goddesses Book 3

A Gods and Goddesses Novelette

A Woman's World Series

A Woman's World Book 1

Lost Powers Book 2

A Collision of Worlds Book 3

ACKNOWLEDGMENTS

Writing is far from being a solitary process, or at least it shouldn't be solitary. As Ernest Hemingway said, "We are all apprentices in a craft where no one ever becomes a master." This is absolutely true. I'm still learning so much in this trade and there are so many people to thank. Thanks so much to the wonderful writers in my critique groups, one of the most recent being Lisa McDonald. She pushed me to fix the start of this book. Thanks to her I finally found a good way to introduce readers to this new world. Her motivation and continual striving to learn as much as possible inspired me to do likewise.

Many thanks to my preliminary readers and thanks to my fellow writers in my marketing group. Writing books is one thing but selling them is another matter entirely. I would be lost without all of their guidance. Writers tend to be a generous lot — always willing to help a fellow writer; for this I'm eternally grateful and indebted!

I'm very blessed to have my amazing editor, Marcia. I pray she never retires! Of course, I can't forget the unwavering support of my friends and family. I love you all very much!

ABOUT THE AUTHOR

Lynne Hill is the author of the *Lords and Commoners* series and the *Woman's World* series. She made the short list for the Chanticleer Book Awards and was awarded a 5 Star Reader's Favorite Award. She was born in Colorado and raised in a small town of eight hundred people. Lynne holds a Doctorate of Psychology in criminology and justice studies. She is an advocate for Restorative Justice, a theme that is incorporated into her novels. Her extensive travels overseas and her work as an American Peace Corps Volunteer in Jordan helped to inspire her writing.

Find out more at www.lynnehill.com and sign up to her email list to get a free eBook. Plus, never miss a new release.

www.ingramcontent.com/pod-product-compliance
Lightning Source LLC
Chambersburg PA
CBHW030624310726
48979CB00003B/865
* 9 7 8 1 7 3 6 7 2 4 9 8 9 *